Ainsley St Claire

VENTURE CAPITALIST
Book 8

Enchanted

A Novel

OTHER BOOKS BY AINSELY ST CLAIRE

Venture Capitalist Series (in order)

Forbidden Love

Promise

Desire

Temptation

Obsession

Flawless

Longing

Enchanted

Fascination
September 2019

Holiday

Gifted
December 2019

Tech Billionaires

House of Cards
February 2020

Tilted
April 2020

chapter

one

QUINN

*M*y other work phone is ringing. I check the caller ID before I answer. "Hello, handsome."

"What are you wearing?" he rasps into the phone.

"A black silk robe. I love the way it feels against my nipples." I breathe heavy for effect.

"Are you touching yourself?"

"I am. My pussy is wet. Can you hear me play with it? But what I want to know is if you are touching yourself?"

"My dick is so hard right now. What would you do if you were here with me?"

"Mmmmm… that's easy. I'd get down on my knees—" I pause for dramatic effect. "—then I'd lower the zipper to your jeans, and I hold on to your hard cock nice and tight." I moan my appreciation. "It's so big; I'm not sure I can take it all in my mouth. What should I do?"

"Take it deep in your mouth," he whimpers.

"Ohhh… my tongue swirls around the end. I love the way you taste."

"I want you to take it deeper in your throat."

"Can I play with my pussy at the same time?" I say in my best coquettish voice.

"Only if it's completely hairless."

"Smooth as a baby's bottom. Tell me what you like. I want to please you."

"Play with your nipples and your pussy."

"Oh, that feels soooo good. Can you feel me take you deep in my throat?" I hear his breathing increase and I know he's close, but I don't want this to end yet. I whisper, "Don't come yet. I want to suck your balls."

He moans into the phone.

"I'm licking and sucking on your balls—swirling my tongue around and pulling gently."

"Pull harder," he commands.

"You get me so horny. My hand is so wet. I neeeeeed you."

"I want to hear you come for me."

"I'll only come for you if you will come all over my tits when I'm done."

"Jesus, woman, I don't think I've ever been this hard before."

I begin to moan my orgasm for him.

"Ahhh," he grunts into the phone. "Gawd, you're amazing. I can't sleep anymore without you. Are you working tomorrow night?"

I'm panting for added effect. "Yes."

"Can I call you again tomorrow?"

"I think I'll have recovered by then." I giggle seductively into the phone.

"Goodnight, Cinnamon."

"Goodnight, handsome. You'll haunt my dreams tonight."

He hangs up, and I walk into the kitchen, wearing sweatpants and a giant ratty old wool sweater I got years ago. I grab a Diet Coke from the fridge before my next client calls for his evening naughty talk.

Sitting down at my computer, I look at the project plan for my newest client. We've just invested almost two hundred million in a company that is working on a cure for Parkinson's disease, and I'll oversee the office manager on-site and coordinate the recruiting and other operational sides of the business.

I pick up my phone, and it lights up, showing I've been on the phone with one of the partners for over a half hour. I quickly push the red button to disconnect the call. Fuck! I'd called William to leave him a message about his newest client and what he was trying to accomplish when my second job phone rang. I thought I'd disconnected the call. Crap.

Living in San Francisco is expensive. My one-bedroom apartment has a rent more than most people's mortgage, and I don't have a parking space or washer and dryer, and my view is of the street outside of my third-floor walk-up. Plus, I have a school loan payment of over four thousand dollars a month. I'm drowning in debt, so I took a second job that didn't require me to have strange people get in and out of my car or actually prostitute my body out to strange men—eww! I've gotten to know men too well doing the job, but they don't know my actual name and only think they know what I look like from the highly photoshopped picture. I make a dollar a minute plus tips, which means over eight hours I earn about two hundred and fifty dollars a night, and I try to work at least six nights a week. It pays my school loans and puts a dent in my rent, but it's often lonely. I haven't been out with my friends for so long they've stopped asking.

My phone rings again.

"Hello, handsome."

"Cinnamon, do you have some time to talk?"

"Jeffery?"

"Oh, sorry. Yes, this is Jeffery."

"Of course. What's wrong?"

"My company is going public, and I'm freaking out. I just need to hear the calm in your voice to get me off the ledge."

"I'm here for you, baby. Just imagine me cuddled up next to you."

"I love how soft your breasts are."

"You're so naughty when you play with my nipples." I moan into the phone. "I'll promise to stroke that beautiful cock, but only if you tell me what's bothering you."

He goes through the litany of challenges that he's facing. I want to tell him he should have invested with my company SHN, but first that would be too close to home, and second, I'm not exactly sure who Jeffery is, but I don't really want to find out.

Most of my job is to listen to the men who call. Some want to have a physical release when they talk to me, and others just need a sympathetic ear. Jeffery keeps me on the phone for over three hours, and when we hang up, I get a message that he's tipped me five hundred dollars. A good night. I turn my phone off and stop taking calls.

My mind drifts back to my open call with William. I've never wanted my professional job to intersect with my second job. They should never mix.

The bile rises in my throat. I don't know what I'm going to do.

Okay, there are two possibilities. I said goodbye, and he hangs up, and most likely he never listens to all of my message. Or he listens and tells everyone, and not only am I beyond embarrassed, but I'll most likely lose my job, and then I'm in serious trouble with my bills.

Fuckity, fuck, fuck, fuck! I can't believe I was careless. Shit.

What am I going to do? How am I going to explain this to him?

What if he thinks I was talking to him? Oh, gawd! I run my hand through my hair, and I see several strands laced in my fingers, and now I'm sure the stress is making my hair fall out, and I'm going to go bald. Why can't anything be easy?

I have an idea. Maybe I can go in and erase the message. I search "How to erase voice mail messages on someone else's cell phone."

Shit! I'm not a hacker.

Okay. Think, Quinn. Do you know anyone who can hack a phone?

No one.

Cameron from work—maybe? But then I'd have to explain to him why I need him to break into William's phone.

Breathe.

All right. What did I say to the caller?

Think.

I told him how I liked how my nipples feel against silk. *Shit! I'm screwed.*

I'm sure he's the type of guy who would erase the message after I said, "Goodbye." He may not have even listened to the message to that point.

I hope. I pace my small living room and bite at the nail on my thumb. How can I ever go back to work again? What am I going to say when I see him? Can I avoid him for the rest of my life?

Quinn, how could you've been so stupid?

chapter

two

WILLIAM

I roll over half asleep and say, "Alexa, alarm off." I cover my eyes and desperately want to go back to sleep, but it's five, and I need to work out. Pulling on a pair of shorts and tucking my feet in my running shoes, I walk to my home gym in my condo. It's really the second bedroom, but I don't have guests, so I have a decent treadmill that I run on each day as I look out on the Golden Gate Bridge. Sometimes, if I feel up for it, I may go for a run up and down the boardwalk, but this time of year there are too many tourists, and it's just easier to run inside.

Noticing a missed call from last night, I pop my cell phone into the cradle for the speaker on the side table and push play on the message. Once the message is over it will move over to my music. Setting the treadmill for a four-minute mile, I jump on and start running. I love how it clears my head and sets me up for a good day.

"Hey, William. It's Quinn. I met with the team at Worldwide Payments and have a timeline all set up. I think we'll be good with one operations person who can double with our help on the recruiting side. I also"—I can hear a phone ring in the background—"think we may need to look at some of the support staff. Let's talk about it in the morning. Goodnight."

I wait for the call to disconnect, but it doesn't.

Then I hear her, in the sweetest, most sultry, southern drawl. "Hello, handsome."

I almost trip over my feet. It's quiet a moment, and then I hear her describe giving the guy a blow job. Before I fall off the treadmill, I stop it and walk up to the speaker. She isn't talking into the phone's microphone, so I can barely hear her, but I know exactly what she's saying. Her voice is so fucking hot. And since I know what she looks like, I wonder what it would be like to have her going down on me.

Holy fucking shit! My cock could pound nails right now it's so hard.

I know I should disconnect the call and erase the voice mail, but I'm so aroused I can't bring myself to do it. I listen for the entire length of the call, and she finally tells whomever she's talking to "Goodbye," I can't help but stroke myself.

Who could she have been talking to? A boyfriend? I've never had phone sex like that, but I'd sure like to.

I'm not in any serious relationship. I have a few girls I see when I need a date or want some fun, but no one who talks to me like that.

She disconnects from the call, and I then hear her hum the sweetest melody.

I've always thought Quinn was stunning. She's blonde, with an incredible rack and legs that I wouldn't mind wrapped around my waist while I pounded into her. Okay, I only thought that last part since I heard her talking on the phone. I don't mix my personal life with my professional life, so I try to only admire my female colleagues from afar.

Holy crap. How will I ever look at her again and not have a huge hard-on?

I glance at the clock, and unless I get a move on, I'm going to be late for work.

The water is warm as I ease myself into the shower, and I keep replaying her sultry voice saying, "I want to please you." I begin to stroke myself until I shower the wall with my orgasm.

How am I going to be able to get through the day and not want to bend her over my desk and pound her hard from behind?

As I walk into the office, I can't help but look around for her. I don't see her. She has a cubicle on the other side of the office, and we rarely interact.

I finally spot her. Her hair is up in a ponytail — easier to pull her deeper on my cock, I think as I fantasize about her.

She's wearing a black turtleneck sweater and black pants with a pair of sexy stilettos — I wonder what her underwear looks like? I wonder, if I were to tweak her nipples, would she moan in appreciation or knee me in the balls? Probably the latter.

I need to get my mind out of the gutter. I need to forget the message and focus on Worldwide Payments. My deal has been funded, and the goal is to finalize the software with Cameron's team over the next year and prepare to take them public. Without Quinn's help, my deal will go south, and not only will the company be out of their investment, but I'll be out of a job.

She did leave a message saying we would talk about my issue today. I'd also like to include Mason, Cameron, and possibly someone from his team to do some planning. I check everyone's calendars and send out an invite for a meeting tomorrow afternoon to discuss.

As I push send, I look over in Quinn's direction. I watch her pop up and look at me. I glimpse a pink flush cover her face, and even that makes me hard. I look away.

What is this woman doing to me?

QUINN

I turn the lights on as I walk into the office. Looking around, there is a lot of glass and spots of color. This is a cool place to work, and I love the people who work here. They are bright, funny, and a few I would call my friends.

I live in a cubicle. It's a big one by our standards, but it doesn't have a door. At seeing my photos and mementos of clients, tears begin to pool in my eyes. I'm going to miss this place. I brought a banker's box with me, and I begin to pack my things. I'm careful to take only what is mine. After filling it with my personal items, I pop the lid on the box and put it under a chair in the corner of my cube as Mason arrives.

"Good morning. You beat me into the office this morning." He smiles at me and continues on to his office.

"A lot to get done today." I stand, adjust my pants, wiping out the wrinkles, and walk into the kitchen to start the coffee.

If William decides to tell Mason about my side job and they fire me, I can walk out with my head held high. Second jobs are allowed, but we have an ethics clause in our employee agreement, and it's very clear that we can be terminated if we do something that shines a bad light on the company. While I've never told a client where I work or much about me personally, SHN could use this to let me go.

SHN was founded by three guys who went to Stanford together—Mason, Dillon, and Cameron. They were friends who, after finishing school, did really well at three different start-ups. Essentially, they were single with too much money. With their talents in business, finance, and technology, they pooled funds and began to invest in other people's ideas. Now, ten years later and over fifty employees, we've grown, and most of the partners are all listed as billionaires by magazines and news organizations. We are a force to be reckoned with in the start-up world, and there are many companies out there looking to bring us down. Bad publicity will do that.

I dated Mason when we were in business school. I thought he hung the moon, but he was so focused on making money that we'd make plans, and then he'd forget. I finally gave up and broke it off with him. I was hoping that he'd fight for us and beg me to take him back, but instead, he hated me. Everyone said I broke his heart, and after graduation, we went our separate ways.

I started working for "the" venture capital fund right out of grad school—Perkins Klein. I worked my way up, but as the two partners made more money, they got careless. In this business, if you make bad investments, it can destroy you. After a few bad investments and the help of a hacker going after their business, they drove their company into the ground.

Years ago, Perkins Klein attempted to hire Emerson, and that's where I met her, and we became great friends. SHN made her a better deal. The hacker has been hitting most of the venture capital firms in Silicon Valley, so we began to share information. I would let her know how the hacker was affecting Perkins Klein but never shared any proprietary information. When Perkins Klein went under, I was surprised that SHN offered me a job. I took a cut in pay to work for them, but I was hoping to be on a partnership track. Given my history with Mason, I've come to believe that will never happen. Now with my fuckup, I'll be lucky if I can keep my job.

My computer pings to alert me of a meeting request for one of William's clients. He wants to meet with Mason and me. It's tomorrow. Fuck. I'm so screwed. Wait, Cameron is scheduled to join us, as is Parker from his team. Maybe it is about just William's client. I breathe a little bit easier, but not tremendously. I'm going to take my things home tonight. That way if for some reason they let me go tomorrow or next week, all I'll need to do is grab my purse.

" —Quinn? Did you hear me?"

"What? Oh, I'm sorry. What did you ask?"

"I wanted to know if you wanted to have lunch together today. I brought my lunch, but the sun is shining, and we can sit outside under the oak trees in South Park," my coworker Tiffany asks.

"Oh. Sorry. Sure. What's on the kitchen calendar for lunch? I forgot my lunch and am tight before payday."

"I totally understand. It's meatball subs and salad. I totally love the meatball subs, but they are terrible for my waistline." Tiffany has some curves, but the guys all seem to love them, but I understand there is a fine line between curves and fat.

"Mine, too. But the salad will work."

I have an afternoon meeting with Emerson, and on Friday the company is renting a plane for all of us to fly into Las Vegas for our annual client and employee appreciation. I'm so excited; one of the partners has a childhood friend who has built a huge hotel on the strip, and we've rented most of it out to help with a soft opening— for us, our guests, and a few others to try things out without the pressure. We have four chartered flights for employees and clients to fly out, although rumor has it many of our clients are flying private jets in. Must be nice.

This will be three days of fun. I'll still have to work my second job in some of the evenings, but that shouldn't be too bad. SHN always does things first class for our clients and its employees

I hardly slept again last night. I did bring my things home after work yesterday, just in case. I didn't have that much in my desk—hand lotion, a box of tampons, some hairpins, and some mementos that I've collected over the years that mean something to me. I left the pictures up in my cube so no one would ask questions.

I hate waiting for the shoe to drop. Today's meeting will give me an idea of what life is going to be like. I checked with my school loans, and I can opt to pay only the interest. It doesn't pay down the principal, but without my regular paycheck, it will be necessary to have a reprieve. I've been saving my bonuses for a down payment on a condo or small apartment but instead will use that to live on. I may just move home to my dad's in Florida for a while. San Francisco is becoming unaffordable.

I watch the clock tick by all morning, waiting for the gauntlet to fall. All of my project timelines are up to date, so anyone can come in and take over. I realized last night that I may not be able to go to Las Vegas, and that made me cry. Each year our client-appreciation party is better than the last, and it kills me that we're having this kick-ass party over a weekend in Las Vegas and I may not be able, or allowed, to attend. I hate San Francisco so much sometimes. It's too expensive, and it drives me crazy that the cost of living is so high here.

At a few minutes before two, I run by the kitchen to pick up a Diet Coke and head into the small conference room. Parker is there, and it makes me feel better that maybe this is a real meeting, not one arranged under false pretenses. I know why I'm paranoid, but I'm hoping I'm taking this too far.

I sit at the table, cross my legs, and shake my foot, a nervous habit I have. Cameron joins us.

"Hey, Quinn. I saw the analysis of Fickle Communications. I think it's spot-on. Thanks."

I'm grateful for the praise. "No problem. I have two more to finish up and will try to do so before I get on a plane on Friday afternoon for Vegas."

"I'm really looking forward to this weekend. This is going to be crazy."

Mason walks into the room. "Vegas?" We nod. "I've seen the agenda. Tina has been at the Shangri-La for two weeks working with their staff. Between her and Christopher's friend, this is a big weekend. It's going to be a blast."

William comes in and sits next to me. When his knee brushes mine, a jolt of electricity dives through me. He looks at me and smiles, exposing his dazzling pearly whites. He oozes confidence, and it is so attractive. There isn't a woman, married or single—and probably a few men—in our office who most likely wouldn't get on their knees for him. He's flat-out gorgeous. He leans over and whispers, "Sorry."

We walk through the meeting's agenda fairly quickly, and as we wrap up, William asks, "Mason, can you and Quinn stay a moment?"

My stomach drops. This is it.

"Sure," Mason says.

I nod.

We watch Cameron and Parker leave, and I pick at the corner page of my moleskin notebook. I'm determined I'm not going to cry.

"One of the chief engineers of a current start-up has come to me with an idea he'd like to chase. What's our protocol for these kinds of things?"

I sit a little taller. This isn't about my second job. He would have mentioned it by now if he was going to bring it up. I'm beginning to think he may not have heard the voice mail and I'm off the hook.

"It's something we do. Is he one of the founders of his current company or is he an employee?" Mason asks.

"He's not a founder, however he's their first employee and has a significant stake in the company," William shares.

"Then I suggest we walk carefully. Quinn, if William can get you his contact information can you talk to him? I think it's a little less obvious to his current team if you're the one to approach him rather than William," Mason suggests.

"At what point do we get Dillon and others involved?" William asks.

I don't hear Mason's answer.

The guys stand up, and I follow suit to leave when I'm sure I hear William say under his breath, "Thanks for all your help."

"It's my job. Happy to help," I tell him with more confidence than I feel.

My bag is packed, and I'm ready for a fun weekend. I'll still work my second job in the evenings, but I plan on taking in a lot of pool time. I take a seat in the 777 airplane. I've never flown in a private plane. This plane belongs to the Sacramento Kings basketball team, and the leg room is amazing. Each chair is a leather captain's chair. The plane is full of employees, significant others, and clients. William walks up and points to the seat next to me. "Is this seat taken?"

"Help yourself." I smile at him, and my heart beats a bit faster. Reaching into my bag, I pull out my Kindle and try to read a steamy romance I've been working on. I tell myself I read these to spice up my second job, but the truth is, I really enjoy them. I'm reading a particularly sexy scene and my body unconsciously shutters.

William leans over and whispers in my ear, "You're all sorts of naughty, aren't you?"

I turn pink. "San Francisco can be tough for a single woman."

"I have a feeling you do just fine."

I shrug uncommittedly. "Maybe." I then go back to my tablet and switch over to a game of cribbage.

"I hope you didn't stop reading your book because of me."

"And what would you say if I did?"

He smiles and starts to say something, but the flight attendant interrupts him with the announcement we are in our final approach to McCarren Airport in Las Vegas.

Once we hit the ground and they open the hatch, Tina, our party planner, steps on the plane. "Hello, everyone! Welcome to Las Vegas where the weather is a perfect eighty-five degrees." She waves to another person. "I'd like you to meet Jean Marie. If you'll follow her, she will take you to the transportation center and get you your ride to the Shangri-La. Of course, you are welcome to grab private transportation. My team will get your luggage to your rooms, so you don't have to worry about that. Once you arrive at the hotel, there will be members of the staff there to greet you and get you checked into your rooms. You will receive a gift bag, which includes itineraries and other activities you can participate in and enjoy over the weekend. We look forward to seeing everyone this evening in the main ballroom at the happy hour beginning at 6:30 p.m. The troupe from Cirque will be there to entertain you. Dinner will be on your own, but with the badges, which you'll be given at the front desk, you can enjoy any of the top-notch restaurants in the hotel at no cost. Until then, have a wonderful time."

We all disembark from the plane, and William and I walk together. I catch him staring at me a few times, and I want to just to get it out there. If he's going to be a pervert about this, then we need to get this over and done with, but he never says anything, and it's killing me.

After checking in, I take off for the elevator and arrive just as he's slipping in behind me. "We meet again," he says with a seductive rasp.

"If I didn't know better, I'd think you were following me."

"I think they've put all the partners and senior staff on the same floor."

I can't help but be a little disappointed that he isn't following me. We walk down the hall, and my room comes up first, but then he stops at the room next door. "Looks like we're neighbors. Make sure you aren't too loud. I'm a light sleeper." He chuckles and winks at me.

I can't believe this.

I step into my room, and I feel as if I'm transported to Paris. The walls have broad white and blue stripes; the king-size bed is overflowing with a down comforter and plush pillows. As I glance into the bathroom, I notice there are travertine tiles everywhere, including a shower that is as big as my entire bathroom in San Francisco and a bathtub that I plan on enjoying with the complimentary bubble bath and bath bombs.

Sitting on the desk is a huge fruit and snack basket. There's a note telling me the fridge is stocked with Diet Coke. They've thought of everything.

I shrug off my coat and grab an apple and some almonds to snack on as I sit in a chair and put my feet up.

I spot my luggage in the corner, and it makes me feel important. Everyone likes to feel important sometimes. I pull the note from the fruit and snack basket. "Thank you for all you do for SHN. We're so glad you're here." It's signed by all the partners. I stop and stare at William's name and decide I want to check out the pool rather than hide in my room. There's plenty of time to do that later. The weather is perfect. I pull a bikini out of my bag, along with my sunscreen and a big brimmed hat.

The pool is easy to find, and I see a few people from the office who had the same idea. I find a chaise lounge chair under an umbrella and take my Kindle out. The pool seems to be the place to be after a while. I see William arrive, and he's talking to Christopher and his girlfriend. I met Bella once and really liked her.

I go back to my naughty book, and I can't help but imagine it's William doing these things to me. It's getting me hot. Needing a breather, I put my book aside and enter into the pool from the steps. As I watch a pool volleyball game, I splash water on me to cool down. After over two hours by the pool, I head back to my room. On my way out, I look over at William, and find him watching me. I wave, and he waves back. When I return to my room, I lie down for a few minutes, which turns into over an hour. It's really nice to have a quiet afternoon. I don't get these very often.

When I finally get up, I have just enough time to shower and get ready for tonight's cocktail party. I'm supposed to be there on time as part of the leadership team to greet people. I spritz my favorite perfume and check myself in the mirror. I look fashionable with my tight, basic black dress, and I like the color my legs got today in the sun, so my come-hither sandals are perfect.

When I walk out of my room, I hear William leaving at the same time.

"You didn't stay at the pool long this afternoon," he says.

"I was there almost two hours. Too much sun for me. I like the sun but only to a point."

"You look beautiful and sun-kissed this evening."

I blush at the compliment. Emerson and Dillon are at the elevators waiting, and then I hear Mason and his girlfriend talking as they approach.

"Looks like we're all headed to a party," William shares, and everyone seems to snicker.

Mason's girlfriend gives me the evil eye. She's never liked me, but I'm convinced it's because I met Mason before she did, and I've seen him naked. Whatever. It's not like I go around talking about it.

Emerson asks, "How is your room?"

"It's beautiful, and thanks so much for the fruit and snack basket. It was perfect," I tell her.

"We signed those cards forever last week," Dillon complains.

Emerson elbows him in the gut. "You'd think his hand was going to fall off."

We ride the elevator down, and I catch Annabelle scowling at me in the reflection of the mirrors. Jealousy does not become her.

When we get to the lobby, I make a quick exit and head to the bar. I need some liquid courage to make it through tonight.

"What can I get you?"

"A Tanqueray No. Ten Gin and tonic if you have it or just Tanqueray and tonic please."

"Make that two," I hear William say over my shoulder. He places his hand on the small of my back, and I can feel the light touch burn holes in my skin. I'm grateful I have a padded bra on because the girls have high-beams and almost hurt they're so erect right now.

"I have the Tanqueray No. Ten, with a lime or would you prefer lavender?"

"A lime is fine." I smile at him before turning to William. "Okay, you heard my entire voice mail. Get it out."

"I did hear it." He leans in, and his citrus and cucumber smell distracts me. "But there's nothing to 'get out.' I'll admit I was surprised. Do you always talk like that?"

"Only when they ask," I say in my best sultry voice. If we're going to go there, I'm going to dish as hard as he is.

Our drinks arrive, and he throws a fifty on the counter and thanks the bartender. Handing me a drink, he clinks my glass. "To an arousing time tonight."

I lean in and see he has a tent in his pants. I bite my lip seductively. "I think you've already accomplished that." I walk away and make sure there's a bit of sway in my hips.

I've already seen one of the partners naked — yes, well over a decade ago—but I don't need further complications at work. With William being a partner, he controls my destiny at SHN, and I can't muddy that water, and I will not sleep with him to keep my job.

The cocktail hour and announcements are a great kickoff to the weekend. I escape back to my room by seven thirty so I can do a little bit of my second job, changing into my ratty sweatshirt and a pair of leggings. I'm not even logged on for three minutes when my phone rings.

"Hello, handsome."

Several of my regulars call, and I end up working for almost four hours. When I log off, it's after midnight, and I'm exhausted.

I think of William while I lay in bed. He's flirtatious, but he's very dangerous. There's no telling what mess I'll find myself in if I admit that I'm a phone sex operator. I'm going to avoid William as much as I can.

chapter

four

WILLIAM

I woke with a raging hard-on this morning. I couldn't get my mind off Quinn and the idea of her talking dirty to me as she fucks me. Playing with her could be dangerous for my career, but I'm drawn to her like a moth to a flame. As I wander downstairs, I see her standing in line for the breakfast buffet. She looks radiant in a soft blue floral sundress. I don't see any bra straps, and it makes me want to explore—but I don't. I ease into the line behind her and take in her smell. It takes all my self-control to keep from nibbling, kissing, and licking from the thin strip on her shoulder up to her neck until I can bite that delicious earlobe. "You disappeared last night. You missed the Cirque show performers."

She turns to me and smiles. "I heard they were fantastic. I wasn't feeling well, so I went to bed early."

"Funny, I thought I heard you talking last night in your room."

"I was asleep. Must have been a different room. Plus, who would I have to talk to? It's only me in my room."

I lean in and ask quietly, "Who do you talk so dirty to at night?" I want to know who my competition is. I've never wanted something as bad as I want her.

"I have no idea what you're talking about." She puts fruit on her plate and begins to walk to the coffee station.

"I can play back the voice mail you left me if you need a reminder?" My cock is becoming erect, and I need to watch how far I push this with her.

She shrinks back, and I know immediately I've gone too far. "William, if you feel you must share it with the world, you are welcome to do so."

She turns and leaves me standing with a plate of scrambled eggs and sausage getting cold. She sits with some of the leadership team, and I join Mason and Annabelle. They look like I feel—miserable. What they see in one another, I'm not sure.

There are a few tours and activities going on, but I just want to talk to Quinn. I want to know who she's talking to. I love that she's conservative, beautiful, smart, and sexy on the outside but has a dirty mind and is wonderfully naughty on the inside.

Later that afternoon, I head out to the pool and see her reading her book again under a big umbrella. I order two Tanqueray No. Ten Gin and tonics and bring her one. She looks up and scrutinizes me as I hand her a drink. I wish I could read her mind. "Thank you."

"It's hot out, and I thought you might be thirsty."

She points to her water bottle. "I'm good, but this works. Are you going on any of the tours?"

"Nah, I've been looking for you."

"Why me?"

I watch her closely, wondering how do you ask someone if they get off talking dirty? "Who do you talk to when you talk dirty?"

She turns a nice crimson color. "Why? Are you asking to be added to the queue?"

"Is that possible?" I can tell that she isn't taking my flirting as I intend. I want to explore more than her dirty mind.

"Look, you know what I make."

At first, I'm a little confused at the change in topic. I don't really pay attention to how much money anyone makes, but I nod. She gets a bonus each year, and I know she makes a pretty decent living.

In a rushed whisper, she shares, "My rent is $4,200 a month for barely a one-bedroom, shithole apartment. My school loans are $4,726 each month. My take-home is less than $5,000 a month, and I need to eat and get myself to and from the office each day, not to mention other expenses. I support myself without any handouts from anyone else. What I do is legal, and I'm able to pay my bills. If you want to go to Mason and the partners about it, you can do that. They'll probably fire me because it could be seen as a violation of our ethics clause. But until I left you that message, no one knew my second job. That's my fault."

She gets up and walks away.

I feel about two inches tall. Fuck. That was not how it was supposed to play out. She was supposed to laugh and tell me she would talk dirty to me, and we'd fuck each other raw and joke that what happens in Vegas, stays in Vegas. Instead, I realize that she doesn't do it because she gets off on talking dirty to men but because she needs the money to make ends meet. I don't worry about money, and it didn't occur to me that in her position she would. I'm insensitive and an asshole.

I sit by the pool and watch her walk away. I need to figure out how to fix this.

That evening, I hear her hotel door open as I begin to walk out of my own. I freeze and wait to hear the elevator ping, alerting its arrival. I hang back, so she doesn't think I'm stalking her. She's been avoiding me all day.

When I finally make it down to the ballroom, I see it's elegantly decorated with the colors from our logo. There's a big stage up front, and a drum set all set up. It's pretty impressive. It's just starting to get busy when I see Quinn talking to Cynthia and her fiancée, Todd. She is laughing and looks beautiful. Her backless dress shows the beautiful arch to her back, and it takes all my willpower to not go over and pull her close.

As the evening begins, Christopher takes the microphone to get the crowd excited for tonight's band. I was shocked when I learned they would come to play a private show for us. Of course, we're paying a pretty penny for this show, but it'll be totally worth it. In this business, these kinds of events bring good clients.

"Isn't this great being here at the Shangri-La? I don't know about you, but I think this is the most glamorous and beautiful hotel on the strip," Christopher says while the crowd whoops and hollers their agreement. "We are so lucky we get to be the first to enjoy this amazing hotel before it officially opens to the public. Let's put our hands together to thank Jonathan." The crowd goes crazy for a solid two minutes.

"I grew up with Jonathan Best. He was this punk who was the smartest kid in our grade. When he called to tell me he was opening a hotel on the Las Vegas strip, I have to tell you, I didn't think he could pull this off. I've never been so glad to be wrong." Christopher looks at his friend and a smile breaks so wide his cheeks must hurt.

One of our clients yells from down below, "Good thing you didn't have his proposal go across your desk."

Christopher bursts out laughing. He repeats what was said for those of us in the back before continuing his speech. "But Jonathan has been amazing, and it's so great to have family and friends here together tonight. You may be wondering why I'm up here, and more importantly, why I've asked Elvis to join me. Well, the truth is he's up on stage to do something. You didn't realize that by being at the coolest party that Silicon Valley hosts each year, you were also being invited to a wedding tonight."

"Jesus, Mary, and Joseph," can be heard from the crowd.

"I think that was my future mother-in-law," he quips, and I realize what he's doing. They're going to get married in front of everyone. Well, this puts the pressure on the bachelors tonight!

"We'll let you get back to your party, but first, if you wouldn't mind being witnesses to our blessed event before the main event tonight."

The ballroom explodes in applause.

I watch him hand the microphone to Elvis. "Ladies and gentlemen, thank you for joining Christopher and Isabella as they join their lives for now and forevermore."

I have to admit, I'm stunned, but I'm also in awe of their relationship. They really haven't been together for very long, but they seemed to click. I've never understood that kind of relationship, but I've heard stories of how it happened similarly with some of the other partners.

"By the power vested in me, I now pronounce you husband and wife."

The crowd goes crazy, and Jonathan comes up to the stage and thanks everyone for helping to make the opening weekend a huge success. "And it's my great pleasure to introduce Bono, The Edge, Adam Clayton, and Larry Mullen, Jr." The crowd goes completely crazy as U2 comes out on stage.

Christopher and Bella wave and walk off stage as Bono says, "For the bride and groom," and begins singing "It's a Beautiful Day."

Shortly after the wedding, I see Quinn escape out the side door, and I know she's headed to her room for the night. I can't help but be disappointed she's leaving, but I get it. She needs to work her second job.

I dance with many of the girls from the office and some of our clients. It's a fun night. The band signs autographs, and there are T-shirts and other pieces of memorabilia for each attendee. It's well after midnight when I finally get back to my room.

There is a note under my door, and for a minute I'm hopeful it is Quinn inviting me to her room, but it's actually an invite to a surprise breakfast for the bride and groom for the partners and leadership team tomorrow morning. I'm scheduled on the last flight back to San Francisco at 7:00 p.m., and tomorrow will be busy all day, so breakfast will be the last time to spend time with everyone in this relaxed environment.

Lying in bed, I'm sure I can hear Quin talking, but the rooms are pretty soundproof, and it's probably more my imagination rather than what I'm actually hearing. My mind drifts to what she was wearing tonight, and I imagine her sultry voice telling me what she's going to do to me, and I can't help but stroke myself.

The next morning, I oversleep a little bit, making me a few minutes late to the celebratory breakfast. The newly wedded couple is sitting at a head table, and most people have heaping plates of eggs, bacon, sausage, pancakes, fruit, and carafes of coffee cover each table.

Seeing an open spot next to Quinn, I know luck is on my side, and I quickly take a seat.

As glasses of champagne are passed around, Mason stands. "Christopher and Bella, we are so happy you shared with us your wonderful event. May I be the first to wish you much happiness in the new life you're embarking on." He lifts his glass, and we all toast.

I look at Quinn, and she's squirming in her seat; she keeps crossing and uncrossing her legs. It's distracting and I wonder what it would be like to have her legs wrapped around my waist as I pound into her.

chapter

five

QUINN

He pulls out the empty chair next to me and was sitting before I realize it was him. When his knees hit mine, a jolt of electricity runs through me. Shit. He's going to torment me. I'm not going to let him make me feel embarrassed about what I do to pay my debts. I support myself. There's nothing illegal about it, and I refuse to hang my head in shame. If the partners decide to fire me, I'll walk out with my head held high. Living in Florida with my dad isn't particularly appealing; although the idea of sitting out by the pool more often is encouraging. It's much nicer than sitting in the gray gloom of San Francisco.

Several of the partners stand and toast to love. Christopher and Bella haven't been dating long, but I've heard people say, "When you know, you know." As I sit here, it gives me hope of finding my own happily ever after.

"I'm not going to tell anyone," he says to me in a low voice.

I'm taken aback by his candor. I don't want him to think it makes me nervous that he knows, and I can't let him think it's any kind of invitation for some kind of perverse arrangement. "I've no idea what you're talking about."

He just smiles salaciously and says, "It's our secret. No one will ever know."

Jennifer, who is sitting on my right, turns to me and says, "Did you two hook up last night?"

William hears and sits back, leaving me a lot of room. Quickly, I make sure she understands. "No, he's talking about something else. I screwed up, and he is holding it over my head."

She leans in so that he can't hear. "He's pretty cute. You could offer sexual favors to get him to forget."

I'm drinking from my glass of ice water, and it nearly comes out of my nose. Between coughs, I croak, "Why would I do that?"

She shrugs and mouths to me, "I would do anything he asks. Anything."

People around the room are looking at me because I'm coughing and struggling to breathe. I smile and croak, "Water went down the wrong pipe." After everyone turns back to the newlyweds, I lean over to Jennifer and whisper, "I don't think you're alone in wanting to do anything he asks, but unfortunately he knows it."

As the festivities continue throughout the morning, William sits back, crosses his legs, and puts his arm around the back of my chair. It isn't sexual in any way, but I feel the heat radiating from him. Our back is to the wall, and he's subtly rubbing small circles on the back of my shoulder with his thumb. I need to get out of here and away from him because, as Jennifer said, he'd be very difficult to say no to.

Breakfast finally breaks off and we both stand. He looks like he wants to ask me something but doesn't.

"Well, my flight takes off in a few hours. I'll see you back at the office tomorrow."

Jennifer looks up at me sharply. "Where are you headed?"

I don't want William to know, but I don't want to be too obvious. "I'm not sure yet. I may walk the strip, I don't gamble, but I wouldn't mind some sun, so I may head to the pool one last time."

"Have fun." She waves as she makes shopping plans with some of the other girls. William wanders off to talk to some of the other partners, and I head up to my room in search of my bikini, big hat, some sunscreen, and my Kindle. It's Sunday, and I need a break.

I put on my bikini and groan as I catch my reflection in the mirror. My pooch is growing, and I need to do something about it—not to mention these child-bearing hips are just awful. My mother always said I should be proud of them, but I swear they aren't anything worth being proud of. I need to work out more and do some crunches if I want to be naked with anyone. I may not be true bikini material, but I don't care. I throw my cover on and head out to the pool.

There are a few people on the pool deck enjoying the warm weather. Finding a spot under a huge umbrella, I lie back and close my eyes, just taking in the heat radiating off the deck. Life is perfect.

"May I join you?

My heart beats faster when I open my eyes and take in his chiseled chest. The beautiful hair that starts at his belly button and leads beneath his floral-printed swim trunks that I wouldn't mind exploring. I take a deep breath to calm myself. "There are more than fifty pool chairs sitting empty, and you want to sit next to me?"

He gives me a lopsided smile, but I can't see his eyes behind his dark sunglasses. "I do actually."

He's paying more attention to me this weekend than he has since he's started. I know he's heard the voice mail. I can't deny it so I might as well attack it head on and let the chips fall where they may. "Why? Just because you heard me talk dirty to somebody doesn't mean I'm going to talk dirty to you."

He throws his head back and laughs before spreading a towel out on the chair next to mine. "Oh man, what I wouldn't give for you to talk dirty like that to me. Can I tell you how many times I've listened to that recording?" In a low voice he says, "I'm going to wear out my phone. It's so hot."

I turn crimson. It's one thing for strangers to react to what I say, but to think that my coworker gets off listening to me is just miserable. This is why I should never have engaged in this conversation with him. My mind is racing, and I'm not sure what to say to him. He stands before me, and my mouth is right at his crotch, and I don't know if I want to punch him in the stomach or reach into his pants and take him in my mouth.

He leans in, and I can feel his breath on my ear. "Don't worry. It's just between the two of us. You can think about that, and I'll be right back."

Speechless, I watch him walk away, giving me a nice view of his backside—damn it! He looks just as good from behind as he does coming. He's going to kill me yet.

He sidles up to the bar, and a few girls from the office seem to grab his attention, so I turn on my Kindle, and of course, it goes right to a super steamy scene in my book. I can't read this with him so close. It gets me too hot and bothered, and I won't be able to say no to what I fear is coming. I open the cribbage app and start playing. It's a decent distraction. But I still have my eye on him, and I can't help but be a little jealous of how the girls flirt so easily with him. I wish I was half as smooth.

I watch the bartender place four drinks on a tray for him, and I'm shocked when he walks over to me with them. "I got us each two gin and tonics."

"Thank you. I appreciate that."

He hands the first one to me and raises his glass to toast. "To dirty minds and sinful bodies."

I'm not sure if he's talking about him or me, but my mouth is so dry, I can't help but drink several big gulps of my drink. I'm going to be feeling this later today.

"I'm curious, what do you talk about with these guys?"

"You're assuming I only talk to guys."

I watch his cock tent in his swim shorts. "You get women off too? Holy crap, is that hot."

"You make this too easy. You're so gullible. I've only talked to men. Most the time these guys are just looking for somebody to talk to. It's not necessarily sexual."

"What's the most outrageous thing someone's ever asked you to say?"

"I plead the fifth on that."

"Well, I got really turned on by you describing going down on that guy. Do you ever meet these guys in person?"

"Never. It's only over the phone. I get paid a dollar a minute to do this. I told you I have bills to pay, and while you're a partner, you make a lot of money. I'm not a partner. I'm just in leadership, and I took a pay cut to come to SHN." I can see him ready to interject, and I know what he's going to say, so I respond before he can ask. "Yes, SHN is generous with their bonuses, but those are once a year. I have bills, and you know it's expensive to live in San Francisco.

"I understand. I think it's rather ingenious that you found a way to earn money that supplements your income."

"That's the gig economy for you."

"So, back to my earlier questions. Has a guy ever told you to, say, suck his balls?"

I turn a shade of crimson and don't say anything.

"Have you ever had another woman join you when you talk to a guy? I bet they would go crazy for that."

"You're impossible, you know that?"

"Tell me something. Leave me something to fantasize about besides how fucking amazing you look in that bathing suit."

I'm so flustered by the compliment that I can't help but be honest. "I don't know. The weirdest thing a guy ever asked me to do was pretend I was sucking his toes while he played with himself."

He sits up and watches me carefully. "Well, did you?"

"It's what he was paying for. I wasn't actually doing it."

He laughs. "True, what about guys talking about furbies or going backdoor with you?"

"Of course they always ask for backdoor crap, and they ask for threesomes and all kinds of stuff. It's all fiction whatever I say, please be assured of that."

"You know your nipples are hard underneath your swimsuit."

"What do you want to do about that?"

"Will you let me suck them?"

I shouldn't have drank the two gin and tonics. I've lost my filter, and I'm a little too courageous. The bad angel on my shoulder is urging me to take him back to my hotel room so we can ravage one another for the rest of the afternoon. The good angel is telling me the conversation is going nowhere, and it's time to head back to my room before I start listening to the bad angel. I gather up my things. "I need to go. See you tomorrow at the office."

I walk back to my hotel room. There is nothing I can do about his questions, and it's only time until he tells someone else. I'm going to have to quit, that's all there is to it.

Packing up my things, I think of what I need to do to find a new job. Grabbing up my cell phone, I look through the job postings, but none of our competitors have anything open at my level. I send out some emails to friends who work at other VC firms and even send an email to a recruiter. I guess, if I'm going to get serious, I need to network with everyone I know outside of SHN. Looking for a new job is a full-time job, so I'm not sure how I'll swing it, but I'm determined.

chapter

six

WILLIAM

Women usually bend to my will easily, but Quinn isn't bending. Part of me really likes that she's so insistent on keeping our relationship professional, but the other part wants to push her up against a wall and fuck her until we are both satiated. I know I need to dial it back a bit. I don't need a sexual harassment suit to chase me down. I'd be fired for sure, and most likely so would she.

Quinn is one of the last few to get on the plane. Jennifer has already claimed the seat next to me, and while she's cute, she isn't in the same league as Quinn, and I'm a little disappointed when she can't sit next to me on the flight home.

I watch her board the plane and take a seat in the back where she sits with some of the girls from her department and one of her clients. He's a little too friendly if you ask me, and I don't like that one bit. When he puts his hand on her leg, I want to jump back to their seats and rip it off her. I have no idea where this protective streak in me is coming from.

Jennifer talks at me nonstop. Ignoring her, I lean back and shut my eyes and try to get some sleep. I need to get my mind off Quinn, and I don't want to talk to Jennifer. Jennifer finally gets the hint and joins her friends in the back. I'm not disappointed in the least.

The flight is under two hours and is over quickly. Once we arrive in San Francisco, we deplane and get our luggage. I watch Quinn pile her computer bag and purse onto her roller bag. As she begins to walk away, it tips awkwardly and throws her bags to the ground.

I watch her carefully as she rearranges her bags and puts her purse on her shoulder, her determination evident and she starts again. The roller bag tips once again, dumping her computer bag a second time. She looks so cute struggling. I want to step in and help, but she's been firm at putting distance between us. Watching her struggle shows me that, regardless when thrown a curve ball, she works through it, and I'm thoroughly impressed. There are dozens of options that would make her life easier, but she carries on. It takes me a few moments to realize her suitcase is missing a wheel. There is no way she'll be able to maneuver her bag in this crowded place to catch the train into town. Finally I walk up to her and ask, "Can I help?"

She looks at me skeptically. I love how she pushes a stray curl out of her face and takes a big breath to steady herself. "No, thanks. I've got this."

She drapes her computer bag across her body, hikes up her purse on her shoulder, and picks up her suitcase. It's a lot. After about five feet, she needs to stop for a break. Unable to watch her struggle any longer, I pick up her suitcase with ease and hold my hand out for her computer bag, placing it with mine on my suitcase. "Follow me. You can't ride the train into town with a broken suitcase."

"The wheel had been loose before I left, but I didn't think it'd break," she mutters.

As I walk away, I look over my shoulder at her. "Are you coming?"

"I guess I don't have much choice."

"Most woman would say 'Thank you' when a guy came in and saved them."

"I'm sorry, I didn't realize I needed saving. Thank you," she says, dripping in sarcasm.

I stop and turn to her. "I didn't mean to make you uncomfortable by the pool. I was an asshole. Please, let me make it up to you and offer you a ride home. I ordered a rideshare and can get you dropped off at your place."

Softening, she says, "Thank you. That would be very much appreciated."

"My car is this way." I open my arm to usher her to my waiting car service.

"Do you always save the damsels in distress?"

"Only the ones as beautiful as you."

She blushes, and it only makes her more beautiful.

Once we get situated in the car and are speeding our way into the city, I look at her and really see her beauty for the first time. I always knew she was a tall blonde with a perfect heart-shaped ass—very much my type, but I don't play with women I work with. It's just too messy. The slope of her neck makes me want to nuzzle and kiss it softly. Her breasts are perfect—not too small and not too large, with just a hint of her nipple that I yearn to pull and play with. And, her legs are long with flawlessly painted red toes. Before my erection busts out of my pants, I think of my sixth-grade teacher, Mrs. Dennison, and ask her, "Glad to be home?"

"I'll miss that hotel room. It was much nicer than my apartment. What about you?"

"I missed my bed. I'm glad to be back."

She nods and flushes. I'm positive her mind goes to the same place mine does.

Our hands are next to one another, and even though we aren't touching, I can feel an electrical current pass between the two of us. She has luscious lips. I wonder what she tastes like. We don't talk much on the ride into The City, but it's surprisingly comfortable. When we get to her apartment, she opens the door before the driver can get out. Scooting out after her, I offer, "Can I help you take your things up to your place?"

"That could be dangerous. I think I can make it the rest of the way."

"Dangerous?"

I see her nipples pebble beneath the thin cotton T-shirt she's wearing. "Thank you for the ride home," she says breathlessly.

"Any time." I turn to get back into the car to drive the last few blocks to my place when she leans in to the car to give me a hug. She smells amazing.

"I'd suck your balls while you played with yourself," she whispers, and I can't help but grin from ear to ear.

I laugh. "I'm going to hold you to that."

She gives me a devilish smile, and my cock becomes uncomfortable in my pants.

I'm going to dream about her going down on me tonight. I'm sure of it.

My alarm goes off long before I'm ready. I had a hard time falling asleep last night. After what felt like hours of tossing and turning, I eventually had to listen to her voice mail and take care of myself. I've never had a woman affect me like she has.

Putting on some great 70's southern rock, I hop on to my home rowing machine and begin working out to some Lynyrd Skynyrd. At just after five thirty, my phone rings. Who the hell is calling me this early? It's a 215 area; that's my dad's area code in Philadelphia but not his number.

"Hello," I say, trying to catch my breath.

"William Bettencourt, please."

"Speaking. Who's this?"

"William, this is Henry Gray. I'm your father's attorney."

My stomach tightens. "What can I do for you?"

"I really apologize for making this call so early, but there's been an accident." I sit up straight, fully alert. "There was a helicopter crash last week in Tanzania. They've searched the area, and—"

"Why am I just hearing about this now?"

"I understand, I was just made aware of this when your stepmother phoned my office recently. Apparently, your father was on a trip to Tanzania and was last seen with a Sherpa leaving to climb Kilimanjaro. I sent an agent to confirm he was on the helicopter. We know he departed from the Machame base, which is the scenic but steeper route to the top. I'm really sorry to have to call you so early. Your stepmother is in a financial bind, so it looks like she's managed to get a death certificate, which will release funds so she can pay bills."

"I thought my father had everything going into a trust?"

"He made some changes recently. William, you'll need to come home."

"It really isn't a good time."

"I understand, but your father has put a provision in your inheritance. You need to be married to get it. You have some time, but if you don't meet that, your inheritance reverts back to your stepmother and her children."

A headache begins to penetrate my skull. I take a deep breath. "When do you need me home?"

"We'll do the reading in two weeks. I suggest you bring a girlfriend with you. Don't let them think they can get at your inheritance."

"I'll let you know what I decide."

I hang up the phone with every intention of returning to my workout, but now that I've completely cooled down, I can't muster the energy. Why didn't I know my dad was in Africa? My mom died when I was young, and he remarried when I was in high school. I've never liked my stepmother very much, and the feeling is somewhat mutual. She was only interested in my father's money, and she has two of the dumbest twin sons, who I refer to as Dumb and Stupid.

I don't care if I get any of my dad's money, but I don't want Dumb and Stupid to get the money either. Fuck! I can't believe I need to bring someone home. Who can I talk into coming home with me and not worry about them thinking they've got their claws into me?

As I shower and get ready for my day, I think about my father. Although he inherited a lot of money, I didn't grow up in the wealthiest neighborhood in Philadelphia or go to the most expensive schools. We had nice things, but we lived modestly. My father was an engineer and inventor and came up with some patents, but he lived in a world all his own. He was devastated when my mom died, and it took some time for him to remarry, as no one would ever live up to my mom. But when he met Lillian, she somehow got him to marry her quickly, and in the end, she must have gotten him to change his will.

QUINN

The breakroom is buzzing with activity as people arrive and dig into the breakfast burritos. They are by far the most popular item we get. I like them okay, but I discovered a long time ago that I really don't care for the taste of pork green chili, and the burritos are filled with eggs, hashed browns, chorizo sausage, and pork green chili. I pour myself a big mug of hot water and dig out an Earl Grey tea.

As my tea seeps to a dark caramel color, I see Emerson. "Hey! How are you doing?"

"I can't complain. How about you?"

"Busy, but I wanted to check in. The business development team has a few things closing shortly, and I need to get some of your feedback. Are you available today for lunch?"

I blanch. I can't afford to eat lunch out right now, but I smile. "Of course."

"Great, let's go to WetBar and expense it back to the company. I'll see if I can't get us a reservation for noon."

I breathe a bit easier. "I'll meet you by the elevators at eleven forty-five."

My morning is crazy busy, and before I know it, it's time to meet Emerson and walk to lunch. WetBar is a great place on the water where the who's who of San Francisco tech come to be seen. "I'm impressed you got a reservation," I share.

"CeCe knows the owner, so I usually just call him."

"She knows just about everyone, doesn't she?"

"I know. But she's cautious about bringing anyone into her circle of friends. We're part of the lucky few." She winks at me. Emerson and CeCe were college roommates, but they've been kind enough to include me in some of their girls' nights and shopping trips—although I watch while they spend.

"That makes sense." We walk along, and I feel like there is something she wants to talk about, and it isn't the business our team is closing. I guess, if she brings up my second job, then I can just go home from lunch.

"I got a call from Jeannine Murphy." My stomach drops. She's the recruiter I reached out to about looking for a new job. I'm so grateful we're walking, so I don't have to look her in the eye for this conversation. "She mentioned someone on my team was looking for a new job. She didn't tell me who it was, but I'm pretty sure it's you."

"It is me. I'm sorry."

"Why? Is it someone on the team? Don't you enjoy your work?"

Wanting her to see me say this, I stop and face her. "I love my work at SHN. I haven't made any decisions, but I took a pay cut to come to SHN in hopes of getting on the partnership track, and that isn't happening. I've had to pick up a second job to make ends meet, and it's getting hard."

Emerson's face contorts in pain. "Why didn't you tell me?"

"Because I was embarrassed, and I wasn't looking for a handout. You made it clear what the job paid when I took it, and I accepted that. I just didn't realize how hard it would be to pay all my bills."

We've arrived at the restaurant, and the owner is there to greet us. "Emerson, my lovely. So wonderful to see you. I've saved you a table on the water."

"Thomas, you are very kind. Thank you."

He leads us to a table that overlooks Treasure Island and the Bay Bridge.

After looking through the menu and ordering, Emerson pushes, "You're very valuable to SHN. I can't guarantee anyone will ever be a partner—"

"It doesn't help that Mason still hates me since we broke up back in business school."

She smiles. "I can't speak to that, but I can talk to the team about a raise."

"I appreciate that, but my bills aren't the company's problem. My rent's expensive, and my school loans are even more than my take home each month." I watch Emerson's shoulders fall. She knows that doubling my salary isn't an option. "Emerson, when I went to college, my dad had an amazing job. Halfway through my sophomore year, he got sick. He's absolutely fine now, but the treatment was expensive, and my parents went through most of their savings, and they couldn't afford my tuition any longer. I'd much rather have my dad than be debt free. I took out loans and went to grad school. We thought my dad would return to another great paying job, but unfortunately, he wasn't able to return to work. Stanford was a calculated risk, but living in San Francisco in my hovel of an apartment is expensive. It's my own fault. I have an expensive education."

"I'm not sure what I can do, but I'd like to try. Promise me to not take any other jobs until I can figure this out."

"I just reached out to Jeannine to see what she had. At this point, given she called you, I'm not sure I'd trust her." Not to mention, I'm only looking because William could out me at any time, and they'd let me go. If she knew what my second job was, they'd have to fire me, and my looking is only to create a safety net.

"Don't let Jeannine's tactics get to you. She didn't tell me your name, I just figured out who you were."

We spend our lunch catching up on my accounts. It's still fun to hang out with her. As we walk back to the office, Emerson asks, "How's your love life?"

"What love life? I'm single in a city where the men outnumber the women, but I don't have the equipment most of the men here are looking for."

"Don't you dare give up. I was resigned to that same thing, and I met Dillon."

"I think you might have got the last good one."

"Don't tell that to CeCe. She's still single." Being reminded that CeCe is still single is encouraging. She's stunning, self-reliant, funny, and super smart. If she can't find a decent guy, then it isn't us, it's them!

I return to my desk, and I'm a little down on myself. I should have known better; the venture capital community is small. When William pulls the rug out, I'll have to figure something else out.

Wednesdays are my day to spend at SketchIt. They've created a new architecture and engineering design tool, and they're close to going public. The work has been intense in preparation, so I've been going there every week for months. I spend the day with a member of my team who works on-site, helping her however she needs. I also have meetings with the management team and will report back to the partners.

When I arrive, it's still somewhat early, but it's crazy busy, much more so than usual. As I head to Francie's desk, our on-site human resource manager, I hear someone say, "They're a group of Twitter trolls flooding the chat rooms and social media groups with misinformation."

My ears perk up.

"I think someone is trying to breach the firewall."

Seeing the engineering manager, I stop in my tracks. "This sounds like the hacker that has been hitting companies in Silicon Valley. We need to pull in Cameron Newhouse."

"I don't think that's necessary," he says as he blows me off. "That's just Derek. He overacts to everything."

"I'd rather be safe than sorry. This is how it started with Pineapple Technologies," I inform him.

"Well, you can call him and look like an idiot. I'm going to let my team manage this."

I'm stunned. How does he work for this company?

I quickly call Cameron, and he picks up at the second ring. "Yes, Quinn."

"Sorry to bother you, Cameron, but I'm here at SketchIt, and I walked into a bit of a firestorm. They've had their chat rooms and social media sites hit with false information. And then one of the engineers said someone is trying to get behind the firewall."

"Shit. I can be there in twenty minutes. This is how they started with Pineapple. Everyone was looking at how to deal with the misinformation and ignored that someone got behind the firewall."

"My thoughts exactly." I don't want to throw the engineering manager completely under the bus, but I need him to know what's going on. "Tom Hiddle believes the engineer who is talking about someone trying to get behind the firewall may be a Chicken Little. I haven't talked to Rob, I just called you."

"Good thinking. Tom Hiddle isn't the brightest guy. Excellent catch. I'll be there ASAP and will alert FBI Cybercrimes. Let Tom and Rob know I'm on my way."

"Will do."

When I disconnect the call, I see Tom talking to the CEO, Rob Paige. They're busy and don't seem to want to acknowledge my presence. "Rob, Tom, I just spoke with Cameron Newhouse, and he's on his way."

Rob looks at me and then at Tom. "Why is he on his way?" Rob asks.

"This is how things started with Pineapple Technologies. They flooded chat rooms and social media sites with false and negative information on the day they went public. It had everyone focused on that while someone went in behind the encryption and stole all their proprietary information and then posted it, destroying Pineapple. The company died within a week of going public."

"Is there someone behind the firewall?" Rob asks Tom, and he winces.

"I heard someone say there was someone trying to get behind the firewall," I tell him. "I thought we'd be better served with Cameron and his team's help. I reached out to Cameron, and he's reaching out to FBI Cybercrimes."

"That is completely unnecessary," Tom fumes. "Derek overreacts all the time."

"I'd rather we overreact than have no company," Rob declares. "When is Cameron due?"

I look at the time on my cell phone. "He'll be here in about ten minutes."

"Can you excuse us?" Rob says to me.

I nod and walk away. Their voices become raised, but I head out front to reception to wait for Cameron.

Two different rideshares pull up. Cameron jumps out of the first, and Parker launches out of the second, and both men rush inside. "What do you know?" Cameron asks.

"Tom Hiddle is upset you're coming, so prepare for some resistance. Rob is glad you're here." I watch Cameron and Parker exchange looks. "The chat rooms and social media sites are being hit heavily with a lot of misinformation."

"I want you to keep an eye on Tom today. It doesn't make sense that he's not alarmed by this," Cameron says.

"Will do."

Cameron and Parker march through reception and head to Rob's office.

I stop at Francie's desk and quietly give her the update.

"I don't trust Tom and haven't for a while. He hasn't been acting normal for a few weeks," she whispers.

"Anyone else seem a little off?"

"There is Michael Wang, but honestly, I think he's worried about his application for citizenship. He's a Chinese citizen applying for his naturalization."

"Let's keep an eye on him." I look around the large room to where most of the engineers are sitting in front of a huge bank of floor-to-ceiling monitors that span the wall. Three of the screens on the left are black and running all sorts of code that mean absolutely nothing to me. The remaining screens are the user boards and is what seems to hold everyone's attention. Parker is talking to the group regarding the false information, and Cameron is in deep discussions with Craig, while Tom stands close by, listening. As I watch, he looks up, giving me the evil eye.

I walk to the company kitchen to pour myself a cup of coffee. I text the SHN office receptionist on the way.

Me: Do you know how Parker and Cameron take their coffee? They've jumped right into an issue here, and I thought I'd make myself useful.

I wait for a few minutes.

Receptionist: According to Constance, Parker likes it with a lot of cream and two sugars.

As the bubbles rotate, I make Parker's coffee.

Receptionist: Emerson believes Cameron takes it with one cream and one artificial sweetener.

Me: Thank you!

After delivering their drinks to them, which they greatly appreciate, I wander back to Francie. Tom is no longer with Cameron and Craig. "Where's Tom?"

"It looks like he's being dressed down by Rob in his office," she says in a low voice.

"What about Michael Wang?"

"He seems oblivious to what's going on. Either he is a very cool cucumber, or he's not involved, but I'll keep watching."

Taking my place at my desk, I sit back and watch all the activity. Parker has the team broken up into smaller groups, and they are all attacking the hackers who are trying to access our data through the firewall.

Cameron is sitting with Craig, and their fingers are flying across their keyboards and they are working to thwart the hackers.

When Tom storms out of Rob's office and slams the door to his own, Francie stands and says, "I'm going to get a cup of coffee. Can I get you anything?" Before I can answer, under her breath, she adds, "I'm also going to talk to Rob's admin, Alyssa. She'll know all the details."

I nod. "I think I'm good for coffee."

As she leaves, Rob crosses the room toward me. "Quinn, thank you for calling in Cameron and Parker."

"No problem. I understand it's a little overwhelming and can feel slightly intrusive to have someone from the outside come in."

"This company is my everything. I've leveraged my parents' home and my savings, and my friends who work here have done the same, so we could get to this point. We can't afford to have what happened to Pineapple happen to us. Tom is newer and less invested. He doesn't understand."

"I'll just sit back and hang out," I assure him.

"Thanks again. It was a good catch."

I blush at the compliment as he awkwardly pats me on the shoulder. I get it. This is his life, and had I not made the call, he might have lost everything. But at this point, there's still no guarantee that the hackers haven't accessed enough information to destroy SketchIt.

Cameron's and Craig's fingers fly across the keyboards as they yell at the hackers, and it seems like a cyber sword fight.

"He's trying to insert malware," Cameron announces.

"I got the opening closed," Parker assures him.

"He's doing a run at the production files," one of the engineers exclaims.

"I moved them to a hidden folder," another engineer shouts.

I'm amazed at how well they're all working together, and to think, Tom was going to ignore this.

The receptionist calls me. "Yes?"

"There is a Cora Perry here out front. She's here to see the two men that you brought in."

"I'll be right up."

As I jump up, I glance over and see Tom watching everything from the window in his office, his arms crossed in front of him. Our eyes meet, and his lips purse and his stance becomes hard. Not giving his attitude another thought, I whisk myself to reception and find a woman with short curly blonde hair dressed in a navy blue pantsuit and flats. She sees me and smiles. "Hi, I'm Cora Perry with FBI Cybercrimes. I'm here to see Cameron Newhouse and Parker Carlyle."

I extend my hand. "Welcome to SketchIt. I work for SHN and called them in this morning when I heard the engineers refer to misinformation going out to the chat rooms and social media channels and another who was sure someone was trying to get behind the firewall." I turn and open my arms. "Follow me, and I'll take you to Cameron and Parker."

She smiles. "Thank you."

Cameron spots us as we walk in. "Parker, can you come and take over for a moment while I catch Cora up on what we know?"

"Sure, boss."

After they trade places, Cameron joins us. "Cora, welcome. Thanks to Quinn here, we may have prevented a full-on attack. Currently, we're just blocking their efforts. No counterattacks—yet."

"Great. I have Lisa in our lab ready to go. Are you ready to deploy the Trojan horse into their system?"

"I am." He claps his hands, and I can feel the excitement.

As they get to work, I see Tom pick up his car keys and walk toward the door. Grabbing my phone and purse, I follow him out the door.

He heads to the garage, and I flag down a taxi. A few minutes later, I see Tom behind a wheel of a white car as it rips out of the garage in a hurry. I jump in the taxi and yell, "Follow that white Chevy Cavalier."

The man has a thick accent. "No problem."

He steps on it, and we go flying through the streets of San Francisco. Tom starts by heading toward the Bay Bridge and then turns the opposite direction, working his way toward Golden Gate Park. The traffic is thick enough that even if he makes a light we miss, we catch up.

He stops at the early part of the Richmond district in the Avenues in front of a two-story apartment building. Gray with white trim, it's somewhat nondescript, and it faces another building with a grassy courtyard between. As he parks, I quickly throw my last sixty dollars at the driver and thank him before I carefully exit the car and watch where Tom goes.

I pick up my phone and dial Cameron.

"Hey. Where are you?" he says in greeting.

"When you deployed the counterattack to the mole, I saw Tom leave."

"Shit. We've gone into his computer and found some red flags. Where are you?"

"I followed him in a cab, and he's at 2nd and Lake in an apartment building. I'm just hanging around outside watching."

He murmurs something to someone in the background, and then a woman gets on the phone. "Quinn, this is Agent Perry. Where exactly are you?"

"I'm at a bus stop just off 2nd and Lake."

"I'm going to send a few people to you. Be careful. We don't know what you may have stepped into."

I hadn't thought of it like that, and all of a sudden, I feel exposed and vulnerable. Following Tom may have been a bad idea. I walk over to a busy bus stop and try to blend in with the group of riders as I watch the building.

Within five minutes, at least ten big black cars come racing up the street with lights flashing in their grills, blocking the street to all cross traffic in front of the apartment building where Tom went inside. The others waiting with me at the bus stop scatter like cockroaches do when the light comes on.

A tall man approaches me. "You must be Quinn Faraday."

"I am." Unsure what to do, I stand there awkwardly.

"My name is Agent Patrick James." He extends his hand for me to shake. "Do you know what apartment he went into?"

"Not completely, but he went in the second entry in the building on the left."

He pulls a radio from his hip and shares that information. Moments later, agents swarm the building and there is a ruckus before I see Tom with an agent on each side of him escorting him out.

As they lead him to a waiting car, he sees me across the street and yells, "You fucking cunt!"

"That's the best you've got?" I scream back before looking over at Agent James and shrugging. "Sorry, I couldn't help myself."

Holding back a smile, he says, "I was thinking the same thing. Glad it was you who said it and not me."

"We don't know if he did anything," I explain.

"Our team is combing through his computer. His departure during the cyberattack is suspicious, and some things aren't adding up. If nothing else, we will detain him and figure out why he's acting erratically."

He steps away, leaving me sitting on the bus stop bench, when all of a sudden Emerson and Dillon come rushing up.

"Quinn! Are you okay?"

I nod. "I didn't do much, other than see him leave and follow him in a taxi. He owes me though. I had to give the driver my last sixty dollars."

Dillon drops his head back and laughs hard. "This could be big. They're not sure about his involvement from Cameron's perspective, but between him, Parker, and the Cybercrimes team, they'll get it figured out."

Agent James returns to me. "Quinn, we're going through his apartment. We'll need a statement from you. Can you meet us downtown—" He looks at his watch. "—say three o'clock?"

I nod.

"We'll make sure she has representation with her," Dillon informs him.

"That's fine, but we're looking for a statement from her and nothing more. She isn't under investigation," Agent James assures him.

"We understand," Emerson says. "We'll get her there at three."

QUINN

Emerson and Dillon walk me to their car. As soon as we're moving, Emerson is on the phone, and it's piped through the car's speaker. "Hey, girlfriend." I recognize the voice as Cynthia's.

"Hey. Who was the lawyer you used with the FBI?"

"Marci Peterson. Do you need her?"

"Quinn may have found the mole, and the FBI wants to meet with her. Dillon and I agree that having a lawyer represent her would be smart."

"Agreed." Then she rattles off a phone number.

"Thanks."

"Good luck. Quinn, she's awesome, and you'll be in good hands."

"Thank you," I yell from the back seat of the car.

Emerson disconnects the call and dials Marci. "Hello, this is Emerson Winthrop Healy. I'm calling for Marci Peterson."

"I'm sorry she's with a client right now," the receptionist informs her.

"I understand. Can you please let her know that Quinn Faraday, from SHN, is meeting with FBI Cybercrimes today at three? This is in regard to the case she worked on with Pineapple Technologies."

"Can you hold a moment?"

"Of course."

"This is Marci Peterson," a woman says through the car's speaker.

"Hi, Marci, this is Emerson Healy. My husband, Dillon, and Quinn Faraday are in the car with me."

"Hello," she says cautiously.

"We work with SHN, and today Quinn went to a client site and discovered our hackers had infiltrated the client. She called in reinforcements, and when things got hairy, she noticed the engineering manager leave and followed him. The FBI Cybercrimes has apprehended the engineering manager, and the FBI has requested a meeting today at three, and while we don't suspect that anything will go awry, we do think it's smart for both Quinn and SHN that we have representation."

"Quinn, who are you meeting with?" Marci asks.

"I was asked by Agent James. I can't be sure, but I think he may work with Cora Perry."

"Can you meet me here at my offices in about an hour?"

I look at Emerson, and she nods. "I'll see you there." I glance between Dillon and Emerson. "Do you know where it is?"

"I do," Dillon volunteers.

"See you then, Quinn," Marci says before disconnecting.

"We should probably grab you at least a sandwich before you meet with her," Emerson suggests.

"I'll be fine," I assure her.

"Nonsense. I have a feeling you'll have a big afternoon. I know you mentioned giving the cab driver your last sixty dollars, so I'll buy lunch. It's the company's fault you are stuck paying for lunch," Emerson says.

"Thanks." Then I realize something. "Oh, I left my laptop back at SketchIt. Crap. I may need it later for my second job."

"We'll get someone to messenger it to us at Marci's. Not a problem," Emerson interjects.

"What's this about a second job?" Dillon asks.

"We'll talk about it later," Emerson admonishes him.

A few moments later, we pull in front of a building that has valet parking. Only in San Francisco is parking so sacred that you find business buildings with valet parking.

We order sandwiches at the little deli, and as we huddle together at our table to eat, they ask me to recount what happened this morning. This definitely was not how I expected my day to unfold when I got out of bed. Dillon is excited that we may have caught the mole.

After lunch, they walk me up to Marci's office and agree to wait for me.

As soon as Marci walks out to reception, I like her already. She's barefoot and explains to me that she wore a cute but bad-for-walking pair of shoes today and had to run around the federal courthouse all morning, so her feet are killing her. "I know it isn't professional, but I promise I'll have shoes on before our meeting at three."

"Don't worry about me. I'd go barefoot myself if you'd let me."

She smiles at me, and I know we'll be fast friends.

We walk back to a large conference room, and she points to the closest end of the long table.

"Tell me why the FBI has asked to meet with you?"

I walk her through how it started when I walked in at SketchIt.

She asks several probative questions and drills down. Judging from my first impression of her, she came off as a little bit of an airhead, but I can tell by her questions, not much gets past her.

"What could the FBI find against you?"

"Do you represent me or SHN?"

"Right now, I'm representing you."

"Then you should know that I have a second job."

"That happens in San Francisco," she assures me.

"It's doing phone sex."

"That's legal. What's your concern? Are their minors involved? Blackmail?"

"Oh God no! It's just the only thing they can hold against me, and SHN could terminate me for it if it were to become public."

"If you're working for a legitimate business, you should be fine as far as the FBI is concerned, but I don't know about SHN."

"That's what I'm afraid of."

"Well, let's get through today and see what they want."

We agree to meet in reception after hitting the restroom and getting our things together. Of course, I have nothing to get together, but I have a feeling it's going to be a long afternoon.

When I walk into reception, Emerson is waiting for me with my computer bag. "Oh, thank you. You didn't have to wait with my computer."

"You're welcome, and of course I did. I'll go with you to the FBI, as long as you're okay with that. This is a big deal."

"You're very sweet. I'm starting to get nervous, and while Marci's great, I don't know her as well as I know you."

She pulls me into a hug. "You're going to do great. You're a hero. You didn't do anything wrong; we just want to make sure they don't turn anything back on you or SHN."

"I know —"

Marci walks in, cutting me off. "Are we ready?"

I nod. "This is Emerson Healy with SHN. She's my boss."

"It's great to see you again," Marci gushes. "Let's get over to see our G-men."

A car is waiting for us when we walk out, and it drives us to the FBI building. I had no idea it was here. I walk past this building often when I walk to work in the spring, when the weather is the best. It's a plain building in the middle of the financial district, but the more you look at it, the more it seems to stand out from its neighbors—no doorman, no awnings, very plain.

We walk in and find a large woman sitting at the desk out front with two armed guards standing behind her. Marci announces us, and the woman requests our driver's licenses and sends us to a screening area outside the elevator banks before directing us to the fourth floor.

Once we are in the elevator heading to the appropriate floor, I finally find my voice. "Holy cow, this place is buttoned up tight."

"It's not too bad. The federal courthouse is worse, but hopefully this Tom guy will fold like a bad hand of poker and you'll never have to deal with testifying," Marci commiserates.

"Agreed," Emerson says.

We're shown to a nondescript conference room, and Emerson is led to a waiting area. Agent James arrives with an entourage of four other agents, so I'm really glad to have Marci sitting with me.

They walk me through my statement multiple times. Asking the same questions over and over in different ways. Agent James ends our interview with a warning, "Miss Faraday, please be aware of your surroundings." He hands me his card with his personal cell phone number written on it. "You can call me day or night if you need anything."

I'm exhausted when they finally wrap up.

We walk out and find Emerson still waiting. What kind of boss would do this? She's amazing.

Riding the elevator downstairs, Marci exclaims, "I think someone has a crush on our Miss Faraday." She grins widely.

"What?" I say.

"Agent James gave you his personal cell phone number, and you can call him anytime. He must have said that a few times. I've never seen an FBI agent offer anything like that."

"And here you were just yesterday saying that all the good ones are taken," Emerson muses.

"You both are something else. It was completely harmless. He isn't interested in me," I insist.

We walk out to a waiting car, which drops me at my building first.

It ended up being almost a twenty-hour day, and I'm beyond exhausted. I need to get some sleep. I'm letting Cameron and the FBI Cybercrimes team take care of what happened today. I set my alarm for seven—only a few short hours away. My head hits the pillow, and it's like I've hit my second wind. I'm so tired I can't sleep. This is so typical of me. I've been running so hard today that I can't calm my mind enough to find sleep.

My thoughts become like a pinball stuck between bumpers back and forth faster and faster. Lying in the dark, I stare at the ceiling as the time clicks by, and I can't sleep. I think about what happened today and the rush of getting the upper hand against the mole, but the fear also creeps up the back of my throat.

I'm still worried that I'm going to lose my job. The FBI will investigate me and may let my secret out. Agent James will no longer be interested. That'd be a black eye on his future. Then there's William. Every time I glanced at him when I was in the office, he seemed to be watching me. I know he's curious about my second job, and I'll only be able to put him off for so long. Once he gets tired of that, I'm sure he'll be ready to tell Mason. Wouldn't that be just perfect? Mason would have another reason to hate my guts.

I can just see the next B-school class reunion. He'll be celebrated as the most successful of our class, and I bet he'll tell everyone that after working for a VC that went belly up, I decided to become a sex worker. The guys from business school will just love that. They're big enough assholes, they'll all try to start sleazy relationships with me. They always thought the girls didn't belong in business but instead on their backs with their legs spread wide. Okay, I'm overgeneralizing. Maybe one or two did. But in a perverse way, they'd love to see something like that from any of our former classmates. It's good, juicy gossip. I'd have no one to blame but myself.

I'm not sure when I finally fell asleep, but it eventually happened. When my alarm sounds, I lean over and shut it off. Today is going to suck for sure.

I pull the covers back and realize it's cold in my apartment. My heat is electric, and I can't afford for it to run at night. It's too damn expensive. I swear I can see my breath. The cold air usually jolts me awake, but this morning it makes me want to curl up under my comforter and hide.

I look at my phone and see several texts have come in this morning.

Emerson: Excellent work yesterday. Take your time coming in.

Her text makes me feel all warm and fuzzy. I adore her!

Me: Thanks. I shouldn't be too late.

CeCe: Awesome job! Lunch on me next week! We're going to celebrate.

I've gotten to know CeCe through Emerson, and she's so kind. I can't wait to go out with her.

Me: Sounds like fun! Count me in.

Dillon: Truly well done! You figured out the hackers were at a client site, which allowed us to launch countersurveillance. Then you chased down the engineering manager and probable spy so they wouldn't get away. You were amazing. Thank you!

Dillon oversees our finances, and the hackers seems to have given him the most heartache. He wants them to go away more than anyone else.

Me: Thank you.

Greer: I think I can set up an interview with the Silicon Valley Business Journal. Any interest?

That would be a mess. Today I'm a hero, and next week I'm dragging them through the mud because somehow someone figures out I have a second job. No thanks.

Me: Thanks for the offer of stardom, but I'll probably pass. Cameron would be great for that though.

Greer: I can get Cameron in the papers anytime. I want you. I'm not giving up that easily.

Cynthia: You rock! Well done!

I love Cynthia. She's always been so kind to me.

Me: You rock, too! Lunch today?

Cynthia: I'm in. My treat!

● ● ●

68

That's the best news of all.

Christopher: Amazing job. So glad you're on our team.

I'm so glad you said that, Christopher. I hope you feel the same when our peer, William, tells you my secret.

Me: Thank you.

William: Well done, kitten. I can think of all sorts of ways we can celebrate.

I can't help but think of his waterboard abs and where the happy trail leads. My traitorous body wants to enjoy all sorts of debauchery with him. While tempting, that would only make the mess I've created worse.

Me: Dream on.

William: Trust me, since hearing your voice mail, I've been dreaming. When will you understand that you've transfixed me?

Me: I'm a lost cause. Move on to your next conquest. Jennifer?

William: I only have eyes for you. See you when you get in.

I'm not going to respond to that, but it does make my heart beat faster. Eyes for only me? I need to pay attention to reality. He's the type that sleeps with any woman with a pulse. Sleeping with him—if you can call it that— will only get me into more trouble.

Mason: You're a valuable member of our team.

Mason's text makes me laugh out loud. Could it be any more difficult for him to say something complementary?

Me: Thanks, Mason. That must have been really hard to say.

Zing!

Mason: It wasn't hard to say at all. I really mean it.

Me: Then, thank you.

chapter

nine

WILLIAM

The change in the will affects the one thing I've always been hesitant to talk about with my dad. We never had a close relationship, and he once told me that he was putting everything in a trust, and his wish was to give the bulk of it to my mother's favorite charities. My parents had a great relationship, and I've not seen many people have that. They truly complemented one another. My dad was bookish and an engineering nerd; my mother was outgoing and beloved by all. I see that in some of my coworkers and their partners, but so many of my friends settled when they married and are unhappy. I don't want that.

As I drive into the office today, I think about who I might know that I could take with me to Philadelphia.

Amanda is a fun lay. We met in business school in Philly, and we've often played with one another. It's been a while since we've talked. We always had a decent friends-with-benefits kind of relationship. She's usually up for whatever floats someone's boat—as long as everyone is enjoying themselves and providing there aren't minors or animals involved. I love her easygoing attitude. I consider asking her, but then I realize she probably wouldn't go along with a ruse without some sort of percentage in the end. No. She won't work.

I park in the garage in our building, but it's a little earlier than normal, so rather than make a coffee in our office kitchen, I walk across the street and hit Starbucks. As I stand in line, I think about Jody. We went out a few weeks ago. She's adventurous in the sack, but unfortunately, we don't have much in common, and if I'm honest with myself, if she were to light up a joint in my dad's house, that would be the end of it all, and that's her style. She's definitely a free spirit, which can be fun when you're naked, but I like a lot more structure in my personal life. No. She won't work.

As I walk back to the office, I think about Cheryl. She is tall, blonde, and has a knockout figure, courtesy of a plastic surgeon. I'm pretty sure she hates my guts because she wanted more than I was willing to give. She's looking for a husband, and this might give her the wrong idea. Plus, I'm fairly certain she'd throw me under a bus before helping me out. No. She won't work.

While riding up in the elevator, it hits me. Suzanne might work. She's not really into getting serious. She's easygoing, professional, and good-looking. I think she'll work out for what I need. I'm feeling extra tall now that I have this all figured out. It'll be a week of good sex, and she likes a bit of kink, which always makes life interesting. I walk into my office, fire up my computer, and give her a call. She answers after the third ring.

"Hey, Suz. What's up?" I can't just jump into this. I need to work my way into my situation so I can make sure she'll be on board with what I need and not think I'll propose when all of this is over.

"What a surprise. I haven't heard from you in a while. In fact, it's been at least eight months."

"I don't think it's been that long," I tease.

"No, I'm pretty sure because that's when I got serious with my boyfriend."

My stomach drops. This isn't going to be as easy as I thought. "How serious are you with this boyfriend?"

"Well, he's no longer my boyfriend. He's my fiancée, and I'm getting married in a few weeks."

"Married? I guess getting away for a week would be out of the question."

"Without a doubt."

"Congratulations."

"Thanks."

We disconnect the call, and I stare at the ceiling. No. She won't work.

Then it hits me—Vivian. There's an idea. She's smokin' hot and wouldn't ask too many questions. I give her a call.

"William," she purrs when she answers the phone.

"Hey, beautiful. How are you?"

"I'm very good. How about you?"

"Not bad. You up for drinks tonight and maybe whatever?"

I hear her deep, throaty laugh, and usually that gets me rock hard, but instead, I think my testicles ascend into my abdomen. "You lookin' for a taste?"

"I don't know. What do you think?"

"I'd love to meet with you, but I have a date tonight. Can we try another night?"

Feeling relieved, I realize that I really don't want to see her, and I don't want a taste of her, but at this point it would be rude to tell her outright, so instead, I say, "Sure. Another night. I'll call you."

"I can't wait," she breathes into the phone.

Looking up across the office, I see her, and instantly I know that's who I really want to come home with me. Quinn is beautiful by any standards, and she has such an easy way about her. The hard part will be convincing her.

I use the interoffice messaging and send her a note.

Me: You available for lunch today?

She's quick to respond.

Quinn: Sorry. I have plans.

Me: Drinks after work?

Quinn: Sorry. I have plans.

Me: Coffee today. You can figure out how to make it work. This involves that second job of yours.

Quinn: I'll meet you at the Starbucks on Market and 2nd.

That's several blocks away. She must not want to have the conversation where anyone in the office can overhear. That's fine. I don't want anyone to know I have to bring someone home for the reading of my father's will.

Me: See you then. Don't be late.

The morning is slow going, but it gives me time to go through more women on my mental checklist, and it only solidifies my desire to bring Quinn home with me.

Market Street divides the city in half. There's something insanely strange about how people feel they are more special depending on what side of Market they live or work on. The tech hub of San Francisco for start-ups is in SOMA, which is the South of Market neighborhood. Our offices overlook Oracle Park where the Giant's play baseball, and it's a great place, but Market Street divides the city, and where Quinn has suggested we meet is right on the edge of Union Square, and there are a lot of tourists.

I grab a burger from a favorite spot close by and then walk over to Starbucks and secure a table in the front corner. I order coffee for me, and I've seen her drink tea, so I order her a tea with the tea bag out so she can exchange it if she prefers something else.

When she arrives, I can see my request to meet has pissed her off. Either that or somebody outside of our meeting has upset her.

She sits down and softens slightly when she sees the hot water and a package of Earl Grey tea.

"I didn't have them put the tea bag in, so you can exchange it for another flavor if you prefer," I offer.

"No, this is surprisingly perfect."

I smile at getting it right. A good start for my request.

She takes a cautious sip and looks at me. "What do you want?"

"I need a favor."

She looks like she's going to throw a punch, so I carefully explain. "My father was killed in a helicopter crash in Tanzania a few weeks ago. My mother passed away when I was young, and my stepmonster is trying to take my dad's money. I really couldn't care less about the money, and originally it was supposed to go into a trust, but now it seems that my stepmonster was successful in getting my dad to change his will. Instead of his estate going to my mom's favorite charities, it will go to her and me—but only if I'm married. If I'm not married, it will revert to her and her two sons, who I affectionately refer to as Dumb and Stupid."

She watches me carefully. "What do you want from me? Have phone sex with Dumb and Stupid?"

The thought alone makes me worried about exposing her to the two assholes. "No. Not at all. I need someone to join me in Philadelphia next week and play my fiancée. I'm not expecting anything intimate; I just need this help. Please do this for me?"

"And if I don't, are you going to tell the partners about my second job?"

"No, I would never tell the partners regardless of whether or not you join me. I enjoy spending time with you. It would be a small vacation from the office and a break. And I'll pay you."

"But you said you needed to be married to get the money."

"That's true, but they don't know that my dad's lawyer already told me the condition of the will, and if you're with me, it may get them to relax before they spend all my dad's money."

She sizes me up. "When are you thinking of going?"

"I was planning on leaving Monday after work and be in Philly through at least Friday, possibly the weekend."

"What are your plans to do with the money?"

"My mother was a big advocate of CASA. It's a—"

"I know it, Court Appointed Special Advocates for children."

"Exactly. I think the bulk would go there but also to a few of her women's charities that were important to her. I'm not rich, Quinn, but I'm working on making my own money. Dumb and Stupid would buy cars and houses. I don't want my family money to go to them."

"I'll check with Emerson and make sure I can have time off." She takes another sip of her tea before clearly telling me, "There'll be no funny business. I may flirt, but nothing more."

I'm over the moon excited she's going to join me. This will go a long way to convincing the thieves that my dad's money won't be easy to get to. We throw our empty cups into the recycling and start to walk back to the office.

"I suppose we should talk about a few things once I get approval from Emerson to go."

The idea of spending more time with Quinn makes my heart race. Maybe I'll be able to convince her she wants more from me. Because I know I want that sultry voice on my voice mail to do all kinds of naughty things to me.

"Whatever you need. I'm happy to take you out to dinner, drinks… whatever."

"Tell me about your mom and dad."

Taking a deep breath, I consider about all the things I want to say. "My mom died when I was young. I hate to admit it, but my memories of her are beginning to blur. She made me so happy though. I know they wanted more kids, but it wasn't in the cards for them, so she put all her energy into me. She wasn't one of those helicopter parents, but she encouraged me to be a better human being and was so supportive. God, she was funny too. Not only could she tell some great G-rated jokes, but she could laugh at herself if she stumbled or did something silly. What I remember most prominently about my mom is that no matter where we went, I knew I was the center of her universe, but she could make a friend with a complete stranger. People just opened up to her and told her their life story. She just had that kind of personality that drew people to her."

"She sounds like a wonderful woman."

"She was. I miss her every day."

"Tell me about your dad."

"He was different before my mom died. He worshiped her. He did so many things for her. He brought her flowers for no reason. We'd always make a big production of going shopping at Marshall Fields before any holiday, and we'd buy her something she didn't need. There was so much laughter in our house, and looking back, they must have really heated up the sheets because I can remember the looks they'd give one another that I didn't understand at the time. He was devastated when she died. I was young, and he didn't know what to do with me. I remember going to her funeral, and my dad left in the middle without me. He just went home and left me behind. My aunt told me he wanted to cry in private, but I don't know for sure. I don't remember how I got home that day, but from that moment on, we were more roommates than father and son. It was like the day she died, the light went off inside him. He did what he needed to, but we had a housekeeper who made sure I got fed and to and from school. Beyond that, I was on my own."

"He sounds like he was heartbroken without your mom."

"He was. My parents' relationship is something I don't think everyone finds. I think some of the people we work with have it, but I look at friends from B-school, and I think they settled and are unhappy. I don't want that."

"How did your stepmonster and father meet?"

"I'm not exactly sure. I was away at camp when I was twelve, my dad called me and told me that he'd met and married Lillian. It was like he'd bought a car or a watch. There was nothing endearing about how he described their relationship. After camp was over, I went home for Christmas and met her and her two sons. My dad was putting them through an expensive prep school, and they were assholes, so that was the last holiday I spent with them. I'd come home now and again. I went to B-school close to home in Philly, and my dad and I would try to meet up every few months for dinner. Lillian would rarely come. When she was around, dinner conversation was too awkward. I hadn't talked to him in a few months, but usually, he'd send me an email telling me he was traveling or going out of town, so this trip to Tanzania was a surprise."

When she reaches out and touches my arm, I feel an electric charge that sends jolts of electricity to my groin. "I'm very sorry about your dad. I'll talk to Emerson and let you know."

We've arrived at the office. "Thanks. I'd appreciate it."

We part ways, her to her cubicle and me to my desk. I watch as she puts her purse down and hangs her coat. The message light is blinking on my phone, so I pick up my messages and begin to return calls. Before long, the interoffice messaging system alerts me of a new message.

Quinn: I can take next week off.

Me: Thank you. Did you want to talk more tonight?

Quinn: Since I'll be missing five days of my second job, I need to get some work done. How about we talk over the weekend and you can tell me what I should pack, and we can talk on the plane.

Me: Breakfast on Saturday morning? We can hit the Embarcadero Farmers Market and hang out a bit?

Quinn: That may work. Thank you for asking me to join you.

Me: I should be thanking you. Wait until you meet Dumb and Stupid. You'll understand why they have those nicknames.

chapter

ten

QUINN

CeCe picks up on the first ring. "Hey, are we still on for lunch today?"

"I'm still planning on it. Do you want to meet over at the Salad Bar off of Second?"

"That sounds perfect to me. I can't wait. Does noon or twelve thirty work better?" I ask.

"Let's go for noon or maybe a few minutes before. That way we can get our lunches and a table without spending most of our time in line and being stuck scarfing our lunch standing."

"Great idea. See you then."

My morning clicks by quickly. I can't believe how much work I have on my plate. We've got three new companies we've recently invested in and are coming on board. It's my job to help line things up and get prepared for not only an operations team but getting communications between the various departments all in line with what we typically like to see with companies working under the SHN umbrella. We aren't a company that typically writes a check and walks away. If we are investing millions, which we typically are, then we want to be involved.

Since I know I can easily get absorbed in my work and lose track of time, I set an alarm on my phone. I have a terrible habit of getting so involved in my work that, unless I have a reminder, I'll look up at my clock and find that it's three o'clock in the afternoon, or even worse, the person I'm meeting for lunch calls and asks if I'm coming. I really want to sit down with CeCe today. I have some questions for her that maybe as an advisor to SHN she might be willing to answer.

When I walk into the Salad Bar, I don't see CeCe, so I take a seat just inside the door and start scrolling through my personal emails and social media, seeing all kinds of fun things that my friends are doing in other parts of the country. Why am I here in San Francisco? There are no men of any value to meet, the cost of living is off the page, and I'm going into significant debt living here. It's overwhelming. I adore my friends and the lifestyle that San Francisco provides, but beyond that, it seems to be a losing proposition, and I can't determine whether or not it's a good idea to be here.

"Hey, there she is."

Glancing up, I spot CeCe as she approaches. She wraps her arms around me in a tight hug. I can't believe that she has adopted me as a friend. She's gorgeous, funny, beautiful, wealthy, and not only is she a tabloid darling, but she owns and runs a fabulous independent cosmetics company that her mom founded. There are people who would give their right arm to be her friend.

I grew up in Florida. My dad had a great job, and my mother was head of the PTO and involved in a thousand volunteer activities. My childhood was Norman Rockwell normal, and CeCe's from an old monied family and listed on *Forbes* list of billionaires, and we learned recently she is dating a real prince—the royal kind. I bring nothing to our relationship, and obviously that is more my issue than hers because she doesn't hesitate to invite me to things and spend time with me.

"You look fabulous today," she informs me. I'm in all black—my go-to color. It makes my pale skin and blonde hair pop.

"So do you. I love that outfit." She stands back, and she shows it off to me. She's put together unbelievably well in a pair of navy palazzo pants, a beautiful white and navy floral print blouse, and a unique cut navy blazer over it and a lot of chunky silver jewelry. She looks outstanding as usual. "Where did you find that outfit?"

"It was one of the designers I worked with at fashion week last spring, and she made it for me."

"You have such gorgeous clothes. I just want your hand-me-downs."

She laughs. "I usually give them to the abused women shelter that we work with at Metro Composition, but if you really wanted this, I'm sure we can get this for you."

"No, I'm just teasing. It's great all the work you do with such an outstanding group, and they need the clothes more than I do."

"Yes, it's all about getting these women back to work and helping them gain some self-confidence, which hopefully means they don't find themselves in the cycle of abuse anymore."

"Exactly, which is why they need your hand-me-downs more than I do. Let's get some salads before the lunch line becomes too long."

Feeling the pressure of eating healthy because I'm with a beautiful, perfect-figured goddess, I order something incredibly healthy with dressing on the side. This is not my typical MO. My preference is typically burgers, fries, a milkshake, and a Diet Coke. When we sit down at our table, I look at her salad and see it's my kind of salad—creamy dressing, sunflower seeds, cheese, eggs, croutons, and a tiny bit of lettuce. "That looks amazing."

"Lettuce is for rabbits. I like all the toppings with salad dressing, so I like to come here."

I shake my head and chuckle. "You're a woman after my own heart. Next time let's do burgers and fries."

"Sounds perfect."

Between bites, I ask, "Tell me a little bit about what's going on with you. I haven't seen you since the wedding in Las Vegas."

"Oh, you know a little bit of this, a little bit of that. We're preparing for the fall Fashion Week. How are things at SHN?"

"I think we're good. We have several companies going public. We're seeing some growth in Christopher's area in biotech companies, which is new and interesting. William has some great prospects with a big financial company that he'll probably wrap up in the next few days."

"Why didn't you want to be a partner at SHN?"

"I did. I was hoping to be on the partner track, but I've come to realize they aren't ever going to offer me a partnership. When Perkins Klein went under, I wasn't working and needed a job, so I took what I could find."

"Rumor has it, you're thinking of jumping ship." She watches me closely, and I'm sure she'll call me on it if I lie.

"Emerson told you. I'm kicking myself for calling Jeannine."

"Don't kick yourself. You should have been offered a partnership. Sometimes it's good to rattle their cages. You're an asset to SHN, and it's good for them to realize that."

"CeCe, I know why I wasn't offered partnership. It's because of my past with Mason."

If I didn't know CeCe well, I might have missed the look of surprise on her face. "What past with Mason?"

"We were pretty serious in business school. I think I was his first girlfriend. You know how shy he is. But it didn't end well."

"What happened?"

"It wasn't fireworks and drama. He was more focused on money, and a relationship was not even in the top five of his priorities. We got along great, but he wasn't really around much. We'd make plans for a date, and he'd choose not to show up. The first time I just forgave him. The second, I blew up, and the third time, I broke it off. He was in love with making money and not me. I think I was more than fair to give up after three strikes. My mother would say, 'Shame on him the first time it happened. The second time, shame on me. The third time, what the heck?'"

She giggles. I totally get it. He can be hyper-focused."

"That's a great description. But what's the deal with him and Annabelle?"

"Good question. I think we all wonder what's going on with them. He seems rather smitten with her and ignores all of his friends who have been subtle and not so subtle with their warnings about her." CeCe looks around to be sure no one is listening. "For me, I can't quite see the logic in dating her. She seems a little too eager, a little too possessive, a little too driven by him and his wants, and she's very dependent upon him. In the past, he always seemed to prefer an independent woman like you."

"Well, she's kind of a unique creature. I'm totally gossiping when I say I thought she was pretty furious in Las Vegas."

CeCe scoffs. "Yeah, I saw that she was not happy to watch Christopher and Bella get married. Mason and Annabelle hooked up about the time Emerson and Dillon got together. So she's watched his friends couple and get married, and when Christopher and Bella happened very quickly, she went over the edge. She's been vying for a ring and marriage since before they met."

"I know this is terrible gossip," I tell her, "but why is he with her? She must be able to suck a golf ball through a garden hose. I can't help but think she's truly in it for just the money."

"I think that's what a lot of us worry about. Mason and I are great friends, and we talk often. But boy, when things went sideways before the wedding with Bella's business partner and they were held hostage at the office, there I was terrified for him, and Annabelle was nowhere to be seen."

"I know! Isn't that terrible? We were talking about that in the office." I take a deep pull of my Diet Coke.

"Why didn't I know you dated Mason?"

"Well, as far as I can tell, it's not a secret, or at least I didn't think it was. Maybe it is, and he'll be mad at me for sharing that. I believe that's why he put his foot down about me becoming a partner. He's been pretty mad at me for breaking it off with him. He's like an elephant, and he never forgets."

"Why would he be mad at you if he wasn't showing up for dates?"

"Exactly. Why get all worked up over something when he was so focused on something else? He wasn't thinking about our relationship, and I'm not saying that I needed to be front and center all the time, every time, but when you make plans and you don't show up, you're an ass, and I didn't need to put up with that."

"No girl needs to put up with that," she sympathizes.

I need to change the subject. "Tell me more about this prince of yours."

She smiles and becomes a little bashful. "I met him at Fashion Week almost a year ago. He seems very smitten and attentive. But he's not perfect. He's never really worked. His brother is king of their country and has like four kids, so he's number five in line of succession. He doesn't ever foresee himself being king. Instead, his goal is to have a great time. I think he seems a little lost and gravitates to me because I'm not all about what he can do for me. But he doesn't quite understand what having commitments and a job actually means. He'll say, 'Hey, let's go to the Caribbean this week,' and I can't because I have to work or I have a fundraiser, or I just want to stay home and put my feet up after working a long day."

"Oh, the tragedy of being rich." I fan myself as if I'm hot.

"He's spoiled and rich," she reminds me.

"I'll never dispute that. You're amazingly grounded. You have a great outlook on life, and I feel grateful that you're my friend."

She reaches across the table and touches my arm. "And I feel the same way—we *are* friends."

"That means a lot to me. Thank you."

"Promise me that you are not going to leave SHN quite yet."

I debate telling her about my second job and the fact that William knows and could tell the other partners and derail me completely. I'd love to share with her that I'm only looking for a job because I'm afraid that they're going to fire me. Instead, I give her the big-picture answer. "I have a second job. I can barely make ends meet, and the problem with that becomes how much I love this city and how much I love my friends, but if I can't afford to work here and live here, then I shouldn't be here."

"Oh, honey, it's got to get better."

"You've heard the stories about my dad's illness and my school loans. It was hard for my mom, and she left. Honestly, it's not just the money that I owe, it's just I live in a fucking tiny little apartment just so that I can live alone. I'm thirty-one years old, and I don't want a roommate that I don't sleep with. My heat is electric, and I can't even afford to run it for fear that I can't pay the electric bill." I'm whining, and I need to keep my problems to myself—even if CeCe is a good friend.

She leans in and gives me a big hug. "I can't say I truly understand, but I swear, just be patient. Emerson is doing everything she can to help you."

"CeCe, it's not her job to help me change it, and this is not a pity party for me. I just want you to know why I'm looking."

"I know they'd never tell you you can't have a second job, but I also know that you're vital to the success at SHN. Trust in Emerson."

"I do. I worry Mason will use my having a second job against me because he still hates me."

"Quite frankly, he needs to get over that hate because everybody else adores you."

"Well, you're my friend and, apparently, the president of my personal fan club, so I appreciate you more than you'll ever know."

We spend the rest of lunch talking about her prince and where she's challenged by him and what she loves about him. Apparently, he's a dynamo between the sheets, and so I'm happy for her.

When it comes time to go back to work, I'm reminded that her life, even with all the money she has, isn't easy. She faces problems on a bigger scale. Someone takes our photograph during lunch, and two men—handsome of course—stop her on the way out and hand her their cards. She's always gracious when they ask her out. It's a constant battle for her.

WILLIAM

Taking my place in the back of the Cadillac Escalade, I reach for my phone.

Me: We're leaving my place and should be at your apartment in ten minutes.

I'm nervous. This is a part of my life that I don't share with many. Most people look at me and think I was born with a silver spoon in my mouth and don't have anything to worry about in life, but just because I have money to pay for things doesn't mean I don't have significant challenges in other parts of my life. There is a reason I live almost three thousand miles away from my family.

As we pull up in front of her building, I see her standing on the sidewalk. She takes my breath away, and I suddenly find my palms sweating. I'm not sure if it alarms me more that Quinn does this to me, or just how much could be riding on this long week ahead.

I jump out to let her get in. As she moves across the back seat, the driver places her bag in the back. "I hope I packed enough clothes. You didn't tell me what to expect."

"You'll be fine. If we need something else, there are stores in Philly, and I'm happy to pay for it. You're doing me a favor, after all."

She looks at me carefully, and I know she can see into my soul. "I guess we're ready then. What time does our flight take off?"

"As soon as we get settled."

She looks confused, but I've purposely chosen to withhold the information on our flight. Gerald, our driver, maneuvers us out of the city and down the 101 to the private plane terminal at SFO. "What airlines are we taking?"

"Bettencourt Air."

"Your family has their own airlines? I've never heard of Bettencourt Air."

"It's my dad's plane or, really, his company's plane."

"That's why you said that we'd be flying once we got settled."

I nod. "Because of the accident, the board wants me to fly back in their company plane."

Gerald navigates through city traffic before getting on the interstate. We both watch through our windows, anxious for our week together. I hear her ask herself, "What have I gotten myself into?"

"It'll be an interesting week. My stepmonster is the quintessential Disney evil stepmother, and she even has two sons—twins. The older one is Dumb. The younger one is Stupid."

Her nervousness is quickly replaced by slivers of mirth. Her laughter is music to my ears. "I think we're in a lot of trouble then. Make sure you tell me their real names, so I don't refer to them by their nicknames to their face."

"I like how you think, and you're probably correct. They are Brett and Jason, and they're just not the smartest guys, but they've never had to be. I guess by general standards, they're considered good looking, but I don't think you'd ever meet them outside of a gym or spending their time and my dad's money on looking good, but they want to take over my dad's business, and they just don't have the know-how."

"Do you plan on taking over your dad's business?"

"Oh, hell no. It's a publicly traded company; it's not anything the family would get any choice over. I'd imagine when my dad's will is read, they're hoping to take his singular board seat and make it into three seats and become a voting bloc for the board." I run my hands through my hair. "My stepsiblings shouldn't even be in the mix of all of this fight. My dad's lawyer shared his weird requirement, so I'm really grateful that you are doing this for me."

"Happy to help."

As we pull up to the private plane terminal, Gerald stops the car out front and rushes to open the side door. "I'll put the luggage in the plane, sir."

"Thank you, Gerald. We appreciate your help."

Looking nervous, Quinn rubs her hands together. This is a lot to take in. We make our way through the terminal and do the required check-in. The pilots have filed the flight plan, but we must be verified.

Standing at the door is Marjorie, the flight attendant. She started working for my dad before my mother died. She opens her arms and greets me. "William. So wonderful to see you." She hugs me so tight I can hardly breathe. "Don't you just look like your father more and more every day." Her voice breaks, and I can hear the hurt and tears close to the surface. I've often thought she was a little too attached to my dad.

"Marjorie, you look more and more beautiful every time I see you."

She blushes. "Oh, you have your father's charm too."

"Well, if only that were half true." My dad was an introvert, but with Marjorie, she spoiled him, and he flirted awkwardly.

"I'm very sorry for your loss, William. I know this can't be easy."

"No, it was a little surprising. I'm sure you know we haven't had the best relationship in a while."

"He loved you so much. He talked about you nonstop. I hear you're making your own money here in San Francisco."

"Thank you. Let me introduce you to my fiancée, Quinn Faraday." I turn to her. "Quinn, this is Marjorie Williams. She has worked really closely with my dad for many years."

"Very nice to meet you," Quinn says.

Marjorie opens her arms for a hug, and Quinn surprisingly steps in. "It's great to meet you too, Quinn. These Bettencourt men are quite the handful, so I know you're pretty busy keeping him out of trouble."

Quinn glances at me and smiles broadly. "I'm sure you understand even better than I do."

"Oh, I know these boys. Trouble." As she leads us from the gate area and out to the tarmac, Quinn stops short.

I grab her by the hand. "Don't worry, you'll be fine."

"It's a 757," Quinn breathes.

"Yes, but it's not as palatial as you think." I'm trying to be nonchalant.

"Not as palatial?"

"Well, it only seats about a dozen people. Since it's a company plane, after 9/11, none of the board members can ride together. It's the corporate rules that everyone must fly independently, so we do a lot of flying commercially, but given the circumstances, we're taking this this week. The plane was designed to act as a roaming office, so there are two bedrooms with their own bathrooms—including a shower for international flights. There is an office, and there are three groups of four chairs with a table in between for working or meeting. There are couches in front of a television that gets satellite TV."

"Have you ever flown in a commercial plane before?"

"Of course I have. I fly commercial all the time."

She looks at me skeptically. "Have you ever sat in the back of the plane in the seats before the bathroom?"

I laugh out loud. "I'm sure I have. It's not that big of a deal. Why are you so scared? We flew to Vegas on a private plane."

"I was nervous. The other plane was a charter so it's not private and I worry about the maintenance of private planes," she says as we take our places in two of the captain's chairs next to one another.

Marjorie brings us two gin and tonics. "Here you go." She sets a little snack basket between us. It has all of Quinn's favorites: gummy bears, almonds, apples, and peanut butter crackers.

"Wow. Thank you, Marjorie," Quinn gushes.

"William did tell me in advance some of your preferences. I have an Earl Grey tea when you're ready. In the meantime, here is Tanqueray No. Ten gin and some tonic water, and I have plenty of other snacks if you're interested."

I lean over to Quinn and say, "She takes very good care of us."

She beams. "I'm always looking out for you, William. I don't want Jason and Brett on this plane again if I can help it. They always like to bring these girls along and christen them to the mile-high club." She rolls her eyes, and it makes me smile.

"Well, I do refer to them as Dumb and Stupid," I share.

She grins at me. "You're so clever. You have a great sense of humor."

"Have you seen my stepmother recently?" I ask.

"Yes, she went shopping last week in Paris, and so I got to spend some great quality time with her."

"That must've been riveting," I say dryly. Then it occurs to me. "Wait, that was after she learned about dad. Did she go crazy buying things?"

"I can't be sure. She didn't really talk to me. I told her how sorry I was about your dad, and she just said, 'Thank you' and buried her nose in her phone and on her computer."

"I have no doubt that she's looking at how she's going to spend my dad's money."

Marjorie sits up straight, and with all her dignity, she decries, "Well, it should all be going to you."

"Actually, it was supposed to all go to my mother's favorite charities."

Marjorie purses her lips in disappointment. There is a ding over the plane's intercom, signally that we're getting ready for takeoff. "It's go time," I tell Quinn.

She looks terrified. "There's no safety speech?"

I point down. "See these pouches?" She nods. "These have your life vest, but given we are flying over land, I don't think you'll need one."

"You know, you really aren't that funny."

I laugh really loudly. "I suppose you're right. If anything happens, follow me. But given this isn't a commercial plane, its maintenance is better, and our aircraft aren't worked as hard as anything flown commercially, I promise you'll be fine."

Once we've met our cruising altitude, I stand and turn to her. "Hey, we have the new Jonny Demarco film. Do you want to watch with me?"

She looks down at her Kindle, and I can see her debate her decision. "Sure. Why not? I'm not usually a superhero kind of girl, but it sounds like a fun way to pass the afternoon."

As I load up the Blu-ray disc, Marjorie offers us more drinks and then lets us know our options for lunch. I order the lobster bisque and a five-cheese grilled cheese sandwich, and Quinn orders the seafood salad with dressing on the side.

As we sit back and the movie comes on, Quinn turns to me and asks, "What movie is this?"

When I tell her, she says, "This isn't even in the theaters yet."

"I thought you said that you weren't a superhero fan."

"I know what I said, but I can know movies," she patiently explains.

I love it when she gets annoyed with me. "One of my buddies works for Jonny, and this is a screener copy that he was able to get to me. I just got it yesterday, so I haven't seen it."

"Amazing. Is there anybody you don't know?"

"Yeah." I chuckle self-consciously. "I'm sure there are quite a few people I don't know."

As we curl up on the couch and watch the movie, I put my arm around her, and it just feels right. She seems to fit perfectly in the crook of my arm. The movie is action packed, but I hear her softly breathing next to me, and my cock goes rigid. Boy, would it be nice to do more than have her breathing rapidly next to me, but I'm fully aware Marjorie knows what goes on in the bedrooms, and it's not really the time for Quinn and me to get a little frisky.

Four and a half hours later, we finally make it to Philadelphia.

"Is it okay if I use the bathroom quickly before we deplane?"

"Of course," I tell her. When she walks out, she's freshened up. Her hair has extra bounce, and I notice she's wearing makeup. She looks amazing with or without makeup. "You look beautiful." I didn't mean to say it out loud, but when she blushes, I'm really glad I did. I don't think she understands that all my flirting is earnest. I'm disappointed that it took her accidentally leaving a message for me to see her for who she truly is.

She blushes. "Thank you."

At the base of the stairs of the plane, Gerald waits for us with another Cadillac Escalade. He holds the door open, and Quinn is obviously stunned to see him. "How did you get here before us?"

"I was on the plane. I sat in the aft of the plane. You just didn't see me."

She turns to me. "Do you always travel with your own driver?"

"Gerald is not just a driver. He's also a bodyguard of sorts. Given the situation, the feeling is that I should have a bodyguard for a little while."

"What's the situation? What aren't you telling me?"

"My father always believed that, no matter what goes on, we need to be aware, but he was killed in a helicopter crash. The board of his company isn't quite sure what's going on, so I've had a bodyguard ever since the accident. Jim Adelson arranged it for me."

"You're just telling me this now?"

"I think it's a total overreaction, but I've learned it's better to roll with it rather than fight these things. We're totally safe, and let me tell you, Gerald could take someone down with a paperclip."

"If he works for Jim's team, I have no doubt about that."

Gerald looks at us in the rearview mirror and smiles. "Miss Quinn, I look forward to spending the week with you both at a discretionary distance."

"Thanks, Gerald," she says.

We drive across town and into downtown Philadelphia. Looking around, I'm reminded of how gray and gross it is here. Maybe it's because, when my mother died, I always felt like she took the sun out of Philadelphia. I'm lost in thought when all of a sudden Gerald is holding the door open in front of the house I grew up in—a four-story stone building built at the turn of the century that sits on the tree-lined street across from a park. The buildings around the park have been converted to high-rise condos, and a few of the old homes were split into several generous apartments. There are only about four houses left like ours around the two square-mile park.

My anxiety increases as I look up at the house, and I find myself holding Quinn's hand. She gives me a gentle squeeze. "It's going to be okay," she whispers.

I nod, appreciating the strength she's giving to me through the simple gesture.

Looking at the house makes me a little homesick, mostly because this is the last place my mother lived before she died and all my memories of her are from this house. It'll be strange staying here without my father.

Thinking about my childhood bedroom brings a smile to my face. I wonder what it looks like these days, or if it's ever changed. Somehow, I'm sure the poster of Kathy Ireland in a skimpy bathing suit is long gone. Well, at least I hope so. I think Jason is living in that room these days, or maybe it's Brett. Who knows? My dad mentioned once that they've taken over the bedrooms upstairs.

"Are you ready?" she asks.

"As ready as I'll ever be." I turn to Gerald. "I have a feeling we won't be staying. Please hang tight for a minute. Let's see what's going on."

Quinn grasps my hand again, giving me the strength to climb the twelve steps to the front door. My hand raises to knock, and all of a sudden, I look up to see Harriett is standing in front of me. She looks the same as she did when I left. She was my substitute mom, and I miss her and her chocolate chip cookies we'd make together.

"Master William! You're home! You're home!" She gives me a breathtaking hug—so tight that it makes me realize how much I miss her personally, but I also miss this house.

"It's so good to see you. How have you been?"

"We've been good, except we desperately miss your father these days." She reaches for my arm and gives me a reassuring squeeze. "I'm so sorry about your loss."

"Thank you. That's very kind of you. It was quite a surprise. I didn't even know he was going to Tanzania."

"I didn't know either, but I'm not usually in the loop on that these days." She quickly changes the subject. "Thank you so much for the wonderful perfume you sent me for my birthday last month. It's my favorite."

"I can't smell gardenia and not think of you. I hope you enjoy it." I smile as I slip my coat off my shoulders and hang it on the coat rack behind the door.

"You look more and more handsome every time I see you," she gushes as she looks at me. When she spots Quinn, her smile can't be any bigger if it was the Grand Canyon.

"Harriett, this is my fiancée Quinn. We just got engaged."

She clasps her hands together and opens her arms wide. "Quinn, I'm so thrilled to meet the woman who tamed this man's heart. We'll have to share a pot of tea, and I want to know all about you."

"I can't wait," Quinn says enthusiastically. "I'll bet you have some good stories you can share too." And I swear that Quinn winked at her.

I can hear my stepmonster's Pomeranians yipping, alerting the world there is someone in the house that isn't normally here. My stepmonster yells in the distance, "Shut up!"

"This should be interesting," Quinn mutters loud enough that only Harriett and I can hear.

"Who the fuck is at my house?" Lillian snarls.

Harriett steps back and doesn't say anything as we watch Lillian slither down the stairs, perfectly coiffed and ready for a night on the town.

"Why, Lillian, it's so wonderful to see you too," I reply.

"What the hell are you doing here? You aren't even part of this family. You walked away when you moved to the West Coast."

"I didn't walk away, Lillian. I met regularly with my father, and I talked to him all the time. I'm here because his lawyer asked me to come, and I brought my fiancée, Quinn. I thought she might like to see where I grew up." I feel triumphant in my sneak attack. I have a feeling she was the one who talked my dad into the silly provision, thinking I would never settle down. Maybe she's right, but I'm not going to let her win without a fight.

She steps back a little bit. "This is not your house, and you're trespassing."

"This is my family home. I have every right to be here," I share with her, keeping my voice low and calm. "Lillian, I didn't come here to take the house that my mother grew up in from you. I just wanted to come by and say hello."

She looks down and blows on her nails as if the polish is wet. "Get the fuck out of my house. I don't want you polluting the air here."

I can't let her get to me. She's an unhappy person, and it's now my job to make her miserable without her knowing it. "That's fine. Quinn and I have a reservation at the Rittenhouse in Dad's suite. If you need to find us, you know where that is."

"I gave up your dad's suite as soon as we got the news about his helicopter crash. Good luck getting a room."

"No need to worry about us. I took care of it before we left."

"I promise to not give you another thought," she snidely says.

I reach for Quinn's coat, and she steps into it, and Harriett holds mine for me. "I look forward to hearing what my father has in his will. Until tomorrow." Harriett holds open the door. "Harriett, I hope to see you this week while I'm in town." I reach in and give her a quick hug before walking back to the car.

"Your father promised to look out for my boys and me. You'll see," she yells after me.

"I'm sure you're right," I assure her. And I am sure she is right—my dad was a kind man. But I wouldn't be surprised if my dad's lawyer wasn't laying the groundwork for her to not get a thing.

Once the door is closed and we're safely in the car, Quinn says, "Well, that was interesting."

"That is my darling stepmonster."

"She looks like a plastic factory."

I laugh. "Oh my God, she's had it all done—her lips, her eyebrows, her boobs, her ass, her thighs, her belly, her arms, and it wouldn't surprise me if she had her vagina done too."

"Eww! That's quite the visual. But her face looks like leather stretched really tight across her face."

"Yes, and I'm sure those are hair extensions. I'll never know what my father saw in her."

"I bet that mouth could perform miracles on a man's dick."

"I don't want to think about that with my father." I shudder.

"I'm sorry, I shouldn't have said that." She looks down at her hands and seems embarrassed. "Sorry."

* * *

"Please don't apologize. I think it's good to see that your second job comes in handy sometimes."

"You have no idea."

The car drives us to the other side of the park, and we get out. The Rittenhouse Hotel is a five-star hotel that my dad would stay at whenever he didn't want to see Lillian, which I think was more often these days.

As we walk across the marble floor, I take in the grandness of the lobby. It hasn't greatly changed since I was a kid, but it's been updated.

"Mr. Bettencourt, so wonderful to see you."

I recognize the face, but I can't place it. I glance at the name tag, and it says "Jennifer." Then it hits me. "Jennifer Wright?"

She smiles. "You remember me?"

"You're all grown up, but yes. How are you? How's Owen?"

"My brother and I run the Rittenhouse together. I saw you were coming in, so I wanted to be sure to greet you." She leans in and conspiratorially says, "Plus, it's always good to show the team up front here that I know what I'm doing around here."

I burst out laughing. The Wright family has owned and operated this hotel for several generations. Owen and I went to school together and, because we lived across the park from one another, spent a lot of time together. "Well, thank you for making sure that I had a place to stay."

"Owen and I were really sorry to hear about your dad."

"Thank you, it is quite the surprise." Then I realize I've forgotten Quinn was standing with me. "I'm sorry. Jennifer, this is my fiancée, Quinn Faraday."

"So wonderful to meet you. William was quite the heartbreaker when we were growing up."

"Don't believe her. No girls were interested in me. I was a nerd."

"He was a major nerd—comic books, Dungeons and Dragons, Pokémon cards," a male voice says from behind us.

"Owen!" I grab his hand, and he pulls me in for a backslapping man hug. "Great to see you, man."

"You too! Sorry to hear about your dad."

"Thanks. I'm in town to deal with the stepmonster."

"Stay as long as you need. We have a few things of your dad's when you ready. It isn't much. Few papers and some toiletries," Owen shares.

Jennifer hands us two key cards. The bellman has our bags on a cart, and we're ready to go up to our room. To those who don't know Quinn, I'm sure she looks relaxed, but I've realized she bites at her lower lip and picks at her cuticles when she's nervous, like she's doing now. I'm sure she's concerned we'll be sharing a bed. Owen is one of my oldest friends, but I need to keep the ruse up just in case someone is watching. I trust no one in Philly.

"We don't want to keep you lovebirds." Owen smiles and winks at Quinn. She looks at me and gives me a luscious smile, and all my blood rushes to my cock. "I hope we can catch up again while we're in town."

"Sounds like a plan," I assure him.

We then follow the bellman into the elevators. His name tag says his name is Jimmy. "You know the Wrights?" he asks.

"I grew up with Owen and Jennifer. This hotel has been in their family for three generations," I tell him. I have great stories of us getting in trouble, but I would never share that with a member of their staff. It's fun thinking of those days— the days when you thought little things like a math test mattered.

"You may remember my dad. James? He was the doorman for many years."

"Of course. He never ratted Owen and Jennifer out when he knew they were out past curfew. Does he still work here?"

"He passed away last year."

"I'm so sorry to hear that. He was a good man."

"He was. I just wish I had told him that more often." His comment hits me right in the heart. That's how I feel about my dad. Quinn reaches for my hand and squeezes it.

Jimmy opens the door to the suite, and I ask him to just drop the suitcases in the room on the left, and I offer him a healthy twenty-dollar tip. "Thank you, Mr. Bettencourt."

"Thank you, Jimmy."

Once he's gone, I pick up Quinn's bag and move it to the other room. "You have your own room, so you don't have to worry about me laying all over you."

She looks relieved. "Thank you."

"Relax a minute and let's grab a casual dinner tonight. There is a favorite spot of mine that isn't too far from here that we can walk to."

"Great. I'm not hungry right now." She looks at her watch. "I know it's after five already, but would you object to a late dinner?"

"Sounds perfect. Say eight?"

"Perfect." She turns to leave but hesitates. "Thank you for bringing me with you. I know this must be difficult."

I'm stunned because I feel like I blackmailed her into coming. "It's you I should be thanking. Today was the first bite from what is a very bitter apple."

"It wasn't too bad. People are marking their territory right now. I get it." She walks into her bedroom, and I hear her shut the door while I stare out at the setting sun through the big picture windows.

The suite is palatial. It overlooks Rittenhouse Square, which is a beautiful park filled with colonial statues and public art, and directly across the tree-lined park is the state capital building. Shining out over the luscious green park, the sun peeks out from the clouds. Maybe the sun will shine again here because my mom and dad are together again. Wishful thinking, for sure.

* * *

I pull my cell phone from my pocket and call my dad's lawyer. "Henry Gray, please," I tell the receptionist.

"May I tell him who's calling?"

"William Bettencourt."

"Just a moment please." She places me on a brief hold.

"Henry Gray."

"Henry, it's William Bettencourt."

"William, so good to hear from you. Have you decided what you're going to do?"

"I'm here with my fiancée, Quinn Faraday. Lillian kicked me out of the house, so we're in my dad's suite at the Rittenhouse Hotel."

"Well, that's very good news. I'm sure she is quite disappointed you've arrived with Quinn."

"I hope so. You have my cell number if you need me."

"I do."

"Great. One quick question. Are the assets frozen or anything?"

"Lillian doesn't have access to anything. She does have her allowance, which is deposited in her account and credit cards. But she doesn't have access until the death certificate is certified."

"It looked like she was spending money, so I was curious."

"That's probably a pretty accurate assessment. But she won't have access to some of the accounts regardless."

"Thanks. Do we need to meet before the reading of the will?"

"No, I think we're going to be okay. It isn't really a lot different than what I explained to you on the phone."

"The house was my mother's. She was born in that house, as was her father. I'm hoping that there is a stipulation that Lillian can live there, but it belongs to me."

"Yes, it is part of your trust from your mother's estate. All of her money and assets belong to you and have for some time. Did your father ever go through that with you?"

"No."

"Maybe we should meet before the reading. How about two?"

"I'll be there."

I hang up the phone. It's been such a stressful day, so I decide to put some workout clothes on. As I walk out, I see Quinn leaving her room with workout clothes on. "Great minds think alike. Where you headed?"

"I don't know the area well enough to explore, so I was going to hit the treadmill in the gym downstairs."

"Let me call Gerald and see if he's up for a run."

"I don't want to bother him."

"I'll show you both around." I dial Gerald, and he answers after the first ring. "Gerald, we were thinking of going for a run. We can hit the treadmill in the gym if you aren't able to join us."

"I'm ready now if you are."

"We'll meet you in the lobby in five."

He disconnects the call.

"We're all set."

"I hope I can keep up with you both."

"You can set the pace where you're comfortable. Gerald will be behind us. There are a couple of places to see. It'll be a general tour."

"I'm looking forward to getting outside. I feel like, between the rainy weather we've had in San Francisco recently and being on a plane all day, that fresh air is required."

"I agree. It'll be nice to get outside and breathe unfiltered air. I'll warn you, Philadelphia has dirty air."

"You're so funny."

"No, really. I'm serious. The air here is pretty shitty this time of year, but there are a lot of great things to see and plenty of American history is here. You'll have a good time."

"You lead the way."

We meet Gerald in the lobby, and I walk him through my planned route. He lets us know he'll be about ten paces behind us. The room key fits easily in the pocket on the arm of my windbreaker. After a quick stretch, we walk through the rotating doors and head north.

We take it slow as we run the park, starting with the perimeter, and I point out the statues of William Penn who founded Pennsylvania, Benjamin Franklin, George Clymer who was from Pennsylvania and was the first to advocate the separation from Britain, and a depiction of the Second Continental Congress. We just run by the bronze statues.

As we cut through the park, we see four different engineering pieces of public art. These are somewhat new.

Zigzagging our way through the park, we easily cover three miles. Quinn may have shorter legs than I do, but she's a great runner and was difficult to keep pace with.

"That was a great run."

"For someone who was sure she didn't keep a fast pace, I think Gerald is going to be suffering."

"Somehow I doubt that. Are you still good with a later dinner?"

"Yep, I wouldn't mind some rest before dinner. I'll meet you in the living room at about eight. A favorite diner of mine isn't too far, and they'll still be serving dinner."

"Diner translates to casual?"

"Yes. If you're in anything other than jeans, you'll be too dressed up."

"That sounds perfect."

I can hear her phone ringing, and I can't help but wonder if it's one of her clients. She takes the call in her room, talking in a low voice. I wouldn't mind hearing it, but it might be too much—all foreplay and no action. I hate that she needs to work so hard. I somehow need to bring it up at the partners' meeting. I know that by industry standards she makes good money, and part of her strapped living comes from her school loans, but if we were to lose her, that would be a great loss to the company and would affect our bottom line.

After a refreshing shower and a quick nap, I'm ready to go. I pour myself a McCallen twenty-five-year-old scotch—my dad's favorite—over some ice and wait for Quinn to join me. No pressure. Turning the television on to *SportsCenter*, I watch the roundup of today's sports news while I enjoy my drink.

I hear her before I see her. "This is a beautiful hotel."

"It is. I think at one time or another, I've been in all three hundred rooms."

"Did you make a bet with Owen to see if you could bed the most girls in a hotel room?"

A deep belly laugh escapes me. "We weren't that clever. No, I worked for the hotel one year, and they were renovating, so we were moving furniture around."

"Why did your dad have his own suite?"

"My dad had terrible insomnia, and Lillian hated when he wandered the house in the middle of the night, so he started staying most nights here."

She nods and walks to the giant window overlooking the park. You can just make out my family home's roofline across the park beyond the large oak trees.

"Would you like a glass of scotch before we go?" I ask.

She eyes it, debating. "No, I better not. I'm starving, and if I start with that, it'll be a liquid dinner, and I really need more than a hangover tonight."

"I promise to give you whatever you need tonight."

She smiles up at me, catching my double entendre, and pulls her coat on.

chapter

twelve

QUINN

When we took a rideshare across town and William walked me into a dark biker bar, I was both surprised and a little bit frightened.

The biggest, ugliest guy in the bar stood from his chair and approaches us, standing toe to toe with William. "Do you think you belong here?" he growls. The entire bar falls silent. Not even a single note of music can be heard.

"Who do you think you are?" William spews at him.

I have one eye on Gerald, and I'm ready to grab William by the hand and run out of the bar when the big, ugly guy grabs William and pulls him into a big hug. "You motherfucker, why didn't you tell me you were coming to town?"

The patrons in the bar relax and return to what they were doing, and William turns to me. "Mark, I'd like you to meet my fiancée, Quinn."

"You son of a bitch! I can't believe you got engaged." He slaps him on the back, and they laugh. He then turns to me, and I brace myself for my own bear hug. "So wonderful to meet you. Please call me Bubba. If you refer to me as Mark, no one will know who you're talking about."

Gerald relaxes and finds a table close enough that he can intercede if needed but far enough away that he gives us some privacy. He keeps one eye on us at all times and the other focused on the happenings in the bar.

Bubba motions us to a table in the back and sits with us while we order. I learn that Bubba is William's cousin from his mother's side. He inherited a lot of money from William's uncle when he turned twenty-five. He fell in love with motorcycles when they were in school, and the combination of too much money and too little supervision got him into a motorcycle club that skirts the law. "I try to keep us honest, but sometimes it can't be helped." He shrugs. When some voices rise in a far corner of the bar, Bubba stands and says, "You two enjoy your meal. I need to calm those two down, or someone will be calling the cops." He leaves us just as our dinners arrive.

The food is surprisingly good—not because we're in a biker bar but because I expected bar food, where everything is fried. I go for an interesting spinach salad, topped with strawberries, goat cheese, candied walnuts, and grilled chicken with a poppy seed vinaigrette.

"This is really good," I exclaim.

"Bubba's place actually is pretty good. He went to the Cordon Bleu in Paris and learned to cook."

"I'm impressed."

"He's a great guy. He really isn't interested in what anyone thinks about him."

"I wish I had that self-confidence."

William looks at me funny. "I would think you had plenty of self-confidence. You even have pretty explicit phone calls with strangers. That has to count for something."

I put my fork down and consider his comments. "Actually, it doesn't take much confidence to lie to a guy about what you're wearing or will do to him. It takes an overwhelming desire to pay your bills over anything else and still remain doing what you want to do." I don't want to be a downer, so I attempt to change the subject. "What time are we meeting the lawyer tomorrow?"

"Lillian and her kids are due at three, and apparently there is something from my mom's estate I need to understand, so he's asked us to come a little earlier."

"Do you want me to just meet you at three? I don't want to impose or be super nosey."

"You're playing the role of my fiancée, so you need to be with me. We didn't sign a nondisclosure, but I would ask that whatever you learn this week, you don't share company-wide."

"That's not my gig, so you're safe there."

We spend a little bit more time with Bubba. When we're walking out the door, Bubba leans into William and says, "Don't let that bitch take anything that belongs to you. And if you end up needing any help from my friends or me, you call, and we'll be there."

"Thanks, man. I can't tell you how much I appreciate it."

Gerald brings the car around, and we ride back to the hotel. We're sitting so close that the heat is just sizzling off of him. He is wearing me down by his sweet and charming ways, but I must remind myself that he is a danger to me and to my heart.

When we arrive at the hotel, Jimmy opens the car door. "Do you ever go home?" I tease.

"I have newborn twins at home. We need the money, and honestly, I'm not sure I'd get much more sleep there than I do here."

"I've heard that about twins," I share.

William reaches for my hand, and we walk through the lobby to the elevators. When we reach the door to our suite, William turns to Gerald and assures him, "We'll be in for the night, but I may need to go for a run in the morning. I'm jet lagging a bit. Let's aim for eight. I'll call you to be sure."

"Yes, sir. Have a good night." Gerald turns and winks at me, and I suddenly feel self-conscious about what is going to happen next.

"Would you like a glass of wine or scotch?" William asks as we walk into the living room.

"No, I'm hitting a wall and probably need to go to bed."

William steps in close to me. Instinct overcomes reason. He reaches out and slides an arm over my shoulders, pulling me close to him. His body warms me as I sink into him. Warm. Solid. So very real. And when my face turns into his chest, my heart squeezes tighter.

His broad arms wrap around me. "Thank you again for coming with me."

I ease back enough to look up at him, and when I do, those deep blue eyes tug at something in my soul no one before has been able to touch. So soulful and expressive, those eyes have haunted my dreams since the day we met. "Thank you for inviting me."

His hands tangle in my hair as he pulls my mouth toward his. Those tempting lips crush over mine. His tongue, rough and hot, dips into my mouth when I open. Before I even realize what I'm doing, I reach for him. I can't help but hold him, lost in the moment. Nothing tells me to stop as flashes of arousal course through me, erupting in my center and spreading through every limb and nerve ending.

I want to continue, but I can't. I reluctantly push myself away. "I should go."

A flash of hurt crosses his eyes. "I understand. The morning is all yours. We can go to lunch at noon and then head over to the lawyer's office."

"Okay… goodnight, William."

My lips are still on fire following that kiss. Holy shit, can that man make my toes curl. I lie in bed, unable to find the sleep my body needs so desperately. I hate when I change time zones and three hours brings on major insomnia. I wish I would have taken something to help bring on the sleep, but it's too late. If I take something now, I'll have a drug-induced hangover all morning. I guess that's what happens when your body is used to staying up past two each morning.

I stare at the ceiling and watch the shadows of the tree reflecting outside. I opened the curtains to watch the traffic around Rittenhouse Square Park, but it's dead at this hour. Rarely do the lights of a passing car reflect on the ceiling.

My mind wanders to everything that happened today. This was not how I expected my voice mail would turn out. My stomach churns with anxiety for William's future dealings with his stepmonster. If his father's attorney is warning us, then we know it's going to be ugly. And now we are doing an advanced meeting.

I remind myself I need to be affectionate, but I also need to keep an emotional distance. He's the kind of guy who eats women like me alive, literally and figuratively. I have no doubt he's a dynamo between the sheets—and the table, couch, shower, countertop, floor, car, and everywhere else you can have sex—but I also know he dates a lot. I believe he's slept with a few of the girls at work. I can't have my heart broken by him. He would just take all the pieces and grind them to dust, and I'm not sure I could go through that again.

I really enjoy spending time with him, and dinner was fun. It wasn't a place I expected. He seems to be a guy who is more comfortable in a tux at a ball than in a dark, seedy bar, so when he said casual, I was expecting a little café that might be kind enough to stay open for us since we arrived pretty late. He is a man full of constant surprises.

I'm not sure when I fall asleep, but the last time I looked at the clock, it was after two. I won't deny I debated marching into his room and jumping on top of him, but I also kept reminding myself what a mess that would create.

The sunlight shines through the window, and I finally wake. It's eight. Gerald and William were heading for a run about this time, so I wander into the living room in my extra-large T-shirt and panties with my computer under my arm.

I see the table is set with bagels, fruit, and coffee. I need the caffeine to get my brain to put the synapses together — my body clock still is on Pacific time. I log onto my work email and begin working through the three-hundred-plus emails in my inbox.

I don't hear him return. I'm so involved in the challenges with one of our new clients until I hear him say, "You're up."

I look up and see his hair is damp, and he has a post-run glow that makes him so delicious. Pouring himself a cup of coffee, he sits down at the table next to me. Leaning forward, he rests his forearms on the table, his hand so close to mine, if he moves just a fraction of an inch, we'd be touching. But I don't need to touch him to feel the heat rolling off him in waves. The same heat is rolling off of me.

We look at each other, the air thick with sexual tension.

Breaking eye contact, he suddenly stands. "You look like you're working. I should go take a shower."

I watch him leave, and I can't decide if I like the view of him coming or going better. The room feels colder now that he's left.

chapter

thirteen

QUINN

I can't concentrate on my work. I keep thinking of him in the shower, and I wonder what he's doing. I can't help myself. My stomach tight, I rise to see what he's doing. Smoothing out my T-shirt, I try to convince myself I'm doing the right thing. I want this. I want him. I want us — at least for this trip.

Walking into his bedroom and then into the en suite, I see his reflection in the mirror. It's distorted from the steam, but I can make out his beautiful body that looks like it's etched in marble. My body quivers and my nipples pebble. I want to join him, but something is holding me back. It's not too late to turn back. I watch him soap himself and wish I was there to caress him and do that for him. As he strokes his dick, I swear he says my name.

He looks at the mirror and sees me. Our eyes lock, and a shiver runs through me. Too late to run and hide now. "May I join you?" I rasp.

"Please do."

I pull my T-shirt over my head and drop my panties on the floor. Our eyes never stray from each other's. Stepping into the shower brings his face only inches from mine, his breath warming my skin, causing a trickle of awareness to course through me. I smell the soap on his body and feel the heat radiating from him.

My skin tingles, and I turn, trapped between his tantalizing male—very naked—body at my front and the hard, cool tile at my back. My muscles quiver as his lips brush my ear. Electrifying sensations run through my whole body.

My fingers caress his hard pecs, and I can't help but lean in and lick the water rivulets dripping from his nipples, and his moans spur me on. My hand travels down his body, finding his enlarged cock. William lowers his mouth to mine, his body hovering over me. He kisses me softly, and I open my mouth with a low moan, wanting more of him. All of him.

"You look beautiful as always, Quinn."

I wash his body slowly and methodically, pausing to stroke him. I want to get down on my knees, but he stops me. "It's my turn."

He takes the bodywash and lathers up his hands. Turning me around, he massages my back, and I'm quickly putty in his hands. His fingers caress every part of my body just enough to leave me almost begging for more.

When he rinses away the suds, he twists and pulls at my nipples, and my hand instinctively goes to my nub, and I stroke myself and him. "I love how naughty you are," he rasps.

Exiting the shower, he wipes me down with a plush towel. I bend over the counter and present my ass to him, and his fingers tease my brown rosetta and invades my tight channel, pivoting in and out and rubbing at my sweet spot. The slick sounds echo throughout the bathroom. I moan my appreciation. It's been so long. It takes only moments, and my entire body shudders as the waves of pleasure overcome me. He sucks his fingers of my juices, and I'm ready to taste all of him.

Taking his hand in mine, I lead him into the suite's living room. I kiss him deeply, tasting myself on his lips, before I push him back on to the couch. "I'll be out in a minute."

William leans back on the couch, watching me as I disappear into my bedroom. I run my fingers through my hair and grab a condom before walking back out into the living room. He watches me place it on the side table, waiting to see what I do next.

"Are you okay with this?" William asks.

I sit next to him, folding my legs underneath me. This causes the towel wrapped around me to ride up, and his eyes are drawn to my exposed skin. "I'm more than okay with this."

Reaching for my hand, he gently rubs over it with his thumb. "I've wanted this ever since I heard your message." He smiles and leaves a slow and lingering kiss on my palm before releasing my hand. "I don't want you to feel pressured."

"I don't feel that at all. I want this." I lean in and kiss him softly. I only mean it to be a quick kiss, but as soon as my lips touch his, I can't seem to pull back. I straddle William's lap, my wet pussy rubbing against his cock.

His hands slide down my back, pushing the towel away as he cups the curve of my ass. I want him. I want his cock inside me. He lifts his hips, teasing my pussy with his hardness. I moan into his mouth, and he squeezes my ass harder.

I open my eyes to see William's beautiful sapphire blue eyes staring back at me. Our eyes lock as I grind against him. "I'm going to come too quickly, unless you stop."

I don't want to end our night too early, so I stop rubbing my pussy against his cock and begin trailing kisses down his neck and over his glorious chest, following the hairline until I'm on my knees and moving lower over his stomach.

I sit here for a moment, running my hand up and down his thick shaft. It's huge, and I'm not sure how far I'll be able to take it in my mouth. It's been a long time, and I'm just hopeful I don't embarrass myself by doing a bad job. He watches me as I leisurely caress his dick, applying pressure to the underside of the base. I lean forward and slowly lick his tip, and he takes a sharp intake of air. His cock pulses against my tongue, and he lets out a groan of appreciation.

I meet William's eyes. He's even more handsome naked than I imagined. His cock's large and very, very hard. I lick it again and watch his fists clench against the cushions of the couch. "I've wanted to do this ever since Las Vegas." I lick over its entire length, making sure it's nice and wet. Then slowly slide down his cock, enveloping it with my mouth.

William groans my name. "Oh God, Quinn, that feels so good. You're going to make me... Oh shit, I'm going to come."

I ignore his warnings. I want this. My free hand moves to my clit, and I rub it as I stroke him faster with my hand and pull with my mouth. He moans loudly as he comes and spills into my mouth. I lick his cock until it's completely soft and then kiss my way back up his body. I'm only just getting started.

William wraps his arms around me and kisses me passionately. Then he stands, picks up the condom and my hand, and leads me into his bedroom, laying me down on the bed. My eyes are heavy with need as I look up at him. His hands gently caress my breasts, causing my nipples to grow hard, and my body to shudder with delight.

William leans down and kisses me, beginning at my mouth and making his way down while rolling my nipples between his fingers and pulling at the nubs. He laves each one of them with his tongue slowly before resuming on his path. When he kisses my hip, I shiver beneath him. He leisurely caresses my hip with his tongue, and I moan loudly. Then he gently spreads my legs apart and kisses up my inner thighs. When he gets to my bare mound, he kisses my clit. I lift my hips to him and moan.

My breathing is heavy, and when his tongue caresses my bare clit for the first time, bolts of electricity rush through me, and I arch off the bed. He grips my hips, holding me to him. He teases my clit—licking, sucking, and nibbling my hard bud. I'm crying out his name. Then I feel a finger invade my channel, gliding through my wetness. He adds more fingers, working in and out. Wet sounds fill the room as I writhe on the bed below him. He sucks hard against my clit, and my orgasm hits me hard.

As I come down from my high, he slides back up my body and kisses me slowly, and I can taste myself on his lips. "You taste so sweet, Quinn."

Feeling his cock hard against me, I reach down to stroke his length, but he stops me, grabbing my hand and passing me the condom. I waste no time ripping it open. He watches me as I roll it on much more skillfully than I feel.

"I want you inside of me, William. Please, I need you."

His lips find mine, and our tongues dance a delicate tango. William reaches down, aligning his cock with my entrance, and I slowly descend on him, taking it slowly inside me. It takes a few tries before I'm fully seated. I adjust to his size, then begin to ride him. I feel so full. With his hands on my hips, he guides our rhythm, pulling me down hard onto his cock. My head's thrown back, and I'm moaning loudly every time I come down on his rigid cock. He reaches up to cup my tits as they sway before him and plays with my nipples.

My orgasm takes me by surprise, and I cry out, feverishly riding William's cock. He's groaning loudly now, every time I slam against him. I collapse against him, and he rolls us over so that I lay beneath him. He thrusts into me in a hard, demanding rhythm of his own.

"You feel incredible, Quinn, so tight and wet. I can't believe how good it feels to be inside you."

His words turn me on even more. I pull him down and kiss him urgently. His fingers tangle in my hair and he kisses me back just as passionately.

He groans his orgasm as he continues to thrust into me with long, deep strokes. When he's satiated, he collapses on top of me, supporting himself on his elbows so he doesn't put too much weight on me. His cock slips out, and he reaches for a tissue and wraps the filled condom into it before lying next to me. I roll over to snuggle closer to him, placing my head on his chest while we both catch our breath.

We lay like this for some time. "This was unexpected and amazing," he says, breaking the silence.

"I agree."

He looks at the clock. "I'm starved. Shall we order in some lunch?"

I nod in my euphoria. "I guess I should shower, so I don't show up to the lawyer's office smelling like sex."

"I don't mind." He grins wickedly. The mischievousness in his eyes has me biting my lip. Leaning over, he kisses me deeply. "Don't bite at your lip. I can't tell you how hard that makes me, and we'll never get to his office."

"Good to know." I smile and bite at my lip while pulling on a nipple.

He looks to the ceiling. "You'll be the death of me yet, woman."

"I aim to please."

"You did more than please me."

Feeling completely ecstatic, I run off to the en suite in my room and hop in the shower. I'm humming a tune when I look in the mirror and see him watching me.

"You have a beautiful voice," he says.

"I'm afraid if you join me, we may never leave."

"I agree. Lunch is here, and we need to leave in about an hour."

"I'll be ready."

I really want to look good for the meeting with Lillian and her two sons and of course meet the lawyer. I'm swimming above my pay grade here, so I want to make sure I look like I'm somebody that William would date. I wear an expensive pair of black pants and a black top that has some cutouts at the top that make it look elegant. My Christian Louboutin black stiletto pumps are a few years old but still look good. I throw a gray pashmina over my arm and grab my Kate Spade black bag, and I'm ready for the afternoon.

When I walk out into the living room of our suite, my eyes automatically zero in on William. He's dressed in jeans that are baggy in the right places, a nice-looking oxford shirt with his sleeves rolled up, exposing a beautiful-colored ribbon at the seams, expensive loafers, and matching belt.

He stands as I enter the room. "You look amazing."

"Thank you. So do you. I hope I've dressed appropriately for our afternoon."

"Well, as long as you have a fifth of bourbon or scotch in your purse, we'll be good to go."

I shrug. "No bourbon or scotch, but I can see if I can get you a little flask of wine if it's really that important."

"No, I'm just teasing. I just figure today's going to be rough."

"I'm here for you—whatever you need me to do. And, if you'd like me to step out for privacy, please just let me know. Otherwise, I'll stand by you and play the doting fiancée."

"Thank you. I may be distracted though," he warns.

"Well, I'll just try to gauge your reaction and step out if it seems too personal."

His laughter is deep and hearty. "No, I'll be distracted by all the things I still want to do with you."

I shake my head and smile. "You really are very naughty, aren't you?"

"You did promise to suck my balls while you stroked me."

"I'll put that at the top of the list today."

We take the elevator down, and he puts his arms around me and kisses the top of my head. "In case I forget to tell you later, thank you for coming today."

Walking into the lawyer's office, we're greeted like kings. They offer us drinks and snacks and seat us in a big conference room that overlooks downtown Philadelphia. The view is a little bit different than our hotel room but stunning nonetheless.

As we wait for Henry Gray to arrive, William holds me by the hand and guides me to the window to point out the pieces of history here in Philadelphia. "That's where the Liberty Bell is." Pointing to another place, he says, "That's where they signed the Declaration of Independence in Independence Hall."

It dawns on me that this is where America started, and I don't even know the city. "You know, I've never been to Philadelphia before. I'd really love to do some really touristy things this week before we leave. Would that be okay?"

"Of course, I'll be your tour guide."

"I totally understand if you have things to do. I can always take a tour bus from the hotel. I don't want you to have to feel like you need to entertain me. I can do a lot of that on my own. I hate to inconvenience you."

"It's not an inconvenience. In fact, it'd be fun to show you around town. We take it for granted when it is here all the time."

chapter

fourteen

QUINN

"William!" We turn and face Henry Gray. He's an older man, probably similar in age to William's dad, and he's dressed in a three-piece tailored suit. Walking in with a thick file in hand, he greets William. Holding his hand in his, he says, "First, I really am sorry about your dad."

"Thank you. I appreciate that, and I thank you for the heads-up of what's to come today." Turning to me, he continues, "This is Quinn Faraday."

Henry turns to me. "Quinn, it's great to meet you. Thank you for coming."

I extend my hand, and he grasps it. "Very nice to meet you too, Mr. Gray."

"Please, call me Henry."

"All right."

Henry looks questionably at William, obviously wondering whether or not to proceed with me standing there, knowing that we really aren't together.

"No, she needs to stay," William declares.

Henry motions for us to sit, and William reaches for my hand as we listen while Henry talks a little bit about William's mother. Apparently, she was an heiress, and he explains that the home William grew up in was her family home. Therefore, the house isn't part of his father's estate. Under her original trust, his father was to manage the estate until William's 25th birthday, at which time it was to revert to William.

"I had no idea that I had a trust. I thought it all rolled to my father and would eventually roll to me. I was so young, I never thought about it. We didn't really talk about that in my family," William muses. "That would mean I inherited it almost eight years ago. I didn't know that. I assume there are some tax implications."

"You never withdrew anything from the trust, and the trust has been managed by my office, so we've filed the appropriate taxes."

"Well, that's good." All of a sudden, William looks up at Henry. "So, I actually have the right to kick Lillian out if I want to?"

"Yes, absolutely. You should know that there's been an inventory of every item in that house, outside of her personal items, and so she could stay there, and anything that is removed, she would be responsible for paying for."

"Well, that's very interesting. I'm not planning on moving back to Philadelphia—well, at least not anytime soon, and so the idea of her staying in the house doesn't necessarily bother me if you think I can trust her."

"I can't make that estimation, but I would suggest you consider your options very carefully. Now we have to talk about the money that your mother left you because it doesn't sound like your father walked you through any of that."

"No, he didn't," William tells him.

I'm feeling really uncomfortable with all of this information, but thankfully my phone starts to ring, saving me. I look at William, and he nods. "Excuse me." I don't need to know the details of the money in his estate, and, in fact, I'd rather not know.

Stepping out of the room, I answer the phone. "Quinn Faraday."

"So sorry to bother you, Quinn, but we have a small emergency. Do you have a moment?" Francie from the SketchIt office calls.

"Hold on a moment, and let me see if I can get somewhere private." The receptionist overhears me saying this, and he kindly escorts me to a small conference room off the reception area. Taking a seat at the table, I resume the call. Thankfully, it's only a minor issue with SketchIt and doesn't take long to resolve.

As I hang up, a loud, nasally voice can be heard right outside the door. I've only heard that voice once before, but it's easily recognizable. Lillian.

"I've already hired a PI to look into his girlfriend. No need to worry about that. He'll never marry her. I've already learned they are staying in different rooms at the Rittenhouse."

I shrink back. I've already let him down.

"I have an appraiser from an auction house going through all the crap in the house and preparing to sell it. I hate antiques."

"But, Mom, what if—"

"Today, we're just here to listen. Don't react. Don't do anything other than listen and know that it will all be ours in a few months. Tahiti here we come."

I'm stunned to hear what was just said. I quickly text William.

Me: I just overheard Lillian tell her sons they have a PI on me and an appraiser going through the house to sell the antiques.

The voices fade away, and I cautiously step into the hallway, stalling so as not to run into Lillian and her boys. An older woman stops me and asks, "Are you looking for the ladies' room?"

"Yes, I am. Can you direct me?"

"Follow me, I'm headed to the same place." She wanders through the back of the office and out a back door. "When you're ready to return, walk the other way into reception, and they'll get you back into your conference room."

"Thank you."

I stall as long as I can, but there's no word from William. I see it's almost time for the next meeting, so I wash my hands and wander back to reception just as Henry walks out to greet Lillian.

When we walk into the conference room, Lillian sees William sitting there with a few files in front of him. "I demand to know what's going on here," she fumes.

"Lillian, we're just going through William's mother's estate. Nothing to worry about. Please have a seat," Henry directs her.

She sits down with her two boys on each side of her. Another gentleman slithers in behind them.

Turning to the man, Henry asks, "Excuse me. Are you supposed to be here?"

"Yes, I represent Lillian Bettencourt," he says smugly. He's smarmy in a television advertising lawyer way.

Lillian smirks. "This is Arnold Smithers. He's my personal attorney, and he's here to look out for me and my children and our interests."

"Okay, very good." Henry goes through and begins to read the will.

"To my stepsons, Brett and Jason, I leave each five thousand dollars." They sit back, looking rather arrogant.

"To my wife of sixteen years, I leave half of my assets. The assets will be placed in trust, and you'll be paid a flat wage each month of twenty thousand dollars for the remainder of your life." Lillian smiles, waiting for Henry to drop the bomb about the marriage clause.

"To my son, I leave my seat on the board of Bettencourt Industries."

Lillian erupts. "That is supposed to go to me. That's my seat."

"I'm just reading his will. We really don't have much say at this point," Henry offers. "May I continue?"

She smiles at him. "Of course."

"The other half of my estate is left to my son. In order to collect the funds, he must be married within one year of my death, or the funds revert to a trust that will be evenly distributed among these six charities." Henry proceeds to list six engineering-based charities.

Lillian jumps to her feet. "Wait! That is not what he told me. He told me he was going to take care of my boys. If his loser of a son doesn't get the money, it should go to my boys." She leans across the table and sneers at William. "You were a terrible son. And this sham of a fiancée is just a further testament to how low you'll go to get your father's money."

Henry speaks up. "Lillian, the estate is valued at forty million dollars—"

"Forty million? It's much more than that. The house alone is worth over twenty million."

"I think you're probably right, but that is part of Reginald's first wife's estate, and William inherited his mother's estate and several of her other assets when he turned twenty-five. It already belongs to William."

"What?" Lillian screams. "I will fight this. That's my money. I earned it by taking care of your father."

Henry says, "Well, Lillian, you are getting twenty million dollars. I think his thoughts were that, all told, the money doesn't revert back to William upon your death. It remains with you and your heirs, so twenty million dollars should take care of all of you for a very long time."

Lillian can't be reasoned with. "There's more money than that. The house, that's not an asset that I'm willing to split. That and all the contents should be 100 percent mine. I live there, and what about possession is nine-tenths of the law?"

Henry looks at her puzzled. "Didn't your husband tell you that he didn't own the house?"

Lillian stands up. "I'm fighting for that house. That house is mine. I put a lot of blood, sweat, and tears into that house, and I want all of the contents."

William had been sitting here watching her make a spectacle of herself, but finally spoke up at this point. "I appreciate that, Lillian, but the house belonged to my mother and has been in my family for several generations. My mother was born in that house; her father was born in that house. My family lived in that house when the Declaration of Independence was signed here in Philadelphia. That house is mine and belongs to me and my bloodline. I have no problems with you remaining in the house until I'm ready to move back to Philadelphia, but let me be very clear, Lillian. There is an inventory of every item in the house."

William opens the file in his lap and pulls out a list of each item and the condition of every single piece of art and antique in the house, down to the number of silver forks, spoons, and knives.

William passes her the list, which is over an inch thick. Thumping on the paper for emphasis, he says, "Lillian, this is the inventory that says what's in the house, so when you decide to vacate the home, everything that is on this inventory must be accounted for, or it will be billed to you and deducted from your allowance."

"This is my house. They're my things. I'm not leaving," Lillian insists.

"Lillian, I suggest you consult with your attorney. You will be very disappointed if you choose to chase the path of suing for an estate that you have no claim to, and sitting in a house does not give you any claim," William advises.

"Lillian, William's not asking you to leave. In fact, quite the opposite. He's asking you to remain in the house and is allowing you to stay there as long as you need. You will continue to receive your monthly allowance. You'll be just fine," Henry reasons with her.

"That's not acceptable. I want a payout of it all. I want to be done with William."

Henry looks through the papers. "I'm not sure I can make it happen. You need to talk to your accountant. I don't think that's what you want to do. You'll lose over half of your money to inheritance taxes if you do it that way. By giving it to you as an allowance, the taxes are less extreme. Plus, what could you need all that money for today?"

"It's none of your business on how I choose to spend my money," Lillian snaps.

Henry holds his hands up in mock surrender. I realize my mouth is hanging open.

It's interesting to see this spectacle happen up front and center. It's like watching a bad soap opera playing out in front of me—overplayed, too much plastic surgery, and dramatic. I wonder if her eyes can actually shut when she sleeps at night. Can she actually even close her eyes? Does her hairline actually move each time she blinks? Does it hurt to have that much collagen injected into your lips? Can she even close her lips? They don't quite meet in the middle, they're so puffy. It's kind of gross actually. And she's making an idiot of herself, and her poor lawyer is just sitting there beside himself.

Her two sons are just sprawled in their chairs expressionless. They aren't upset. They aren't happy. They're just there, staring at the walls. Then I notice what they are doing—they're each clenching the muscles in their right arm and holding it. I count to ten and watch them move to the left arm and do the same. Then they go back to the right again. I can't believe what I'm seeing. No wonder William calls them Dumb and Stupid.

Lillian stands up and storms out of the room with her lawyer and twin sons trailing behind her. That's fine. She can head back to wherever she came from.

"I think we're going to have a problem," William suggests to Henry.

"Oh, I'm positive we're going to have a problem, but I've already started preparing with some of my team because I figured this might be coming." The three of us sit here quietly, each of us replaying the fiasco that just unfolded in front of us.

Looking at William, Henry says, "It may not make a difference if you two don't marry. The money from your mother's estate and the house will always belong to you. What's at stake is the half of your father's estate and the seat on the board of your dad's company.

"I understand," William says. "I'm positive that my dad didn't want her or her kids to take that seat. The money, as far as I'm concerned, can go to the charities that my mother requested. The house I need to think about what to do with."

"Philadelphia isn't such a bad place to raise your kids. You turned out pretty well."

William stands. "Henry, I appreciate your help. Let's figure out how to manage the house. Quinn overheard them talking about hiring private investigators, which I couldn't care less about. However, they also have plans for an auction house to come in and clear out my mother's things."

"We'll send an injunction over today and make sure she knows that isn't to happen."

William extends his hand. "Again, thank you for your help today. We'll be at the Rittenhouse for the remainder of our stay. Although, I'm thinking of taunting her and going over to the house today. I'd like to make sure to talk to the housekeeper. She'll be a good inside person for us, and I'll make sure she doesn't fire Harriett."

"I don't think that's necessarily a bad idea, but just so you know, Harriett and Marcus are employees of the estate, not of hers. Make sure to take your bodyguard, and don't let her escalate it."

"I understand."

chapter

fifteen

WILLIAM

I can't say that the reading of the will went any differently than I expected. I saw Quinn recognize what Dumb and Stupid were busy doing with their clinching muscles shit. I'm surprised she actually caught on as quickly as she did. It took me a couple of times of sitting with them to realize what they did. They seem to zone out when their mother freaks, or just talks really. Not that I blame them, she doesn't have much to say.

"I want to go by the house this afternoon and spend some time with Harriett. I'd love for you to join me, but please don't feel obligated if you're not comfortable or you have things to do at the office," I explain to Quinn.

"I do have a few things to do for work," she says carefully, "but are you kidding? This is better than anything I've ever seen on television. I definitely want to go to the house. Plus, Gerald will be with us, so I feel pretty safe."

"Gerald, are you up for running by the house?"

"Anything you want, sir," he says.

Looking over at Quinn, I notice how nice she looks. "Do you think we should change and go more casual or go as we are?"

"I think I should go put on some jeans, and we can go act like we're going to really settle in. Too bad we can't bring an overnight bag or something and really freak her out." Her giggle is the sweetest sound.

"You've really nailed it right on the head. Let's just put some casual clothes on and go rattle her cage a bit."

We arrive at the Rittenhouse, and she quickly goes to her room. I look out at the late afternoon sun setting behind the capital building and pour myself a glass of scotch. Maybe a little bit of liquid courage will help me prepare for what I'm sure is going to be World War III. Part of me is excited; the other part of me dreads this. I'm determined to be nice about all of this, but we know she's just a bitch.

When Quinn walks back into the living room, I'm stunned. She looks positively beautiful. She's wearing skintight jeans that show off every delicious curve and a sweater that fits just right in all the right places, along with a pair of ballet flats. She looks dignified yet casual. I know she was worried about being outside of Lillian's sphere, but Quinn has more class than most of the women I grew up with.

"You look great. Are you ready?"

She blushes and bites her lip—that delicious lip I'd like to be the one biting. "May I have a glass of what you're drinking?"

"Absolutely." I stand and pour her two fingers of scotch. "With or without ice?"

"Without is fine."

I hand her the glass of tawny liquid. "Sit with me. We're not in any hurry."

We sit down together, and she fits well in the crook of my arm. I can smell the floral scent of her shampoo.

"I'm sorry about today," she says just above a whisper.

"What do you have to be sorry about?"

"I just wish it was easier, but at least it was entertaining."

I laugh. "Yes, Lillian has always been entertaining. She wasn't always so plastic and over the top."

"I can't imagine that she was. Your dad had to have fallen in love with her to marry her."

"Maybe. We weren't that close after my mom died."

"Well, hopefully, this afternoon will be a little entertaining." She giggles and puts her fingers over her mouth. "Does that make me a bad person?"

I chuckle. "Not after what she pulled this afternoon. But I'd much rather pick up where we left off this morning." I rub her shoulder.

She leans in, and her kiss takes my breath away. Reaching for her perfect mound, I'm hard already. As I play with her nipples, she moans and it's the most exquisite sound. My phone rings, interrupting us.

"We have all night," she whispers.

I begrudgingly reach for my phone. The caller ID tells me it's Henry. "Hello?"

"I've set up the auditor to go through the house and take an inventory and compare it to the one we have from a few years ago. If we find anything amiss, we'll take it from her inheritance. I've discussed your father's will with one of my colleagues, and we believe that if she takes her inheritance in a lump sum, then she will need to vacate the house. Are you okay with that? We just feel it's the only way to protect your assets."

"I'll defer to you on that. If that's your recommendation, I'm fine with that."

"Would you like me to tell her or would you like to let her know?" Henry asks.

"I'll talk to her. In fact, Quinn and I were just talking about heading over now."

"Let me know how it goes."

"Will do. Thank you, Henry."

I disconnect the call and tell Quinn what he said.

"Let's head over, and we can decide what to do afterward."

I can't help but be disappointed that we aren't going back to what we were doing before he called, but we have all night to explore.

She crosses the room and gathers her purse. She's graceful and never complains—yet another reason to really like her. As we ride down the elevator to meet Gerald at the car, I smell her perfume, and it makes my dick hard. "Should we come up with a signal for you to tell me you need some time alone with Lillian?"

I snort. "I will definitely not need any alone time with *her*."

"I'm sorry. I didn't mean that kind of 'alone.' I just thought, if there was something you wanted to say, something you didn't want me to hear."

She's so cute when she's trying to be gracious. "Thank you. If anything, I think I need you as a witness to what's said."

She nods. "That's probably smart." She has something else to say, but we've arrived in the lobby, and we see Gerald waiting for us.

Once we get situated in the car, I reach for her hand. "First, let me say thank you again for doing this. I know this is above and beyond what we agreed to."

She leans over and gives me the softest kiss, which makes me fall even harder for her. I've never felt this way about anyone, and it's almost disconcerting.

"Second," I continue, "the plan is to make it clear what she can and cannot do. The house is full of antiques, and she can't sell them off."

As we pull up in front of the house, I smile because I see Harriett peeking out the window where she usually does when she knows I'm coming.

The front door opens before we are both out of the car. She has a look of concern on her face. "Master William, I'm so glad you're here. Miss Lillian has broken two vases."

I take a deep breath. This may not be as easy as I was hoping. "Well, that's not good. Can you please let Lillian know that I'll be waiting for her in the salon?"

As we enter the house, we walk past a huge table that has been in that spot my entire life. I remember the huge bouquets of flowers my mother would decorate the table with. Today it's covered in what looks like junk mail, several pairs of shoes beneath the table, and multiple high-end bags. It's chaos. No wonder my dad was living mostly in Rittenhouse. I look up as Harriett disappears around the corner upstairs to the master suite. There's another loud crash, and then I hear, "What the fuck is he doing in my house?"

"Maybe it wasn't the best idea to leave Gerald outside. Should we at least invite him in to remain in the foyer?" Quinn murmurs.

"I just texted him."

"Great minds think alike." She winks at me and reaches for my hand, and it oddly settles me. "I'm ready to call 911 if I need to."

Gerald slips into the room, taking up an unobtrusive post by the door. He nods in greeting, but before they can say anything, Lillian stalks into the room wearing silk pajamas and a silk bathrobe that flows behind her as if it was a cape. "What the fuck are you doing in my house?"

"I think it was made abundantly clear that the house belongs to me. I'm the one who pays the utilities, the property taxes, and the salary for the staff. You're welcome to stay rent free until you choose not to and live on your allowance. But there was an insurance audit two years ago of all the household items, and they must be accounted for, which means the two vases, possibly a third that you have destroyed today and anything else that may be missing is going to be withheld from your inheritance."

"You can't do that!"

"I spoke with Henry after you left, and he made it clear that I could."

"I'll sue you."

"If you can find someone who will represent you when you vandalized turn-of-the-century antiques, by all means, do." She's steaming, so I put it out there just so she knows. "Lillian, please, also know that should you chose to take the lump sum of your inheritance, you will immediately be evicted from the house."

The rage in her eyes is evident. "Fuck you."

"I have set up an auditor to come in and go through everything. It's the same person who went through for the insurance claim. They'll be here tomorrow morning at eight."

"You can't do that. What about my things?"

"They'll be completing the inventory all week. If there is something that you feel doesn't belong to the estate, just make a note. They certainly won't be going after the clothes in your closet. They're looking for the antiques that are part of this house."

"I won't allow them in the house," she sputters.

"You have a choice, Lillian. You can live here happily for free, no property taxes, no utilities, with Harriett and Marcus to help you maintain the house, and enjoy your monthly allowance to go shopping and maybe have something left over to give your sons. I'm not pushing you out. You can stay as long as you want. Heck, if you even want to redecorate some of the rooms with your own money, I'll have everything packed up and stored. I have no problems doing that, but let me be abundantly clear. My house. My things. My rules. It's been that way since I was twenty-five. I've been kind and allowed you to live here. That will only change if you decide you're going to be destructive. Do you understand?"

"I'm going to fight this. Your father promised me this house."

I laugh because I know that isn't the case. "I'm positive he didn't do that given what he did with his will. But even if he did, it was never his to promise you, and no court will tell you otherwise. Sure, you can hire an attorney who will represent you for hundreds of thousands of dollars, but that is your precious inheritance that pays for that."

"Well, you and your sham girlfriend will find that I'm a viper and I bite. I'll take it to the Supreme Court if I have to."

I can't help myself, and I laugh out loud.

"It'll be a waste of money," Quinn inserts. "Your stepson fucked my brains out this morning, and I expect that tonight we will do a repeat. You can take your sham relationship theory and go to hell. We work together, and it isn't for public consumption that we're dating. William may not tell you this, but I have no problems telling you that you're behaving like a small child. Your husband died. His father died. All you care about is the money, and that's truly sad."

Lillian's mouth visibly drops open in shock. In my head, I'm pumping my fist high above my head and thinking this is a drop-the-mic moment. Lillian has underestimated Quinn, and she's in for a rude awakening if she thinks she can go toe to toe with her. Not only is Quinn book smart, but she's street smart, and that'll take Lillian down about eight pegs and quick.

"I don't have to fucking talk to you," Lillian retorts.

"You're right, you don't have to talk to her, but you do have to talk to me. Let me be clear, tomorrow morning the auditor's coming in and going to inventory everything. The vases you destroyed and anything else they can't locate will be deducted from your inheritance. And as for what you broke, I really hope they weren't one of the Ming vases that my mother had, because right there, that's a $5 million deduction."

Clenching her fists at her side, she screams something inaudible and marches out of the room. This is a woman who's definitely used to getting her own way and is absolutely beside herself, but that is not going to happen now.

Harriett steps into the salon. "Harriett, can you grab Marcus and meet me here?"

"Yes, Master William." Harriett scurries off with a smile on her face.

"That was way too much fun," I tell Quinn.

"I know. I'm sorry I said anything. I should have kept my mouth shut, but she was so belligerent and hateful to you, I felt like I needed to step in and set her straight."

"I thought it was brilliant. Thank you."

Marcus and Harriett join us in the salon and stand at the door. I invite them to sit down. "Marcus, what shape are the grounds in?"

"Very good, sir. Your mother's hydrangeas are preparing to bloom, and I'm fertilizing with today's watering."

"Good. It looks great to me. All the equipment is in good working order?"

"Yes, sir. I have an account at the hardware store if I need anything."

"Wonderful. How are the cars?"

"They're fine. I know Miss Lillian would like a newer vehicle, but it is only two years old."

"I agree. Let's hold off on buying a new car. If she wants to buy something new, she can do that with her own money."

A large smile erupts on his face, and I know he's happy with that.

Turning to Harriett, I ask, "What is the shape of the house?"

"I will admit I do struggle to keep up. Miss Lillian is a bit of a whirling dervish."

"I see that. The auditors will be here tomorrow to check the inventory of the house. Is there anything you are aware of that is missing?"

"There are a few things. I can make a note for them just in case they've been put away somewhere I'm not aware of."

"I don't want you to feel like you are in any danger," I stress. "So, if you feel uncomfortable, please let us know, and I'll make sure that you have your own help and escort here at the house, but I really need you to stay here. I've no problems hiring a security team to join you."

"There's nothing that women or her sons can do to hurt me. I know jujitsu," she informs me.

I raise my eyebrows in surprise. "That sounds good. I hope it doesn't come to that though." I look around the room and survey the house I grew up in. It would look great with a bunch of kids running around. I'm not sure where that thought came from. "You know how to reach me. Currently, I don't have any plans to move back to Philadelphia, so I'm depending on you both to care for the house as if it was your own."

Harriett sits up and proudly states, "Not a problem, Master William."

I stand and open my arms, and both Harriett and Marcus step in and give me a hug. "I would never have made it through my teen years without you both. You're welcome to remain here as long as you want. You're family."

Harriett wipes a tear away. "Thank you, Master William."

I reach for Quinn's hand, and as we walk, I tell Gerald, "I think we need to make plans to have someone here at the house tonight. Can you help me with that?"

"Yes, sir. I'll make sure that happens. Give me two minutes." Gerald seats us in the back of the car and then puts up the partition between the front and the back as he calls somebody. Over the intercom, he announces, "Jim Adelson has a team that will be at the house within the hour and will remain in shifts twenty-four hours a day for the next few weeks."

"Thank you, I appreciate it." Turning to Quinn, I take her hand in mine. "What would you like to do for dinner?"

"I'm very flexible. It seems everyone wants you for something. I hate to be one more in line."

"I think it's me who wants something from you." Her lips call to me—those sweet, luscious lips, all plump and pink and parted and so damn tempting. Suddenly, the only thing I want is to taste her and take her and make her mine. I lean over and kiss her. My hand wanders to her warmest spot, and I rub back and forth over her jeans. Her hips move restlessly as I touch her precious spot. Her hand glides across my chest, causing my skin to tingle beneath the thin fabric of my shirt. The casual touch sends a jolt of electricity through my entire body, spurring a host of memories from this morning. I want her hands on my skin, her lips pressed against mine, her body below, above, and against me any way she'll have me, as many times as she wants.

The trip to the Rittenhouse is short. Gerald has stopped the car and opened the door before I realized we've arrived. Quinn discreetly wipes her mouth and gets out of the car. She's a perfect shade of crimson. Gerald winks at her, and I see her smile back.

Taking her hand, I'm ready to race her back to our room and ravish her, but Jennifer stops me. "Are we still good for dinner tonight? Owen is bringing his girlfriend, and I thought I'd introduce you to my husband." She turns, drawing attention to a man in his early thirties dressed in a suit with shoulder-length blond hair and a two-day-old beard and piercing blue eyes. I think he's a good-looking guy, and I'm not sure I want him anywhere near Quinn.

He steps forward and extends his hand. "Jefferson Mills. Nice to meet you."

"Great to meet you too." Mills? I wonder if he's related to Francis, so I ask.

"Yes, she's my little sister." He smiles. "I was ahead of you and Owen by three years in school."

"So nice to meet you, Jefferson. We were just heading upstairs to change for dinner," Quinn informs them.

My cock automatically deflates. She squeezes my hand in assurance that I hope says that we'll eventually pick up where we left off. "We had some drama with the stepmonster. I'll tell you all about it over dinner if you're interested."

"Sounds great," Jefferson says. "We can reminisce over some predinner drinks."

"Owen's always late, but his girlfriend should be here any time," Jennifer shares.

Quinn rushes me off to the elevator and waves. "See you in a few."

The elevator door closes, and I back her into the corner and nuzzle her ear. "This isn't how I imagined our evening going."

"If you think dinner gets you off the hook from being fucked hard, you're going to be sadly disappointed." She bites her lip, driving me crazy.

"That's the kind of disappointment I can live with," I tell her.

QUINN

Jennifer turns to me and says, "Oh my gwad, you should see the crap these two pulled when they were in high school."

"Be nice," Owen warns.

"Don't hold a thing back," Monica interjects.

I like Monica. She's Owen's girlfriend, and I have a feeling they're more serious than we are led to believe. She's beautiful and exotic with dark hair, dark features, and big black eyes. I particularly like that she's wearing off-the-rack clothes from a department store and, like me, has a Kate Spade bag—nice but not over the top.

"Owen was playing with one of the young housekeepers, and William was covering for him." There are some protests from the guys, but they're hardly believable. "When our mom found out, she went crazy. She made Owen apologize to her."

"Apologize? She did a lot more than that. She grabbed me by the ear and marched me down to housekeeping, and I had to apologize to the girl in front of all of the housekeepers," Owen says as he rubs his ear. "She then made William and me sit in her office and lectured us on how to be respectful of women. She gave both of us condoms—which was humiliating."

"That's right. We could never use those condoms either. That would have been just wrong to use condoms bought by your mom," William reminisces.

"I think that was her point." Jennifer laughs.

"Oh, no, she was very clear that she wasn't forty yet and didn't want to become a grandmother at such a young age," Owen informs us.

We are all laughing so loud that we're distracting the other diners to the restaurant. "What happened to the housekeeper?" I ask, keeping my voice low.

"She's now the head of housekeeping." Looking at Monica, he is quick to add, "She's married with a bunch of kids too."

"There must be more stories," I ask.

"Do you remember what you guys did to Brett and Jason on their sixteenth birthday?" Jennifer asks.

"I have no idea what you're talking about," William answers in such a way that we know he recalls exactly what they did.

Jennifer leans into the table and, just loud enough for the table to hear, says, "They were having a big party with all the who's who of Philadelphia, but William and Owen were on restriction and weren't allowed to attend the party. So they snuck into the kitchen and put chocolate-flavored laxatives in their milkshakes."

Both Owen and William are laughing so hard, they are almost on the floor.

"What happened?" Jefferson asks.

"Brett and Jason had big speeches to give to thank everyone for coming."

"They'd been practicing for weeks at home," William injects.

"Both the guys had dates—the head cheerleader from school and some other girl that was way cooler than the rest of us—and they were planning on getting laid. Brett walks to the front to make his speech and lets a huge fart go, and it got picked up by the microphone, so everyone heard it. Then Jason was laughing so hard, he blew out his pants. Not only was it an ugly sight, but it smelled bad. Needless to say, they didn't get laid."

"We didn't know that we put too much laxative in their shakes and that it would take effect so quickly."

"You didn't?" I exclaim.

"Everyone was sure it was us, but they couldn't pin it on us since we weren't anywhere close to the party," Owen says, laughing.

I look at William. "Lillian must have been super pissed."

"It was almost as bad as what we saw today—almost."

"What happened today?" Owen asks.

William walks him through what happened, giving them the highlights.

"Your dad was so smart," Jefferson remarks.

"He was. I know he loved Lillian once, but if I'm honest, he wasn't over my mom, and he must have known she married him for the money."

"When's the funeral?" Monica asks.

"I'm not sure. My dad's will didn't even specify what he wanted. Of course, right now with the crash, we're having problems getting his remains," William says.

I put my hand on William's leg and rub it to console him as best as I know how. He puts his arm around me, and I know this is hurtful.

"Jennifer, how did you and Jefferson meet?" I ask to change the subject.

She glows when she talks about him, and I love seeing them look deep into each other's eyes. They're head over heels in love. Once she's done with her story, she deflects to Monica and Owen, and they are quick to share their story.

"When are you two getting married?" William asks. "I want to be there."

"We won't be getting married," Monica says. "I know it seems crazy, but my mother married six times, and not only do I not have a good reference, but things are good as they are. We're happy with our relationship. We can have kids and do what everyone does without a piece of paper."

I nod. I know a lot of people who say that.

"I support you," William says, "but I'd still like to take him out for a good bachelor party. Get him nice and drunk and in a bit of trouble."

"Don't pay any attention to him," I warn Owen.

"He's only saying that because he's worried I'm going to do that for him, which I fully intend to do." Owen gives William a warning look.

"We haven't set a date," I share.

"I hope you'll do it here at the Rittenhouse," Jennifer says.

"We still have a few things to work out," I tell them.

"Pish, pish," Jennifer discounts. "When you know, you know. You two know."

I'm a bit taken aback. I could see myself with William for a while, but I don't know about forever. The longest boyfriend I've ever had was Mason, and that was two years, and look at how that ended.

Dinner begins to break up, and I hug Jennifer and Monica goodbye before we head up to our room. I feel like I've made two good friends. "I like your friends."

"They like you." He backs me into the corner of the elevator, kissing me deeply as he lifts my skirt and slips his hands in my panties, immediately going for my special spot. "You're wet."

I nod. "You have no idea how hard it was to sit next to you all night and want you to bend me over the table and fuck me hard and fast from behind with them watching."

"You want to be watched?" He's excited at the prospect.

I giggle. "Not particularly, but you do something to me that makes me want to fuck you, and I don't care who sees."

"I feel the same way." The elevator stops, and he sucks my juices from his fingers. "I don't think we're going to get much sleep tonight." He shuts the door to our suite behind him, and our lips crash together.

He unzips the back of my dress, and it falls into a pool on the floor. I start to slip out of my stiletto sandals, but he stops me.

"Leave those on."

I'm standing in a sexy pair of white silk panties and matching bra. Feeling self-conscious, I start to cross my arms over myself, but he grabs my arms and opens them wide, taking in a long look. "God, you're beautiful."

I look down and turn crimson. I've rarely ever heard that before. I step forward and kiss him. Right now I want him inside me. Not wasting any time, I undo his belt and slide his pants off. His erection tents in his boxer shorts, and I start to get on my knees, but he stops me. "Tonight is going to be all about you."

He unbuttons his shirt, watching me as he does each button, and I quiver with anticipation. Dropping the shirt to the floor with the rest of our clothes, he grabs me by the hand and leads me to his bedroom. He sits on the bed with me standing between his legs. He takes a big sniff. "You smell so good." Leaning forward, he kisses and licks at my breast over the silk while his hands reach around me, unhooking my bra and releasing my generous breasts. He attacks one nipple with his mouth, swirling his tongue and sucking the nipple deep into his mouth while his hand pulls and pinches the other. Moaning my appreciation, I try to get on my knees again, and instead he insists, "Lie down on the bed. I'd like to give you a massage."

I comply, and he focuses mainly on my back, chest, and hips. He avoids my sex, and the touch is making me more and more eager for him to be inside me. Gradually, he works the tension out of me.

I roll over, feeling relaxed and like jelly, and his hands slip lower, his fingers running over the smooth spot between my legs. His teasing only increases my need. I groan softly.

"I feel like I'm going to just... melt."

"Can I touch you?" he asks.

"God... yes, please touch me." I open my legs wide to give him plenty of access.

With the lightest of touch, he runs his fingers at the edge of my slit. I gasp at his touch. My hips move up to meet his caress, wishing for more.

He delicately slides his hand up and down, one finger on each side of my wanting and wet opening. My breathing gets heavier.

"William... I think you're going to make me.... Keep doing that...."

As his hand reaches the top of its arc each time, he squeezes his fingers together, just enough to tease and trap my clit for a moment. Then he releases it and runs his fingers back down, varying the speed each time so I can never quite know when that pressure would be back, keeping me on edge and begging for more.

With his other hand, he gently toys with my nipple, making it hard and wanting.

"Oh... this is so much better.... I had no idea...."

He pushes one of his fingers between my legs more firmly downwards, forcing my lips open and running the finger lightly up and down through the slickness.

"Have you played with yourself while you've been here?" he whispers into my ear. "Have you laid on your bed and made yourself come?"

I nod, unable to speak.

"Did you think about me?"

"Yes... I thought about the first time you listened to me having phone sex and what it did to you.... When you told me what it did to you... I knew then I wanted to get you to... fuck me. I just needed to... figure out how...."

"I wanted to fuck you long before I heard that. But hearing your naughty voice did me in," he murmurs. "My fingers are on your wet pussy, and soon I'm going to slide myself into you and feel how tight you are."

"Yes... I want you to do that."

He tips his finger inside me and rubs at that special spot, causing me to jump.

"Is that okay?"

"Yes... that's... really nice. God, I'm so wet. I can't believe how wet you make me."

He slowly and ever so gently fucks me with the tip of his finger. He puts the finger in his mouth, and I watch, my chest heaving, and I'm breathless.

"It's delicious," he says. "I want to taste you with my tongue."

"God... William... you can do whatever you want to me... just please do something. You're driving me crazy." I start playing with my nipples, pulling and stretching them.

He slides down the length of my body until his head is just below my waist, and I spread my legs a little wider apart to give him room to get comfortable. His tongue starts at the top of my inner thigh and moves upward at a leisurely pace. "I love that you're so smooth." Then he travels back down the other side. While he does this, he teases my opening with his finger, pushing my lips open and then together again, entering me briefly and then retreating again. I can hardly stand it, and I grip the sheets.

He bows his head lower and runs his tongue up the length of my entrance.

"Oh, Jesus... nobody's ever done that. That feels amazing."

He licks his way around me carefully, just delicately flicking his tongue over my hot spot once or twice but focusing most of his attention around my labia and thighs. His fingers and hands remain busy, stroking and playing with me constantly. I'm lost in my own euphoric world, eyes closed, occasionally pushing my hips upward to grind myself a little more firmly into his face.

"Quinn," he says. "I'd like to fuck you now."

"Oh God, yes, please, William. That was incredible, but I really want you inside me."

He moves away and grabs a condom from somewhere before sheathing himself. It's so big, and it makes me nervous. I'm still a little sore from earlier. Moving over my body, he rests above me, looking down into my eyes.

"Put your hand around me," he says. "Make me wet as well."

Stroking myself, I coat my hand with my own wetness and then begin to stroke him before guiding him to my entrance.

I gasp as I stretch to accommodate him. "You're already good for me. Now please let me fuck you or I think I might explode," he groans.

I smile, and we push our bodies closer together, fully seating him deep inside me. It's a tight fit, and I'm not sure I can take any more. He slowly backs out and then moves back in again, picking up speed. The only sound heard is the slick noise of two bodies colliding again and again.

"Oh God, William... that is just... oh yes!"

I shudder and quickly wrap my arms around him. "Just let me feel you like that... for a second... oh yes... don't move... oh God!"

A tremor courses through me, and I cry out. "Oh fuck!" I gasp. "Oh that's... oh fuck! Oh God, William, you made me come through penetration."

He has a smile of complete satisfaction as he watches me ride out my pleasure for a few moments before kissing me softly.

"You're the first person to make me come through penetration, do you know that? I've always had to... do it through direct stimulation. Holy shit... that was amazing."

"You're incredibly responsive."

I gasp again. "Oh God, I loved that. And you feel so big inside me. You hit my G-spot perfectly. I just... God, I just want to stay like this forever."

He kisses me again. "That sounds nice, but I was hoping it was my turn next."

"Oh, yes... fuck me, William. Do whatever you want. I want you to fill me with your seed," I say, grinning wickedly, knowing how much he loves it when I talk dirty.

"You're a naughty one, aren't you?" He pushes back inside me, picking up a steady rhythm, concentrating on his own orgasm. Moving my body with his, I feel my own orgasm begin to build again.

"Fuck me, William. I'm going to come again." My hand moves to my clit, and he gives me the room to rub.

My muscles contract hard on his cock. "So close now...," he grunts. "Just want to feel you come again. Come on my cock, Quinn."

I groan again and again, the tremors rippling through me, my pussy milking his cock, and together we come.

"Quinn," he calls as he spurts deep inside me.

We're both satiated, and he collapses on me, breathing heavy, my pussy a vice not willing to let him go. "Holy shit, that was incredible," I whisper. "You're all mine now—for a while at least."

My pussy finally lets him go, and he gets out of bed and throws out the used condom before joining me in bed again and holding me tight. We fall asleep in postcoital bliss.

chapter

seventeen

WILLIAM

I wake slowly with my body intertwined with Quinn's. The light is peeking through the blackout curtains of the hotel room. I loved last night. Quinn was incredibly responsive, and I love the way she really seemed to blossom and become more comfortable and confident as we continued. Usually, I'm more a get in and get out kind of guy, but for some reason, last night I wanted to enjoy myself with Quinn and take is slow. It was worth it too.

I need coffee. My head is pounding, probably from the lack of sleep, but I'm going to pretend it's just the lack of caffeine. I carefully extract myself from Quinn. She's sleeping far too peacefully in our bed—yes, it's our bed. The thought brings a smile to my face. Eventually, I'm going to need to think about all these strange new feelings that I'm experiencing for the first time in my life.

I walk into the living room and fire up my computer to see what's going on. There's an email from Henry explaining a few things that I need to get done for the estate. He also included a spreadsheet covering the details and expenses of the house. Everything looks somewhat copacetic, but it'll take some looking it over eventually. It's a seven thousand plus square foot house built in the 1800s, and it probably keeps in more of the cold than it keeps out. I remember the drafts that my mother used to complain about.

My cell phone rings, and I don't recognize the number, but it's a local number. Figuring it might be the auditor, I answer. "William Bettencourt."

"Mr. Bettencourt? This is Agent Michael McGraw with the Federal Bureau of Investigations."

"Yes, Agent McGraw? What can I do for you?"

"We were wondering if we could come by and meet with you this morning?"

Why would the FBI be calling me? "What is this in regard to?" I ask, wanting to tell them I'm not interested, but curiosity gets the better of me.

"This is in regard to your father."

I stop short. My father? What has Lillian done?

"We can meet at my lawyers, Henry Gray's office. He's at Gray, Wilcox, and Holmes."

"We'll meet you there at eleven."

"What's your number, Agent McGraw? In case there's a conflict or we need to change venues?"

He recites a number, and I write it down on a scrap piece of paper.

I disconnect the call, and when I look up, I see Quinn standing there, her hair a matted mess, and she's wearing my shirt from last night. All the blood in my head rushes down to my cock. She looks beautiful, and I'd like to go back and join her in bed.

"Who was that?" she asks.

"It seems the FBI wants to talk to me about my father."

"What do you think that could be about?"

"They didn't say, and I'm curious." I put a call into Henry and let them know that the FBI is calling about my father and that I've asked them to meet at his office at eleven and ask if he could join me. Thankfully, he agrees and suggests bringing the white-collar attorney in their offices who has dealt with my dad as well.

I look at Quinn. "Well, it looks like we're all set. I would've much preferred time with you in bed, or the floor… maybe the dining room table, or pushed up against the couch."

She blushes, and I wonder if she'll always be embarrassed that she enjoys sex. Her shyness is beautiful. "Well, we'll still have lots of time later, it's not like we're rushing back to San Francisco. We have a few more days here."

"I'm hoping this last longer than just here. This has been rather nice."

She smiles but doesn't say a thing, and it sticks with me for half a second that she doesn't agree, but I keep moving on. I call Gerald and let him know when we're looking to leave.

Quinn asks, "Would you prefer I stay here? I have no problem being here alone. I have plenty of work to occupy me."

"No, please join me. I'd love your company and support today. Maybe afterward we can go out for a nice lunch and do some exploring around Philadelphia. Independence Hall is really quite spectacular."

"Do I have time to shower and get ready? I'd hate to show up smelling like sex."

"You smell like a rose. But yes, you have plenty of time. We can head out just before eleven."

She disappears into the bathroom, and it takes all my willpower to not follow behind her like a dog in heat. She emerges smelling amazing and looking beautiful.

She throws her computer in her bag and says, "I'm ready when you are."

I really like that she's always so accommodating but yet able to stand up for herself when necessary.

On the drive over, I see the trees in the downtown area as people walk with a spring to their step and enjoy a little bit of sunshine after what was a long, cold winter. My thoughts keep drifting to my father, and I can't help but wonder what the hell he got himself into. "Gerald, when we get there, can you make a few calls and find out if our people have learned anything about the accident and any remains? It just seems odd that they don't have anything to report at this point. "Please text me if you learn anything new."

"Yes, sir. Not a problem. I'll get that taken care of."

When we arrive at Henry's office, Gerald opens the car door, and we get out. I spot two Lincoln Continentals with government plates, and I'm sure the FBI is already here and waiting. It is twenty minutes to eleven, which piques my curiosity further.

The receptionist lets us know that they've arrived and they're waiting in the conference room.

Henry joins us, and a short, stout woman with warm eyes follows quickly behind him. "I'd like you to meet Marie Abraham. She worked with your dad on criminal defense work."

"Hi, it's nice to meet you," she says. "Your father has told me a lot about you. He was very proud of you. I'm sorry for your loss."

"Thank you. Do you know why they're here?"

"I don't really have any idea what this could be regarding. We were dealing with some issues with his company, but I can't see why they'd want to meet with you. It was regarding some union issues."

"Could Lillian have done something?"

"That's not likely," Henry assures me.

"Let's play this cautiously," Marie says, then proceeds to map out our plan for meeting with the FBI. "We want them to do most of the sharing, and we want to do most of the listening."

The four of us walk into the conference room, and Marie introduces me, Quinn, and Henry. We sit down, and I quickly realize Marie's familiar with both of the agents.

Before they start, I ask, "Did you both come together?"

"Yes, we came together," Agent McGraw says with a puzzled look.

"Then where are the other two agents?" I ask.

"I'm sorry?"

"I noticed two cars out front. I was just curious."

"We are executing a search warrant on your father's house at this time."

"Technically, it's my home and has been for almost ten years." That still doesn't tell me where the other two agents are, but I smile brightly. "That must just be sending my stepmother, Lillian, over the edge."

They continue. "We've also executed a search warrant of your father's offices."

"Why wasn't I notified?" Marie interjects.

"These searches are in regard to the possibility of SEC violations," Agent McGraw says.

"SEC violations? How is that possible?" I ask.

"It's believed that your father may have shared insider information regarding Bettencourt Industries with several individuals."

"Bettencourt Industries has been public since I was in preschool. What could he have done that constituted stock price manipulation and insider trading?"

"We didn't say stock price manipulation and insider trading."

I roll my eyes. What else could it be? "All right, so why did you need to speak with me?"

"Tell us about your relationship with your father."

Marie interjects, "Is this really necessary?"

"Yes. We see there are a group of phone calls between you two."

"They're father and son," she reminds them.

"We're looking to see how close they were."

"I hadn't spoken to my father in probably three months. He recently passed while he was in Tanzania in an accident."

"When do you expect to get his remains?"

"Well, it was a helicopter crash, and right now we're having problems getting his remains—if there are any—because he died in a foreign country. It looks like the crash happened in a deep ravine off Kilimanjaro."

"Mr. Bettencourt, tell us why there was a large transfer of money into your bank account and you were added to several existing accounts."

Henry speaks up. "He inherited money from his mother. We began moving money around and adding his name to the accounts attached to his inheritance, which he came into when he was twenty-five years old. This was necessary to pay some of the fees associated with the home on Rittenhouse Square."

"But this was done before you read the will yesterday," the agent counters.

Henry looks at them a little surprised. "Yes, but the will of Victoria Bettencourt stipulated that William inherit at twenty-five years old. We didn't realize that this hadn't been done until we began digging through James Bettencourt's estate."

The agents look at me. "Why didn't you ask for your rightful inheritance at twenty-five?"

"I was eleven years old when my mother died. No one told me of her will. As far as I knew, her estate went to my father upon her death."

"We understand Lillian Bettencourt and William will split Reginald Bettencourt's estate. What are the provisions of the will?" Agent McGraw asks.

Henry says in broad strokes, "Half goes to Lillian and half goes to William. They both have some things to take care of. Meanwhile, William owns the house on Rittenhouse Square, and Lillian is living there rent free."

"She's been moving a lot of money around. Are you aware of that?" Agent McGraw asks me.

"It's not surprising. She's been a little panicked given my father funded her lifestyle, and currently, she has no income until the will is read and his estate is through probate."

"She does have quite a bit of debt. Are you aware of that?" Agent McGraw inquires.

"Again, not surprising given my father financed her life, and she hasn't received anything from him in almost two months at this point," I explain.

"Mr. Bettencourt, would it surprise you to learn that we believe your father is the mastermind behind a Ponzi scheme," Agent McGraw presses.

"Ponzi scheme? My father? He wasn't in investments. He was an inventor and entrepreneur," I explain.

"He was collecting and paying out money as he went to investors as he received other investments," the other agent interjects.

I'm trying not to lose my cool. "I work in the venture capital world, and to me, that sounds like he was raising capital for one of his inventions, and when people were unhappy with how long it was taking to recoup their investment, he bought out the previous investors with new investors. That wouldn't have been a Ponzi scheme but managing investors."

"Mr. Bettencourt, we know exactly who you work for, and we know that Miss Quinn Faraday here works with you. We're quite aware of who you are and what you both do at SHN."

I don't know if that's supposed to scare me, but it seems like a bullying tactic, and it just irritates me.

The FBI continues to ask questions about my father that I can't answer. I have no idea what he was doing in Tanzania. I have no idea what's going on with his company. I have no idea what his current creation or invention could be. I have no idea of anything going on.

They eventually finish all their questions and leave. "That seemed strange to me. Did it seem strange to all of you?" I ask Henry, Quinn, and Marie.

"It definitely seemed strange, and why the warrants to search?" Marie questions.

"I haven't been to my dad's office. I guess I should probably go over and meet with the company."

"Let me see if I can help you set that up," Henry offers. "I know the chairman of the board, and maybe we can arrange that for tomorrow or the day after."

"That sounds perfect. I promised Quinn I would show her around Independence Hall today after lunch at Pat's King of Steaks."

"Well, Quinn's in for a treat. Sounds like you guys have a good afternoon planned. I'll send you an email letting you know when to meet with the board and if it's tomorrow or the day after."

"Thank you, Henry. I'll look forward to talking to you soon."

When we get in the car, Quinn exclaims, "What was all of that about with the FBI?"

"I know. That's just crazy. I can't imagine my father was involved in anything illegal like a Ponzi scheme; it just seems a little strange and offhanded."

"Exactly, and a Ponzi scheme? That just seems ridiculous. I can't even imagine it would stand up against a good defense attorney. He's an inventor, and it makes sense that he's raising capital. You said exactly what I was thinking when you said that he was, of course, raising funds. It just doesn't make any sense."

When we get closer to Pat's, I see the corner is crazy with people and there's no parking. "Gerald, you can drop us here. I'll grab you a sandwich and fries with a coke?"

"That sounds perfect."

"Eating here is a challenge. We'll get it to go and head toward Independence Hall and eat over there."

"I'll be waiting."

Quinn and I get in line, and it goes quickly. When it's my turn, I ask for three wiz wit, three fries, two cokes, and one diet."

The employee yells to the crew behind her, and I pay for our lunch.

While we wait, I tell Quinn the story. "Supposedly, Pat is the inventor of the cheesesteak sandwich. He had a hot dog cart and one day got strips of beef from a butcher and fried it up on his grill. A cab driver thought it smelled good and asked for one, and then the next day he had a line of cabbies getting sandwiches. No one knows for sure if it's the real story or not."

Our lunch is ready, and we head back to Gerald and drive to Independence Hall. It isn't far, and we sit on the grass and enjoy our sandwiches. "You mean the cheese in a real cheesesteak is Cheese Whiz?"

"Yep. That's what makes it so good. What do you think?"

"I love a good Philly cheesesteak. This is amazing—the bread is perfectly crunchy on the outside and soft on the inside, melted cheese, and fried onions. What's not to like?" Together we share our fries. "I'm so glad we don't live here. I'd want to eat this every day for lunch, and I'd weigh 700 pounds."

I laugh. "You'd look beautiful no matter what."

Blushing, she looks down at her sandwich. "You shouldn't be bashful when I tell you you're beautiful."

She looks up at me with her head tilted to the side and says, "I'm just... I don't hear that very often."

"Well, that needs to change."

Her smile is radiant. "Thanks."

I know she's not sure where we're going as a couple. I'm not sure either, but I like that we're together, and I like her. I want to explore this further.

We head off to Independence Hall and enjoy a great afternoon of exploring.

chapter

eighteen

WILLIAM

It was a glorious afternoon wandering through Independence Hall, showing Quinn the Articles of Confederation, the Declaration of Independence, and the Constitution. Despite the long line, she enjoyed seeing the Liberty Bell. I love that she was excited like a young schoolgirl—just eager to take it all in. Having never been to Philadelphia, she kept saying, "I need to come back. There's so much to see and do here."

When we get to the car, we decide to go over to the Reading Terminal Market, and we wandered through stall after stall of bright fruit, stunning cut flowers, delicious meats and sausages, and every kind of art for sale.

I picked up a mishmash of dinner, and we split a roast pork sandwich, doughnut, an apple dumpling, a soft pretzel, a whoopie pie, and scrapple. It was quintessential Philadelphian and the perfect dinner. Quinn is comfortable at Lacroix eating a Michelin three-star dinner or eating out of paper food containers.

"What a great junk-food-filled day," Quinn gushes. "I feel fantastic; this is exactly my kind of day."

As I look at her, I see everything I've always been looking for in a woman. When we get in the car, Gerald informs me that he's forwarded a report regarding the helicopter crash to my email. "I wanted to alert you, so you didn't miss it tonight."

I had hoped for a little bit more exercise in the sheets when we returned to the hotel, but it's quite fine to wait so I can read this report.

When we arrive at the hotel, Quinn excuses herself and leaves me to read the report on my own while she has some work to do. She escapes to her room with her laptop. I watch her retreat, and I really hope she's not going to have phone sex with strange men tonight. I'm really not sure I want her doing that anymore. I'd like to see her using that dirty mind with me and not sharing it with anybody else. Call me selfish, but I don't want to share her. Before I get lost in that rabbit hole, I open up my email and download the helicopter crash report.

It's partially in English and partially in Swahili, and I struggle to cut and paste passages into Google Translate. From what I can piece together, it looks like the crash is being attributed to foul play. They believe that there are three bodies plus the pilot, but they can't determine anything about them. I know we sent copies of my father's dental records and a DNA sample, but apparently, the fiery crash left nothing but ashes in a pile of rubble in a difficult to reach location.

This report confirms my belief that there's foul play involved in the accident. That then raises the question of why the FBI is involved. It doesn't make sense that they're looking at SEC violations.

"What did you learn?" Quinn asks.

I look at the clock on my computer and see it's been several hours. I sigh deeply. "They think it's foul play, and the crash is in an area they can't easily get to."

"I'm sorry."

"Thank you. Any chance you'd want to Netflix and chill with me tonight?"

She smiles. "We don't have to watch Netflix to chill."

"I like the way you think, but I wouldn't mind seeing a show on Netflix."

"That's fine." She shimmy's up to me on the couch, sitting close. I love her body heat, and she fit so well next to me.

We watch the movie that caught my eye, but it isn't very good. Oh well. We do get a little bit of chill with our Netflix and enjoy our evening together. Crawling into bed just after midnight, we fall fast asleep.

My phone rings, waking me from a fitful sleep. I glance at the time before I answer. It's never good when the phone rings in the middle of the night.

"Hello?"

Quinn sits up, waiting for the bad news. "William," Lillian slurs, "your father never loved me. The money is payback for everything I did to make him look good. He's now haunting me. I swear, his ghost is here." She's been drinking, and apparently, she's drunk dialing. Big mistake.

"Lillian, I don't need to know this. I understand." She's crying into the phone, alternating between brash defiance and victimhood. Sitting up, I drag my hand through my hair. "I'm sorry if he hurt you. Twenty million dollars is plenty of money for you. This is my father's estate. This is money from his family. The house comes from my mother."

"You don't deserve this house. My lawyer tells me I can fight you." She continues to cry, and I can barely make out anything she says. Pulling herself together, she declares, "There's no way that you two are actually involved. You like to screw women over, just like your dad. Quinn will never love you."

"Lillian, I love Quinn." I don't know what else to say to her. "You should get a big glass of water and get some sleep."

"Never."

Quinn can't look at me, and I know she thinks I made it up to placate Lillian, but I realize that is exactly how I feel. I may have thrown that out a little bit faster than expected, but I feel comfortable with her. I need to tell her how I feel directly. Quinn lies down and pretends to sleep as I continue to try to extricate myself from the phone call, but Lillian is rambling, and I need to know what she knows, so I listen to her nonsense.

When she becomes too incoherent, I finally disconnect the call. "I'm really sorry about that."

Quinn doesn't respond, but her breathing isn't steady enough to show she's asleep, and I know I need to have a talk with her about how I'm falling hard for her. I just hope she feels the same way.

My sleep is troubled with nightmares, mainly about losing Quinn. Finally, I just lie there in the dark, I replay my dreams in my head. The thought of losing Quinn causes me physical pain and leaves me worried. Strangely, I also dreamed about my father telling me to go paint the garage white. Not only do we not really have a garage, but he's never asked me to paint anything—not even a room or a canvas.

I must have dosed off, because when I come to again it's after nine. I need to get moving, or I'll be in bed all day. A wicked thought of being in bed all day with Quinn crosses my mind, bringing a smile to my face and hardening my dick. My head is throbbing, probably from the lack of fluids and caffeine, so I go in search of coffee. Thankfully, our continental breakfast was delivered — coffee, juice, tea, bagels, and fruit. Food doesn't sound appealing right now. I pour myself a large cup of coffee and drink it black, hoping not to dilute the caffeine, and go in search of Quinn. Peeking in her room, I find her asleep in the bed. I wonder why she left last night.

Firing up my email, I see what I was expecting from Henry. It looks like the board wants to meet this morning at eleven o'clock. So much for a day of relaxation. The morning will be spent with the board of directors of my father's company. That doesn't sound relaxing in the least. I debate whether or not Quinn should join me but decide in the end it's probably best to have her there. I rationalize that it shows her how I feel about her. There is acting like you're in love and being in love, and I think we're both the latter.

I'm studying my computer when I hear Quinn walk out of her room. She looks beautiful in a big shirt and her long, luscious legs. Her hair is messy and sexy as hell. "Hey, you, what happened last night?" I ask.

"Sorry. I couldn't sleep, so I worked for a few hours and then fell asleep about four."

"I missed you when I woke up this morning."

She smiles at me but doesn't tell me she missed me too.

"I got an email from Henry," I inform her. "The board would like to see us at eleven this morning. Does that work for you?"

"I need to shower, but I can be ready quickly."

"Feel free to bring your computer, and you can work if it gets too boring."

"Thanks." She's putting up walls, and I need to work on pulling them down, but right now I need to shower, or we'll both be late. I drop a text to Gerald.

Me: It looks like we will need you in about an hour.
Gerald: No problem.
Me: We're headed to Bettencourt Industries. Do you need the address?
Gerald: Nope, I got it. See you downstairs.

When Quinn emerges from her room, she's a vision of beauty. Usually, she wears black and looks great, but today she has a navy pair of wide-legged pants, a white shirt, and a deep red jacket. "You look like you belong here in Philadelphia."

"Too much?"

"Not at all. I like you in colors."

"CeCe tells me that all the time."

"You should listen to her."

As we ride the elevator down, my phone rings, and I deal with an issue with an anxious founder of one of our most recent acquisitions. The phone call lasts the entire drive to my dad's office, but on the way, I watch Quinn stare out the window, and I wonder what she's thinking.

When we arrive, we are escorted up to the twelfth floor. A woman runs over to me and pulls me into a tight hug. "Look how grown up you are."

I recognize Mitzi immediately. She's been my dad's secretary for years. I remember my dad telling me how she is a whiz at patent applications. "Mitzi? What a wonderful surprise to see you. You look the exact same. Please share with me your secrets to stop aging."

She blushes. "You're such a flirt." She looks beyond me and spots Quinn. "And who have you brought home with you?"

"Mitzi, this is my fiancée, Quinn Faraday."

"Oh my goodness." She brings Quinn in for a hug. "I'm so happy to meet you."

"Thank you."

"I'm sorry. I've known William since before he learned to walk. He would sit with his dad and help him with his inventions."

"I think I was a bigger pain than a help."

"Nonsense!" She points us toward the boardroom. "I think the board is all here, and they're preparing for the meeting this morning."

She leads us to the boardroom.

The CEO comes rushing over. "William, so good to see you."

"Thank you."

"Please, take your father's seat."

I sit down, and someone pulls up a chair for Quinn to sit behind me.

I'm handed a copy of the financials, but I know from working with Quinn that no one can find the weaknesses in financials faster than she can. I move over and motion for her to sit next to me. I can tell the men at the table aren't crazy about Quinn being at the table, but I don't care. They won't challenge me, yet.

They present me with a report about my father's death. It includes photos of the accident site. The belief is that it was caused by pilot error, and my father, along with three others, was killed quickly.

"I know this is difficult to hear, but we wanted to show you the due diligence we did."

"Thank you."

As I study the photos, I notice there is a plant growing between the two burnt-out front seats of the helicopter. That doesn't make any sense.

"As we understand it, your father has given you the family seat on the board," the CEO throws out.

I nod. "He has."

"What are your plans?" the sole woman on the board asks.

I'm not sure what I'm going to do, but I don't need to tell them I don't have a plan yet. "I have no immediate plans to move back to Philadelphia."

"Then you'll be resigning your seat?" one of the board members asks, a little too excited for my taste.

This is the company my grandfather founded. There's no way I'd give up my seat. I've reviewed the rules that they've established, and I know what the requirements are to keep my seat on the board. "No, why would I do that?"

"We meet regularly. The bylaws state you can miss up to five meetings a year," the board member tries to explain to me.

"Yes?" I want to watch the asshole squirm. I may be fifty-years his junior, but he's crazy to think I've not studied up and worked with other companies.

"Well, if you don't live here, then you will miss many more than five meetings a year," he tries to make his point.

"Why? Are the planes no longer going to fly? I've read the bylaws, and there is nothing that says I can't Skype or Facetime in for meetings. I shouldn't have any problems."

"That would require a change in the bylaws, which needs to be voted in by the shareholders," another board member attempts to share.

I'm not sure why they want me off, and that alone makes me want to stay. "I don't think so. Plus, I own the largest number of shares between my father's options and my mother's options."

The men are uncomfortable, but I'm not going to make them squirm for long. "Look, I'm not here to make waves. I have some instructions from my father, which I will carry out. My hope is to be here for regularly planned monthly meetings, and I will be available for impromptu meetings via Skype or Facetime."

We walk through three issues on their agenda. Lunch is brought in, and we are served lobster bisque, a broiled swordfish, sautéed vegetables, and a fancy scalloped potato with a decadent cheesecake. I'm a little surprised by the extravagant lunch. This kind of luxury is out of character for my dad.

After lunch, we finish up the last three items on the agenda. I notice a few raises proposed for the executive staff.

"My understanding is that this requires a unanimous vote. I'd like to wait until next month to review and look at some salary surveys. Given I work in this area, these seem a little high to me, but maybe it's the difference between east and west coast."

Some of the board members look ready to shoot me, but I'm also a stockholder, and if they're out to rape the company, then I need to stop them.

After the meeting, I return to Mitzi. "Can you show me my dad's office?"

"Of course." She picks up a set of keys and opens the door. "No one has been in here—not even the cleaning people—since your dad left."

I stop at that statement. The FBI told me they were executing a search warrant of my father's office. If they weren't doing that, what were they doing?

The office looks the same as it did when I was growing up. There is his desk in the corner and workstations throughout the room with computer equipment and thousands of prototypes. Some are his and others by the engineering team. Mitzi unlocks several cabinets and drawers.

"Thanks, Mitzi." She leaves, and Quinn and I look around.

"What are you looking for?" Quinn asks.

"I don't know, but I guarantee that today's lunch was not normal. My dad would not have approved of that, and I'm positive that the salaries they were looking at for the leadership team were way off."

"I agree. I made some notes about the financials that seemed a little off."

"Thank you. I figured you knew your way around a financial statement better than anyone in that room."

"Well, I don't know about that, but there are a few of those guys who are yes-men to your chairman, and that's an invitation to malfeasance."

"Agreed."

We poke around for a few minutes. Finally, I stick my head out of the office and ask Mitzi if she can help me find something.

"Right away." She jumps up and joins us in the office. Mitzi was one person my father trusted implicitly.

"I'm sorry, Mitzi, I wanted to ask you a few questions without raising anyone's suspicions."

"Sure, what can I help you with?"

"What was the feeling around here after the announcement of my father's crash?"

"It was pretty normal. The chairman stepped in and started with a few changes I think your dad had been hesitant to make, but that didn't seem out of character. He got along well with your dad."

"Today's lunch seemed a bit over the top. Is that normal?"

"No, not at all, but I think it was more for you than anything else."

"Okay. Are you hearing any rumblings about my seat on the board?"

"Quite the opposite actually. They'd love to have you here more often, so the plan of your being her once a month really has some of the board members excited."

"Well, that's good news."

Mitzi walks over to a cabinet and points to a file marked with my name, and I grab it and tuck it under my arm. "I guess we'll head out. I think there are a few things I need to take care of."

"We'll need to set up the banker to come in and meet with you so a few things can be transferred to you."

"Let me know when." I lean in and quietly tell her, "Mitzi, my father trusted you with his innermost secrets. I need you to keep an eye on things here and keep me posted. Anything that seems a bit off, I need you to let me know."

"Absolutely. I have a few projects that I work on to keep me busy, but I'd love more, so if you need anything from me, please don't hesitate to let me know."

"Thank you, Mitzi. I look forward to working with you."

QUINN

Lying in bed, I look up at the ceiling of my room in the hotel. It's quiet. There are no sounds from the living room, so either William is out or still sleeping. I like sleeping with him, but I sleep a bit better by myself. Plus, it makes it easy to confuse things. I'm confused enough as it is. My mind wanders to all my bills that are quickly becoming past due. I haven't worked my second job all week, and I know that I'm losing some of my regulars by not being on every night. That will hurt me financially.

I begin to wonder how my dad is doing. After my mom left my dad and disappeared last year, he's been a little lost. I realize I haven't talked to him in a few weeks, and he doesn't know where I am. Brilliant, Quinn!

I pick up the phone and give him a call.

"Hey, sweetie," he answers in his typical upbeat voice.

"How's it going?"

"Oh, you know, typical ailments."

"Typical? Enlighten me," I prod.

"A little bit of arthritis in my knee and back. You know, old creaky stuff that tends to happen after the age of fifty."

"You're funny. How's Maggie?"

"Running me ragged."

"That's why you have her, right?"

"She is going to eat me out of house and home at this rate."

"Are you feeding her your food? You know you're not supposed to do that."

"No, she has her own special diet. But she likes to go for walks on the beach and is getting better about staying close and not wandering off."

"Is she making a lot of friends?"

"Everywhere she goes. She's generous with her love and kisses."

"As Labradors are supposed to be. What did the doctor say at your visit last week?"

"I'm all good. I'm watching my diet, and my blood pressure is good, so you don't have to worry about me."

"You're my dad. I'll always worry about you. How are things going on a personal level? You can tell me. Have you had any dates recently?

"I could ask you the same thing," he retorts.

"I'm in Philadelphia right now without my current l'homme du jour."

"Really? That sounds serious if you've gone home with him."

I need to back him away so that he doesn't get it in his mind that this thing with William is a long-term possibility. "Actually, it's somebody I work with. It's not really that serious. He lost his dad, and he has a real spitfire for his stepmother. So, I came more for reinforcement than as his girlfriend."

"Well, that sounds promising though." I love that my dad is an optimist. He always sees the bright side of things.

"Good to know I can fool you so easily," I tease. "Tell me more about what's going on with you. How are the dating apps and stuff that I set you up with on your phone?"

"All the women there just want to get married again. Some of them are working on their fourth or fifth marriage, and I'm not sure I want to remarry."

It breaks my heart to know that my dad is like me and has given up on love. He had it great with my mom, but now that she's gone, he's giving up. "I know it's kind of tough after Mom, but it'll be okay to date and find someone to hang out with."

"I know, sweetheart. I have Maggie to keep me occupied. Don't worry about me. Really. I'm managing just fine."

I can hear the emptiness and a little bit of loneliness in his voice. "Dad, you're not going to believe this, but I'm thinking of leaving San Francisco and moving to Pensacola."

"Really?" he answers quickly, and his excitement breaks my heart, reminding me that I've left him alone to fend for himself in Florida.

"Yeah, I think I'd like to be close to you, and San Francisco is becoming so expensive, and work's a little overwhelming."

"You're welcome here. But I know you like the bustle of a busy city, and this is a wonderful quiet beach community. Why don't you just come for a visit? Don't quit your job before checking it out and making sure it's what you want."

"You're right, Dad. That's a good place to start. I do want to come for a visit. I promise it'll be soon."

"What's on your agenda today?"

"We wandered Independence Hall a few days ago, and I saw the Liberty Bell. I loved the history. I need to come back and really spend some time. But today will be low-key. William has some things to take care of with his father's estate. So I plan on working out this morning and getting some work done before everything gets too crazy here."

"That sounds like a good day. I love you, sweetheart. Plan your visit soon."

"I love you too, Dad. I'll work on that once I get back. Have a great day. Call me if you need me. I always have my cell phone and will take your call no matter what I'm doing."

"Promise." He hangs up, and I wipe a small tear from the corner of my eye. I miss him so much, and I've been so worried about him ever since my mom left.

The idea of moving to Florida sounds more and more appealing. I get out of bed and splash some water on my face. Looking in the mirror, I see I have an ugly pimple right in the middle of my forehead. Of course, I thought once I was done with puberty, I'd have that behind me. I pull my yoga pants on and put my hair up in a ponytail. The sun is shining, and it's a beautiful day. I'm going to go for a run. Rittenhouse Square has some great paths, and I can run around the park, run diagonally through the park, and through the middle of the park without going far.

I wander into the living room. William is somewhere, but I'm not sure where exactly. After scribbling a note letting him know that I've gone for a run, I tuck my cell phone in an armband and grab my earbuds. I wave to the doorman as I walk out the door. As I'm adjusting the volume of my music, I see a wall of chest blocking the way. It's Dumb and Stupid. I guess they've been waiting for me. Great. Can this day get any better?

"Yo, bitch," I can read on Dumb's lips.

I pull my earbuds out of my ears. "Are you talking to me?"

"Yeah, you. You tell that boyfriend of yours that he needs to let our mom have her money. She earned it," Stupid says.

They're standing a little close and trying to block my path, not letting me get by. "I think she has access to her money. But regardless, this has nothing to do with me. I don't think William has anything to do with it either. Have her talk to the lawyer if she's having problems. I'm just a guest."

Stupid walks into me and grabs my arm. "You're hurting me," I tell him, my voice quivering. He doesn't let go, and I'm beginning to get alarmed.

In a menacing voice, Dumb informs me, "Yeah, we know you're not really engaged to William. Your secret's not safe with us."

Trying to keep my bravado and hoping that the doorman sees us, I say, "I wasn't aware it was a secret. It's pretty much common knowledge we're together and looking at dates."

"You're not wearing a ring," Stupid points out.

"That's because I'm rather simple. Unlike your mother, I'm not interested in William's money, and I'm just looking for a plain platinum band. I don't need big giant diamonds to know that William loves me."

Stupid jerks me to the side, and I almost fall. The hair on the back of my neck stands up. "You and William need to leave Philadelphia. Now."

"Excuse me, Miss Faraday. Is there a problem?" I'm flooded with relief knowing that Gerald is here.

Stupid releases his grip but both of Lillian's sons stare me down.

"No, I don't think so. I was going to go for a run, but maybe now I'll just head to the gym in the hotel."

Gerald steps between me and Dumb and Stupid. "You two boys need to move along before I call the police and we have a problem."

Dumb glares at me "You better have heard our message."

I give a single nod, and Gerald steps forward, his arms wide, making sure that they don't cross into my personal space. When they walk away, he turns to me. "Are you okay?"

"Yes, I'm fine. I just wanted to go for a run."

"You should have called me so I can go with you."

"You're not here for me. You're here for William," I reason.

"No, I'm here for both of you." He looks around and types something into his phone. "If you wait a moment, I'll join you."

I don't want to take him away from William. He's much more important in this area than I am. "Gerald, I'll just go upstairs to the gym and get on the treadmill."

He looks out at the park before turning back to me. "It's a beautiful day, and I'd love a run, but I just need to put some clothes on other than the suit and the shoes I'm wearing. Can you give me a few minutes?"

"What about William?"

"Don't worry. He'll be covered. I have help, you just don't always see it."

It only takes a few minutes before Gerald is back and ready to run with me. As we stretch, he says, "You set the pace."

"I feel silly making you run with me. I'm really okay going upstairs."

"What? Are you kidding? This is one of the best parts of this gig. I get paid to work out." His smile puts me at ease.

"Okay, we'll head out to the park. My plan was to run the perimeter, then run the diagonal each way and then through the middle. I figure that will be close to three miles."

He nods. "Let's not run with your earbuds in. They're distracting, and we need you fully aware of anything that's going on around you."

"Understood." I take the earbuds out and put them in the pocket next to my phone. "Did you let William know you were with me?"

"Yes, he knows. I sent him a text message. Now set whatever pace you feel most comfortable at."

I set out at a decent pace. Since I don't really know Gerald, I feel silly running with him. "Where are you from?"

"I'm from North Carolina."

"Really? Whereabouts?"

"Halfway between the Virginia border and Raleigh."

That doesn't really narrow it down. "That's a beautiful area. I love Raleigh. I've always wanted to live there."

He doesn't say anything. I see Gerald is a man of few words.

"I love Durham. It's pretty spectacular too."

"Yes."

I give up. He's not here to be my friend but to protect me. Moving on.

We fall into a nice pace, and as we circle the park, my mind drifts to William. When he said to Lillian that he loved me, it surprised me. I don't know why. We are supposed to be engaged. But I think I'm freaking out because I'm beginning to have real feelings for him. I would love his admission of love to be real. But why would he love me? He can have anyone. Why would he want me?

I'm starting to worry that, when this is over, he's going to decimate my heart. It's too late. I've jumped off the cliff. It wasn't hard. He's god-like in appearance. He has money—not that that matters, but at least he's not swimming in debt like me. His confidence is what's really super attractive about him. He doesn't seem to care what anybody thinks, and he excels at everything—he's great at his job, he's great with friends, he handles Lillian well, and he handles the lawyers well. The guy just has it all together. Why would he want a mess, like me? I'm drowning in debt. Obviously, I'm not great at my job since they're not even considering me for partner. My love life is a disaster. I'm a disaster in every part of my life.

As we finish the last leg of our run, I remind myself of the things I do have going for me, trying to rid the self-doubt and to protect my heart.

So he told Lillian that he loves me, that doesn't mean that it's true. He's probably the type of person who uses that term easily. A lot of people will just say "I love such and such" when it actually means "I think such and such is amazing, or you're great." And we are playing at being engaged, so of course, he's going to throw the L-word around.

We stop at the corner, and I admire one of the engineering statues. An older gentleman is admiring them too.

"Isn't this amazing?" he says out loud, maybe to me, maybe to the wind.

Gerald is carefully watching.

The old man looks at me. "Look at how the wind powers the sculpture and makes all these other parts move."

"You're right. I didn't notice that." I stare at it and start to see all the fine details of the art piece. Then I notice the small solar panels. "Look at that, the sun is making the little people run around."

"I didn't even notice that. You've quite the eye for detail," he marvels.

"Thank you, but only things that fascinate me." We stand side by side and point things out to one another. He seems to be a little lonely.

"Are you from around here?" he asks.

"No, I'm visiting with a friend."

"Philadelphia offers so much to see and do."

"I want to come back. Of course, I'd like another cheesesteak too."

"I hope you got one from Pat's."

My mouth waters at the thought of the decadent sandwich. "We did."

We talk briefly for a few more minutes, and he tells me about his wife, who died many years ago and how he misses her, and his son, who is getting married soon, and how he hopes for grandchildren.

"Well, enjoy the rest of your stay," he says as we say our goodbyes.

"Thank you." Such a sweet old man.

When I return to the room, William has left me a note saying he and another bodyguard have headed over to the lawyers to discuss what happened at the board meeting yesterday. It's nice to have a little bit of time to myself. I can, hopefully, cross a few things off my to-do list.

After a quick shower, I fire up my laptop. As I look through my emails—all two hundred and eighty-seven that have all come in the last day—I try to eliminate the junk mail, those that are CYA copies, those looking for my input, and those that need an immediate response. It's overwhelming the amount of work that I have, then add the stress of this mole going after our clients, I start to feel a little nauseous. Sometimes just walking away and going to live with my dad in Pensacola sounds incredibly appealing. I'm on a break, and I already need another one. I can't do this much longer.

chapter

twenty

WILLIAM

Loosening the tie at my neck, I take a deep breath and look out the car window. What a week so far. I got through everything I needed to with the lawyers regarding my dad and his company, and we set a plan for the estate. Lillian is going to be a train wreck. I still think the FBI is up to something, but I'm not letting it out of the bag to anyone.

As I watch the crowds of people walking along the sidewalks heading to their individual destinations, I think about Quinn. I'm beyond pissed that Dumb and Stupid accosted her this morning, but thankfully Gerald was there to intervene. I need to talk her into making a report with the police. It was an assault from what Gerald tells me. Fuckers.

I missed her today. She is the steady in this storm. I'm actually really excited to see her tonight. I thought about checking in with her all day but never really had a chance. Tonight we are going to relax, so I call the concierge and order pizza and beer. We can watch some Netflix, and I hope to get some chill time in. I don't want to pressure her, but I also want to wake up with her tomorrow morning. Our little hideaway is going to end soon, and somehow, I need to figure out how to make this last longer.

I walk in and see she's dressed casually and working away at her computer.

"You're back. How did it go today?" Quinn asks.

"We set our plan on how to manage Lillian."

"I'd call that productive." She smiles and pushes an errant strand of hair behind her ear.

"Gerald told me what Dumb and Stupid did today."

"They were more words than physical," she tries to reassure me, but I can tell they frightened her.

"What did they want?"

The color rises in her cheeks. "Just to get you to give your money to their mom."

I snort. "That only confirms that we have the right plan in place to deal with Lillian."

"Please don't worry about them. They're assholes." She comes over and kisses me softly, and I can't help but wrap my arms around her.

"I hope you don't mind, but I've ordered in some pizza and beers."

Reaching up, she rests her hands on my shoulder. It isn't like she grabbed my cock or anything, but I still feel a jolt of electricity at her touch. I bask in the feel of her warm body pressed to mine. She lingers in my arms for just a moment before drawing away. "No, that sounds perfect. Go change, and I'll put some makeup on so I don't scare people and we can meet back here."

I nod and watch her disappear to her room. God, I love watching her coming and going. Running my hand through my hair, I wonder how I can convince her that I want more than this make-believe world we've built.

I change into a comfortable pair of jeans. I've had them forever, and they have tears in the knees and holes in odd places, but I love them. I'll have to throw them away eventually. I walk into the living room and see she's wearing one of my button-down shirts. I unconsciously groan. She looks sexy as hell.

"I hope you don't mind. I'm out of anything but dress clothes."

I shake my head. She looks amazing, and I can't help but stare.

"What do you want to drink?" Her voice is just above a whisper.

"Beer, please," I manage, and she turns around and makes herself a drink and pops the top on my beer. I can only see her legs from just above the knee down, but they look smooth, like she's just recently shaved and moisturized. There is just the barest hint of color, but I know from Gerald she was in the room all day today. She is blessed with a fantastic ass, and I want to reach for it when she bends down to place the drinks on the table in front of me. Her ass is hiding its full grandeur beneath the baggy shirt, but the wide neck of my shirt has slipped over one of her lovely shoulders and shows me another fun fact.

She's taken off her bra too. I swallow what feels like a bucket of sand in my dry mouth as she sits next to me. I do my best to maintain eye contact and not look at her body or reach for her tits, which look as if they're dancing under the shirt. Who the hell cares about Netflix and dinner? My cock is ready to chill now.

I want to reach out and put one of her nipples in my mouth while I play with the other. My cock makes itself known as it grows in my pants, only restrained by the button fly. I try to think of things that will deflate my cock—my stepmonster, my apartment, Owen laughing at dinner. Thankfully, it works.

Taking a sip of my beer, I try not to choke on it as she pulls her feet up and crosses her legs. The shirt hikes up a bit more, and as she leans back and sips her drink, I notice the shirt press against one of her breasts, her nipple poking the shirt. I'm a goner—and hard as a rock.

A knock at the door interrupts my naughty thoughts, and I get up and accept our room service. It's a welcome reprieve from my desire to bend her over and fuck her hard. The pizza is outstanding, and I share with her all I learn today.

When she's done eating, she gets up and moves back to the couch, where a random movie is playing on the TV. I know if I join her, I'm going to jump her, no doubt about that, so I hang back, willing my cock, which is at half mast, to be patient and just wait. I don't know why I think it'll listen to me since it hasn't since I was twelve.

"Are you going to just sit over there or are you going to join me?"

"If I join you, it won't be to watch the movie," I rasp.

Biting at her lower lip, she looks up at me. I'm done. In two strides, I'm sitting next to her.

"Well," she says, drawing out the word as she kicks her leg over me and settles astride my lap. I can feel her rock-hard nipples as she slides her body down mine. The heat between her legs settles over me. With her face inches from mine, she runs her fingers through my hair, and I struggled to breathe. My hands move by instinct, settling on her smooth thighs and pulling closer to me. She kisses me lightly on the upper lip, her half smile there again.

"What do you think?" she says in a whisper.

Fuck.

We move at the same time. Our lips part and our tongues dance, gently at first. The desire between us is animalistic. My heart's beating so hard I can hear it in my head. My cheeks are on fire, and I'm sure if I'm not careful, I'll pass out. Her skin's so hot as I move my hands up her thighs, stopping at the crease where her legs meet her little sexy panties. I let my fingers gently roam as our kisses become harder and more urgent. Her hips rock against my bulge, grinding on my cock, and I know her wetness will leave a spot on my pants. What a turn on.

She finally breaks our kiss as I palm her ass, spreading her bare cheeks and caressing them roughly. We're both breathing really hard, and our eyes lock as she moans and rolls her hips against me, keeping an agonizing pace—not too fast and not too slow. With one hand on her amazing ass, I run my right hand up the front of her shirt to her generous breast. She drops her forehead to my shoulder as I massage her tit, her rock-hard nipple poking against my palm as I gently but firmly squeeze, pinch, and pull at the erect nipple.

"Fuck," she breathes against my neck. "You do the most amazing things to me."

Three layers of rapidly soaking fabric is all that separates us from fucking, and that makes the tease all the sweeter, all the hotter as she continues to rock and swivel on my cock. Her pussy feels like it's literally on fire as she increases the pressure, and I'm in heaven. My hand spreading her ass open is no doubt causing her lacy thong to ride against her clit, which is pressed between us.

"This feels so fucking good," she moans. She closes her eyes and sighs, her mouth dropping open. I can hear a wet noise from between our bodies as she moves. Her panties are completely soaked, and my dick can feel the wet spot she's leaving on the front of my pants.

"You have no idea how hot you are, how sexy you look right now," I say honestly.

She pulls back and takes my head in her hands, kissing me deeply, running her skilled tongue against mine before breaking the kiss and sliding back off my lap. A large wet spot on my tented crotch is evidence she's just as horny as I am. My cock is so hard it feels like it'll break if it isn't freed from my jeans. She kneels in front of me and begins to undo the button fly.

"I'm gonna say sorry in advance," she says in a whisper as she gets the last button undone. "I'm not sure I'm very good at this, but I love the taste of your cock." I lift my ass off the couch as she pulls my pants down and off.

I'm not sure how to tell her that she is a rock star at giving head. As I try to formulate the words, I get distracted as she takes my cock in her hand and strokes it up and down. My cock is leaking precum pretty bad at this point. I've never had anyone who can hold a fucking candle to Quinn.

"Does that feel good?" she whispers as I watch her through half-lidded eyes, and I nod dumbly as she brings her other hand up to gently play with my balls. I try not to scream when she suddenly leans forward, opens her mouth wide, and takes half of me in her mouth. Her cheeks hollow as she bobs up and down on the top half of my cock. I try not to come right away, but my cock is already on fire and twitching in her mouth.

There is something otherworldly about when a woman has your cock in her mouth, but it's so much more awesome if she seems to really be into giving you pleasure. The pressure builds after a few minutes of her orchestrations on my cock. Her cheeks hollow each time she bobs, and her tongue rolls around the super sensitive head, and, God, it feels so good. She lets out a moan from deep in her throat, and I notice her other hand, which has been on my bare thigh, is now nowhere to be seen, but I can see her arm working down below her waist. The sounds of wet skin on skin can be heard just above the wet slurping sounds as she bobs faster.

"Fuck, babe, I'm really close," I manage to say as she pulls off, sucking so hard at the mushroom head as she comes off it actually makes a pop sound. Like a tower of purple want, my dick is twitching, so full of blood and begging for release. She stops right at the cusp of my orgasm. Closing my eyes, I take a deep breath and think of anything to keep from exploding.

"You're really close, aren't you? Right at the edge...." Squeezing my cock again, she runs her flattened tongue against the underside, just below the head, and I bite my lip hard to keep from coming. She's toying with me, and it feels so fucking awesome.

"It's my turn to play." I'm going to eat her pussy.

She cries out as I hook my fingers in the strings of her sopping wet thong and yank it off.

"Wait," she says, probably thinking I'm just gonna saddle up and pound her. Oh, she's in for a treat.

Her next words are lost as I grab her amazing ass, pull her cheeks apart, and clamp my entire mouth over her swollen-lipped pussy. God, I've missed this today—all of it, the taste, the smell, the texture of wet skin swollen with lust parted on my mouth. I lance my tongue as deep as I can, and I hear her catch her breath and then let out a long "mmmmmmmmmmm" as she reaches back and pulls my head into her.

I slap her right ass cheek, not hard enough to hurt her or make too much noise, earning a little yelp followed by a moan. I give her left cheek equal treatment and then slip my middle finger between her lips without any preamble. She's soaked, her lips engorged and a little bit open, bent over as she is. She groans as I add another finger and sawing my arm back and forth, fingering her pussy. The wet, slopping sounds are crazy hot. She drops her head to the couch, and I hear her groan into the cushion as her pussy grabs my fingers like a vice and clenches them in a hard, wet rhythm. The muscles in her ass flex, and her little toes curled tight. I keep on until she pulls forward and dislodges my fingers, falling onto her back before surging up to her knees and ripping her shirt off.

This woman is my kryptonite. She has poise and authority, and sex is literally dripping off her. She brings me to my knees.

"Lay on your back," I command in a stern voice.

She looks down at my cock, still mostly hard and quickening back to its full rigidity at the sight of her sexy body.

"Stay right there while I get a condom."

"I'd love to feel you inside me. I'm on the pill and have been for years. I haven't been with anyone in almost a year."

My cock is hard. "I was just checked, and I'm clean. Are you sure?"

She bites her bottom lip and nods. I grab her hand and lead her to the bed in her room. Although her smile is still there, I can see the seriousness in her eyes. I take hold of one of her nipples and gently squeeze it as she kneels on the bed and takes my head in her hands, pulling my lips to hers. God, she's sexy.

She laughs and drops back onto the mattress, presenting me with the most glorious view of her from behind.

As I position myself between her legs and run my cock through her slit and over her only recently claimed clit. I sigh as my fat cock head rubs her clit again. Skin on skin is amazing.

"I don't want to come right away. I want to savor this," I confess.

"It's your turn. You've given me three orgasms already. I'm going to be sore in the morning. Trust me, it's fine. I want you inside me. Now."

So direct. God, I love this woman. Yeah, I'm going to fuck her really good and hard just the little bit makes me almost shoot my load.

As I thrust my hips forward, I can see her reflection in the mirror behind the dining room table as she closes her eyes, and we both open mouths and groan together. Fuck. I'm completely seated in one push, like slipping into a warm, soft glove that holds on just tight enough.

"Oh, yeah...," she sighs as I dropped the full weight of my pelvis down on her, pushing as much of me as I can inside her. God, she's wet and grips me just right; it's incredible. I sit, buried up to the hilt for a second as I push myself back and see she has her eyes closed, pinched shut actually. I don't want to move; I just want to be like this for a whole day—savoring how she grips me, how wet she is, how hot her skin is. All of it. I pull back a bit and push forward again. Her eyes are still closed.

"You okay?" I ask, not sure if I've been too rough.

She laughs. "No, I'm good. It was just a lot all at once, and I haven't had... this much great sex... ever," she admits. As she speaks, I move in and out of her just the last inch or so, back and forth, rubbing the head of my cock and shaft as deep inside her as possible. She groans again, and I bite down on my lip as her pussy walls grip me, clenching around me and pulsing a bit.

"Yeah," she whispers, "like that." I pick up speed, still giving her short, even strokes.

"Yeah, faster...," she pants, her eyes clenched shut, and she's holding on tight to the duvet. The sound of our skin slapping is building, getting wetter with each pass. I can feel the pleasure mounting higher and higher.

She's facedown in the duvet, groaning and moaning into the blanket to muffle her cries as I continue my merciless pounding. Her ass jiggling as I lunge into her as hard and fast as I can. Sweat's pouring off me now, and I can feel how slick her skin is under my hands too.

Slap, slap, slap. Over and over.

"Quinn!" I gasp, my eyes wide as I feel my balls tighten all the way up and my strokes get even harder. My hands grip her hips so hard, I'm sure they'll leave marks. The duvet balled in her fists, she pushes her ass back into me as hard as she can.

"Now, oh fuck, please," she cries out. I feel her clench, clamping down like a spongy vice around me, and all the muscles in her sides seize up. I feel her cum. The sensations intensify and build as she gets so much wetter, and that's it. I'm right there. I slam into her one last time, as hard and deep as I can, grinding my pelvis against her. With my cock as deep as it will go and her pussy pulsing around me all wet and wonderful, my whole world explodes like a bomb.

She gasps and drops her head into the duvet, and I hear her muffled scream. Her back flexes and her whole body goes rigid as she tries to push back harder into me. I've never come at exactly the same time as a woman before, so this is without pale.

Unreal.

"Holy shit." I hear her say as she raises her face out of the blanket and turns to look over her shoulder at me, my cock still buried to the hilt in her ravaged pussy.

"Yeah, that was so awesome."

I hiss as her pussy clenches around me again, and then she reaches back underneath her and between her legs, and I feel her fingers on either side of my cock, brushing her soaked lips, and she tenses again.

Feeling my rising cock, she smiles and shakes her head. "You need to behave. I'm going to be so sore in the morning." She moves forward, causing my cock to slip from her body, and leans up and kisses me once really hard. "So much for the movie."

"We can still watch it."

She snuggles in, and her eyes close. "Maybe another night."

I kiss the top of her head. "I want to wake with you tomorrow morning."

She's already asleep, and I hold her tight. I'm absolutely, without a doubt, in love with this woman. Nothing will ever change that.

chapter

twenty-one

QUINN

I look out at the park for the last time. I'm ready to head home to San Francisco, but I've really had fun here in Philadelphia. I'd love to spend more time wandering the city and exploring where my country began, and I wouldn't mind a few more cheesesteaks. They're the perfect food with a large side of fries. As I daydream about cheesesteaks, William pops his head into my room. "Ready?"

"I'll be ready in just a few minutes. Let me just pack up my final things."

"Great. Gerald will be downstairs in fifteen minutes. Do you think that will work?"

"It'll be no problem."

"I have a few things to throw in my bag myself. I'll meet you in the living room." He pivots to walk away but comes back. "Thank you again for coming with me. I would have been lost this week without you." He reaches for my hand, and I let him hold it. An electric jolt runs through me, but it also causes a bit of heartache. As hard as I tried, I couldn't stop myself from falling for him. "It was very kind of you to invite me. I'm happy I was of some help."

"I need to get you back to San Francisco before you realize there are other places to live."

I yearn to hear him tell me he loves me and can't live without me, but I know reality. He doesn't do relationships, and he most certainly doesn't want a relationship with a woman who is almost two hundred thousand dollars in debt and works doing phone sex as a second job. Rather than let him decimate my heart when he wishes me well and tells me he'll see me around, I jump in. "Are we taking that big plane back again?"

He chuckles. "Yes, it's the only plane the company has."

I nod. "It just feels like such a waste of money in so many ways."

"I agree with you. But this way we have Gerald and his team with us when we travel." He starts to say something else, but his phone rings. Before he answers, he says, "I'll meet you in the living room when you're ready."

William is on the phone all the way to the airport and while we board. I get it. We've been out of the office for a week on short notice. Life doesn't stop when we aren't in the office. I wasn't as busy, so I was able to keep up a little better each evening, but I never had time to do my second job. That is going to bite me in the ass hard when I get home.

As we enter the plane, the flight attendant is blubbering again about William's father. He finally disconnects from his call and talks to her. I get myself set up on the Wi-Fi and put my headset on to listen to a little bit of music while I go through my emails.

William finds a spot on the other side of the cabin, doing essentially the same thing. He's so handsome it makes my heart hurt. I know I'll fall into a pit of blackness that will pull me in if I don't protect myself. Wishing our circumstances were different, I wipe away a tear from my eye.

When we land in San Francisco, Gerald brings the car around. It takes only a few minutes, but we're hardly on the ground when William's phone rings. The office knows we've landed, and they've tracked us down. He's on the phone all the way to my apartment. Gerald stops, and William gives me the one finger hold-on-a-second motion.

I smile warmly at him before kissing him softly on the cheek and mouthing to him, "Don't worry about it. I'll see you tomorrow at the office." I get out of the car and climb the stairs to my tiny one-bedroom apartment.

Having lugged my suitcase up three flights of stairs, I'm out of breath as I push my door open, ignoring the note from my landlord that was pushed under the door. My rent's late and he's looking for it. Nothing like the oppression of overdue bills to greet you after having spent a week in a five-star hotel.

I'm exhausted. Despite my apartment's tiny size, I have a bathtub—a big, beautiful bathtub. I start the water and begin to fill the bath with glorious bubbles that I took from my bathroom at the Rittenhouse.

As I soak in the tub, I realize I feel like I've broken up with William without a big argument or fight. The lack of drama leaves my heart with the option of the possibility of more. I begin to cry, feeling the heartbreak of not being able to be anything more than what we are. I knew this before I left, but I think in the back of my mind, I hoped for him to fall madly in love with me and save me from my mess. Unfortunately, it's my mess. I made it, and I have to clean it up.

The water is becoming tepid, and the bubbles are almost all popped. I hate to get out, but when my phone rings, I figure it's time. Glancing at the caller ID, I'm happy to see it's CeCe.

"Hey," she says.

"Hey, yourself."

"I hear you're back in San Francisco."

"We just landed, and I'm decompressing."

"Any interest in getting together for dinner tonight?"

My finances are a mess, but I quickly realize I have a good excuse. "I don't know. I've eaten out so much this week. I was just going to have a sandwich here."

"I have a better idea. Why don't you come over here and have dinner at my place? I'll invite the girls and, we'll make it a girls night. I'm not totally lost in the kitchen, and we can catch up."

I laugh. "You cook?"

"I didn't say it was going to be something you'd find in a restaurant; I may not cook every day, but I can make a mean grilled chicken."

"Sounds perfect. What can I bring?"

"If you have a bottle of wine at home, you can bring that, but otherwise just bring yourself. I may invite some of the other girls over if that's okay?"

"Sounds good to me." I hang up, and the cloud of depression steps back as I remind myself that my love life may be a disaster, but at least I have friends, and I know they're good friends. Also, if someone likes CeCe can be in this city and still not be married then you know there's something wrong with the city.

After I throw on a pair of jeans, boots, and a sweater, I grab a bottle of red wine in one hand and white in the other and catch a rideshare to CeCe's. She lives in the posh neighborhood of Pacific Heights. Her beautiful home overlooks the bay with a stunning view of the Golden Gate, Alcatraz, and Marin. When I ring the bell, she answers the door herself in jeans and bare feet. She looks like she has money, but you'd never guess she is one of the richest women in the world.

"You made it!" she gushes.

"I did." I step inside the foyer, and she takes my coat and both bottles of wine.

"White and red. We could mix them together and make rose." She giggles.

"Just don't tell Greer."

"You're so right. Come on back. Emerson just arrived, and Hadlee and Cynthia should be here any time."

I walk back into the kitchen, and Emerson stands and gives me a big hug. "So, how did it go?"

"I feel bad for William. His stepmother is a piece of work. I don't envy his position." I don't want to say too much and share things that are inappropriate.

"Oh, good grief," CeCe says as she rolls her eyes.

"His father was rather clever actually. He was generous to everyone so no one could contest the will saying they were left out," I share.

"Oh, that is good." Emerson nods.

"I got to explore Philly a bit and wouldn't mind going back and really playing tourist. William showed me around one afternoon, and I saw so much, and some of the food was to die for."

"Did you have a Philly cheesesteak sandwich?" CeCe asks.

"I did, and I'm grateful they aren't made here. It was amazing. I'd be as wide as I am tall if I ate them every day."

"What are your plans with William moving forward?" Emerson asks.

I shrug. "We really don't have anything else in our plans. I believe Mason called as we were leaving the hotel, and they talked all the way as we drove to the airport and until we had to close the door. I think we said ten words to each other this morning. We're already back to our routine. We go back to work and ignore one another."

"Well, that sounds pretty sucky," Emerson chides.

I agree, but it's the best way to work together and not fall apart. Once the girls all arrive, we all talk about our men. CeCe is getting pretty hot and heavy with her European prince. I've seen them in the tabloids, and they are a striking couple.

When Emerson announces she's pregnant, that's the end of boyfriend talk.

"I had better be your pediatrician," Hadlee admonishes.

"Don't you worry. You're the one."

"Will you find out if it's a boy or a girl? It makes it so much easier to plan showers that way," Cynthia muses.

"I'm just past the twelve-week mark, so we can find out shortly. I figure it's a surprise when you find out regardless of when."

"You don't have to tell us the name, only the sex," CeCe assures her.

"Well, I may need reinforcements. Dillon is looking for strong Greek names."

My brow furrows. "I'm confused. I thought he was Irish?"

"He is, but he's got it in his head to call a boy Marcus Aurelius and a girl Copernicus," Emerson says in exasperation.

"Okay, wasn't Copernicus the man who was first to say the world wasn't flat? I thought he was a German philosopher."

"Thank you! That was him, and the fact that Copernicus is German helps," Emerson agrees.

"And Marcus Aurelius was a Roman Emperor who was part of a century-long prosperity and peace in Rome if I remember correctly," Hadlee hesitantly shares.

The evening moves on like this all night. I sit back and listen to the girls. If I leave San Francisco, I'll really miss them.

It's after midnight when Emerson drops me at my place. "Have a great night. I'm looking forward to seeing you in the morning."

I wave goodbye. "Congratulations again! I'm so happy for you and Dillon."

It's really late for me, and I'm exhausted. I'm just barely able to wash my face and brush my teeth before I fall into bed. It's fun to think that this morning I woke up in Philadelphia and I'll fall asleep in San Francisco. Thankfully, I'm so tired that I only give William a half second of thought before I crash.

chapter

twenty-two

WILLIAM

I'm kicking myself for not having the conversation I wanted to have with Quinn. On the flight home, she definitely started putting up some serious walls that I need to work on taking down.

Once we hit the tarmac and got in the car, my phone rings. Mason and Dillon's call couldn't have come at a worse time. All the way into the city, we discussed some of the challenges we're having with one of my most recent acquisitions. It's good to be back though. I'm glad to be away from Philadelphia, and I can think about something other than the chaos that comes with my father.

Our flight attendant is awfully upset. I know she cared about my dad, but I find it hard to believe they were involved. She insisted on sending me a recording of a phone call she had with my dad before he died. First, my dad was always super professional. I find it difficult to believe that he'd have an affair. I remember when a member of his leadership team had an affair with his secretary. He fired the guy and told everyone that Bettencourt Industries had no room for people with questionable ethics. He believed in the sanctity of marriage. Despite the challenges he might have been having with Lillian, I just don't see him having an affair.

Gerald drops me at home and informs me he and another gentleman will be rotating shifts and someone will be with me at all times. If I want to go anywhere, I need to give them about fifteen minute's notice. I'm too tired to think about anything other than my bed calling my name.

I have mail on the kitchen table. How do I get so much junk mail? I don't even look through it. Instead, I head right to my room, leaving my suitcase in the front hall. I'm ready to take a quick nap, and then I'm going to call Quinn.

As I lie in bed, I formulate my plan. After my nap, I'm going to take her to dinner at the Italian restaurant nearby, and I'm going to convince her that she needs to move in with me. It'll take the pressure off her so she can quit her second job. She won't have to worry about rent anymore, and she can concentrate on paying off her school loans while living here for free, and if I'm lucky and things go well, we'll talk about what our next steps are. I'd happily pay off her school loans, but I know how proud she is, and I doubt she'd ever allow that. I want to take care of her for the rest of our lives.

I drift off to sleep, and when I roll over it's dark. Glancing at the clock, I see it's after nine. How did I oversleep? Shit! It's too late for dinner. She's most likely eaten and is in bed. Dammit! If I call her now, it'll sound like a booty call. My cock stiffens in my pants at the thoughts of Quinn and a booty call. All the sex we had all week was amazing. I've never felt such a connection with anybody. I can't resist. I want to see her. I don't want to wake her just in case she's gone to bed, so I pull out my phone and text her.

Me: Hey. You up for a late dinner tonight?

Crickets. She's not responding. Bummer. She's probably gone to bed. She probably didn't do what I did and crash as soon as she got home. Damn! I'm mad at myself for missing her.

Then I remember Marjorie insisted on sending me that recording of her conversation with my dad. I have no idea why, but I wouldn't mind hearing my dad's voice. It seems a little too convenient that she just happened to have a recording while the FBI are conducting an investigation. I listen to the message, and it's nothing that I expected. I listen to it a few times, and some things strike me as funny. The naughty talk between the two of them grosses me out. I mean it's my dad, of course there's a ick factor, but there's something wrong with it.

"Hi. What are you wearing?" a female voice says.

"I am naked. What are you wearing?" says a voice that may be my father. I've always preferred to think of my father as asexual. As I listen carefully to how they speak instead of what they're saying, I realize the conversation doesn't seem to flow naturally. They aren't using contractions, and the conversation is stilted. My best guess would be that they're reading something. I've never heard my father have phone sex with someone, but it doesn't seem relaxed. There is no chemistry between the two supposed lovers.

"I love it when you make me come."

"You are the only one who can get me erect."

Who the hell says "erect"?

This is not a real call.

They both have orgasms that would make a porn star blush. This is just awkward. Then without a second thought, they change subjects. No afterglow. No heavy breathing. "I spoke with Tully Fitzgerald today. He is going to give me two hundred thousand dollars. That will give me the money to pay back Mercer Miller."

"That is really great. You have been worried Mercer would tell everyone he could not get his money out of the scheme."

"I think I have Johnathan Raymond on the hook for almost a million dollars," my dad says.

"That would be a relief. Do not forget you promised me a shopping trip in Paris," she says.

"I am in love with you, bunny. We will take our money and go hide in Paris, and you can buy whatever you want. Bettencourt Industries will go into bankruptcy, and we will be far away from it."

"Oh, lover, I am yours forever. I cannot wait to be with you all of the time."

As I listen to the recording over and over, there are a couple of nuances that don't add up. The person on the tape uses a hard T in Bettencourt. My father always used a soft T. It would sound more like Bettencore.

I don't know what to do with this. I wish I could call Quinn and ask her her opinion. Plus, I still can't understand how somebody "accidentally" recorded a phone call. I don't have any idea on how to do it on purpose, let alone do it on accident. This just doesn't make any sense to me.

I forward this to Jim Adelson, the security guru at the company.

To: Jim Adelson
From: William Bettencourt
Subject: Can you help?

Jim,

Can you have your experts look at this? They claim this to be my dad, but there are a few things that aren't making any sense, and quite honestly, it doesn't sound like him. Can you help?
William

It isn't even two minutes later and my phone rings.

"Sorry to bother you so late," Jim says, "but I got your message and my team's happy to work on this. First, let me tell you how sorry I am about your dad. I lost mine a few years ago, and it was really tough."

"Thank you. I don't think it's fully hit me yet."

"I know it's late, but before I send this off to my audio team, I was hoping for a little bit of background."

"The FBI approached me while I was home in Philadelphia this week for the reading of my father's will. They said he was participating in a Ponzi scheme. This voice mail was given to me by the company flight attendant. She was visibly upset on our flight to Philadelphia, and on the return flight she said she found this call that she had accidentally recorded."

"Accidentally recorded it? I don't hear that very often."

"It does seem to confirm the claim about the Ponzi scheme and say that my father had an affair, but it seems a little off. Most importantly, it doesn't sound like him. I'm hoping you and your team can dive into the recording and help me out."

"Do you have any voice samples of him?"

"You can find copies on the company website and also on YouTube."

"We should have some answers for you in a few days."

We end our call, and I glance at the clock. It's after eleven, and I need to try to get more sleep. The morning will be here quickly, and it's back to work for us.

Rolling over in bed, I glance at the clock. It's just after three. My internal clock tells me it's time to get up. I shut my eyes and think about Quinn. I love the way she smiles. Her whole face is animated. Her eyes sparkle like diamonds, and her mouth showcases her lush lips and perfect teeth. It's infectious. Then there is her killer body. Just the thought of what she looks like underneath me makes me hard. She's also kick-ass smart, and I love how quick she is with an important analysis, a witty retort, or just a senseless factoid.

I can't sleep. Thinking of her only reminds me that she isn't with me, and I hate that. I justify that I've had nine hours of sleep and I'll make it through today.

I dress in workout clothes. It's too early to go outside, so I head to my rowing machine today. I need a good ab workout. I start with my favorite voice mail. I just need to hear her voice. When it's over, it reverts to my workout playlist. I'm sweating hard when I'm done. I can't wait to see Quinn in a few short hours. I'm going to take her to lunch, and I'm going to lay out my plan for us and do whatever I can to sell her on moving in with me.

Arriving early at work, I turn the lights on and start the coffee. I'll probably be mainlining it by two today, but a few cups this morning would be nice. It's relaxing being here before everyone else. It makes it easy to get a lot done. Before eight I've gone through all of the papers that were sitting on my desk and through my work email. I even manage to set up a few things with some of my potential investments. As the morning wears on, people begin arriving.

Mason drags me into a meeting with the acquisitions team. We haven't met as a group in a few weeks, and he likes to get a feel for what we're working on. Dillon and Cameron usually join us because it affects their teams, but today it's just Christopher, Cynthia, Mason, and me.

"The former developers from Pineapple and Change Technology connected at the annual party we just had, and they're looking for investment," Mason shares.

"That's great. What are they proposing?" Cynthia asks.

"It's a finance piece," Mason says, and everyone looks at me. That's my area.

I throw my hands up. "They're your connection and a previous client. They don't belong to me."

"I brought Pineapple in a few years ago with help from Dillon, and Change Technologies was just bought by one of the big five. I don't have the bandwidth to take on a client. Would it bother any of you if I gave this over to William?"

Christopher and Cynthia don't even think twice, and now I have a new client. "You'll have to go out and meet with them. This will be somewhat like what we did for Christopher's new client company, and you'll need to help them with their business plan. Both Tim Johnson and Dana O'Neil will each own a third, and we'll own the final third."

I nod. Christopher's new wife was part of a start-up where her original business partner brought a piece to the table that he stole. He attempted to push her out by stealing her work, but that didn't work out. With our help, we put together the original developer of the stolen work and Christopher's then-girlfriend and helped them build a new company. He's been swamped getting it off the ground, but these are great deals for us. We invest in them, and they focus on what they are developing.

Throughout the morning, I've looked for Quinn, but I haven't seen her. So much for lunch. I text her.

Me: How about dinner tonight?

I don't see the bubbles bouncing, so that means she hasn't seen the message and she'll answer me when she has time. I can't help but be a little disappointed.

An appointment shows up on my calendar, and I see Mason has scheduled a meeting with the new company for me tomorrow over lunch at one of the best restaurants in Palo Alto. I'm grateful for the handoff of what will be a very profitable venture for the company and me personally, but I can't help but be disappointed that it takes time away from Quinn.

What's wrong with me? This is not how I am usually.

As I slog my way through my work, the receptionist sticks her head into my office. "William, there are two guys from the FBI here for you in reception. Do you want me to tell them you're not here?"

I look at her and smile. "That would be great, but they won't go away. It's something to do with my dad. Are any of the conference rooms open?"

"I believe the large room is open. Would that work for you?"

"Sure."

She heads out, and I run over to the kitchen and grab a few sodas and head in to meet them. I'm stunned when I walk into the conference room and see it's Agent Michael McGraw and someone I've never met. I notice he doesn't introduce himself.

"This is a surprise. What brings you to San Francisco?"

"We still had a few other questions for you, and we wanted to talk to you a little bit further about your dad."

"Okay," I say with reluctance. "I'm still not convinced this is a Ponzi's scheme, but ask your questions."

"What do you know about Bettencourt Industries?"

"It was founded by my great-grandfather as a mercantile business. In the late 1800s, he transitioned to the steel industry, which really took off for my grandfather. My father inherited the business and kept the steel part of it going, and as an amateur inventor, he started putting his inventions through the company. His biggest invention with the most commercial success was the levered trash can. While not glamorous, he invented the foot pedal and the pop top. It made the company an obscene amount of money."

"Do you have a seat on the board of directors?"

"I didn't before my father's death, but I've inherited his seat. Why?"

"When was the last time you looked at the company financials?"

I think a minute. "I saw them last week when I was in town."

"And before that?" Agent McGraw insists.

"I'm not sure. It's been a while, but really, I'm not sure I've ever seen a proper profit and loss statement from the company. Why?"

"Were you given a recording of a phone call between your father and his mistress?"

"Yes. Why?"

"Have you listened to the recording?"

"I have. Why?"

"What did it say?"

"I'm not answering any other questions until you begin to answer mine."

"Mr. Bettencourt, we're here to ask you questions, not the other way around."

I stand to leave. "Then you can direct all questions through my lawyer."

"Mr. Bettencourt, please take a seat. Tell us what you know about the recording."

I think for a minute. They're here to throw me off balance. I know more than they do. I'm not convinced the recording is my father, but if it is, it incriminates him. "It's supposedly a recording of my father and one of his employees. It begins with them having an intimate conversation, and then it talks about an embezzlement scam."

"What makes you think that it may not be your father?" the other agent asks.

"To start with, it's a little out of character for my dad to have somebody on the side. He was truly in love with my mother, and I know he never cheated on her."

"Yes, but we're talking about today, and from what we can tell, your father and his second wife were estranged. Things can change," Agent McGraw suggests.

"Yes, they can, but I don't think you understand. My father was an extreme introvert. He could probably go weeks without talking to a single person. And, not only was he an introvert, he was shy and sometimes had a hard time looking people in the eyes."

"He was the majority shareholder and CTO of a Fortune 1000 company. I find that hard to believe," the other agent says.

"I guess what I'm trying to say is that my dad was the quintessential nerd. He didn't have good emotional relationships with people. He was all about his inventions and his company."

"But he had a suite at the Rittenhouse Hotel," Agent McGraw insists.

I sit back in my seat so that I answer this carefully. "Yes, but I think that was more because my father didn't manage conflict well, and there was conflict with his second wife, Lillian."

"Have you heard from your father?" Agent McGraw insists.

"No, I'm not usually accustomed to talking to dead people."

"Has anything odd happened?" the other agent interjects.

"What are you trying to ask me?"

"Will the government of Tanzania provide anything more than a certificate of your father's death? Because to be perfectly honest, we're beginning to wonder if it was an actual accident, or if he paid someone off with all the money he embezzled and faked his death."

I carefully debate my next answer. I'm sure they know all of this, but I feel like it needs to be put out there. "You do realize that my father left an estate of forty million dollars. I find it really hard to believe that if he was going to go hide in another country that he would be leaving forty million behind. Not to mention, he also never touched my trust, which he had full access to, and I've gone through all of the paperwork. My inheritance from my mother in cash alone is close to a billion dollars. He could've taken all the money, and I never would have been the wiser."

"I think it would have been a lot more difficult for him to get access to your trust."

"I truly had no idea about the money until I sat down with our estate attorney."

"We have an inside source that's shared some pretty specific information, and we would like to get a copy of the recording that was sent to you."

"It's on my phone." I can make them wait and get a subpoena, but since I've already sent it to Jim and he's working on it, they can have it. Jim's lab will be much better at getting it figured out. Agent McGraw gives me his email address, and I send it over to him, and then we listen to the recording together.

"What alarms you about the recording?"

"It doesn't sound exactly like my dad. For example, he pronounces our last name differently. There's no chemistry between the employee and himself. Come on, you guys. The last time you had phone sex or had an orgasm, everyone was breathing heavily. These two seem like they're reading a script, and they jump from phone sex to this supposed Ponzi scheme. And the amounts of money they are talking about are nothing compared to what he already had. I have my security team looking into this, and we'll let you know what we find. I'm not convinced this person on the recording is my father."

"We'll investigate. Thank you for your time. We'll be in touch."

"Of that, I have no doubt." I walked them to reception and wait with them for the elevator.

The agents enter the elevator that Mason has just exited. "Everything okay?"

"I'm not 100 percent sure."

"Come on back to my office and tell me what's going on."

We weave our way through the office, and I can tell people are waiting to talk to Mason, and I feel silly talking to him about my personal life. There's no room at work for personal lives.

"Mason, it looks like there are a lot of people waiting for you. This can wait. It's just stuff with my dad. How about drinks tonight?"

"Hold on a second and just give me the overview."

I walk him through everything that's going on, my concerns, and I share that I've sent the recording to Jim.

"It sounds like the FBI isn't sure that your dad is dead."

"I agree. The lawyer hired someone and got some confirmation, but my stepmother's behavior about the money is strange. It could be completely unrelated, but even her boys threatened Quinn when she tried to go out for a run."

Mason looks alarmed. "They threatened Quinn?"

"They did. She shared that you two dated once, and it's far in the past, but I'm sure you don't want any harm done to her."

"No. I hear from Emerson and CeCe that I need to move her to partner."

"It would have my vote."

He sits quietly for a few moments, taking in everything I've shared. "Let's call Jim and get his thoughts." He pushes a button on his phone, and it rings one time before Jim answers.

"What can I help you with, Mason?" Jim asks.

"I know you're working on William's voice mail that he sent. We were wondering if you had anyone who could fly to Tanzania and help him out."

I walk Jim through the whole story. "My dad's company hired a local investigator, and for all I know, they could've been paid off, but he was recommended by the lawyers. I'll send you what I have right now." With a few clicks on my phone, I sent him the report.

"I got it, and I have Paul here who can head out tomorrow."

"I appreciate that. Something doesn't add up, and I'm grateful for the help."

"I've got you covered. We'll keep Gerald as your bodyguard with you until we get this figured out for you."

"Thank you." We disconnect the call. Now I know that there are many people waiting for Mason's attention. "I really appreciate your help."

"This is what I'm here for."

chapter

twenty-three

QUINN

I've been successfully avoiding William for the last three days. I know I won't be able to do this much longer, let alone forever. He'll eventually get upset and tell Mason about my second job. I've received a few text and voice mail messages from William but ignored them. I need to protect myself and my heart.

I know he just wants to get together, have dinner, and pick up where we left off—friends who have great sex. And great sex it is. I honestly don't think anyone has ever played me like he has. My body still hums every time I think of him. He's probably ruined me for all men.

I finally went through my bills last night. It's depressing. For the first time, I'm receiving collection calls. I received eleven overdue bills while I was gone. I'm so far behind that I feel like Indiana Jones and the big boulder is ready to run me over. I'm current with only one bill—my cell phone because I need it for work. I sent my last two hundred dollars to my landlord and explained I'll have the rest soon, but I don't get paid until Friday.

I stand in my kitchen and look at what I have to eat. There's nothing fresh in my fridge, and the pantry is pretty bare unless you want to eat oregano or garlic salt. For the next month, I'm left with only meals I can get at work.

Dropping my things in my cubicle, I head to the kitchen in the office. I'm in desperate need of coffee. I'm out at home, and I was up late last night working my second job. I knew I wasn't doing a great job when the tips were small or nonexistent, but I kept going. I make money every minute I'm on the phone.

As I watch every drop of the extra strong Nespresso fall into my cup, my anticipation builds, as does my caffeine headache. "There you are," William says as he saddles up to me.

"Hi."

He looks and smells delicious. He's wearing a blue, patterned shirt with the shirt sleeves rolled up and khaki pants and my favorite loafers and matching belt, and he smells like sandalwood and citrus. He's oozing sexuality, and women literally stop and stare at him when he walks by.

Under his breath, he asks, "Where have you been? I've sent you a few texts, but you haven't responded. Can I take you to lunch today?"

It's tempting. "I wish I could, but I have meetings straight through today." It isn't exactly the truth, but it will placate him—for now.

"Then tonight. Let's go to dinner tonight. I'd like to update you on what's happened, and… maybe catch up?"

"I don't know, William. I didn't work my second job for over a week. My rent is late, and I desperately need to work. Maybe in a few weeks after I get caught up."

"Well, that's part of what I want to talk to you about."

My heart stops. Great, now he's going to tell Mason. "Please, I need to work. Can we try for lunch—maybe tomorrow will work?"

He smiles at me. "You look beautiful, and I miss hanging out with you. I don't want to put any added pressure on you, so I'll be patient. But you'll never believe this—I still don't believe it. Lillian has moved out of the house."

"What? What about Dumb and Stupid?"

"They're out too. She insisted on the lump sum. Harriett and Henry are working with the auditors and going through the inventory. They'll pay out her inheritance in a lump sum by the end of the week."

"What if she tries to come back?"

"Harriett is changing the locks. My guess is that she must have some serious debt collectors after her to get the money and run."

I know that feeling. "Well, that must be a small relief for you."

"Maybe a little. I was thinking of going back in a few weeks. I hope you'll come with me." He caresses my arm, and an electric jolt goes right to my core. "We can christen a few of the rooms in the house." He wiggles his eyebrows.

I smile at him. The idea of being close to him and having more hot and steamy sex sounds amazingly appealing, but I can't be his beck-and-call girl. "We'll see."

One of his team members call his name from the doorway, letting him know he's needed. He raises his finger, indicating that he'll be there in a moment, and them he turns to me and says, "Mason scheduled a business lunch for me tomorrow—I have a new client coming on. I know you want time to work your second job, so I'm putting you down for lunch the day after tomorrow. Make a plan on it."

I nod and smile. I'm going to be off-site the day after tomorrow with a client, and I'm determined to not be alone with him again. I can't trust myself. I can't do it. My heart hurts. I can't even be his friend right now. It's too hard. I close my eyes and will the tears to go away.

I work through the day and eat at my desk. I'm so grateful the company provides at least two meals a day. It's after six, and I need to get home if I'm going to get the east coast crowd. The office is almost empty. I see William is meeting with Cameron and Dillon, so I quickly shut my computer down and head out. I detour by the kitchen to see what might work for dinner tonight. There isn't much. I grab a few pieces of fruit and a few snacks. It isn't the most nutritious meal, but it'll have to do for tonight.

As I head to the elevator, I see William waiting. I'll change my mind if he asks me out tonight for dinner or for sex. I can't afford that, so I turn around and take the stairs. I must work tonight.

Walking home, there is a fine mist falling. It's dark, cold, and wet. It isn't a quick walk, but it isn't too far. I can't afford a bus pass, and I certainly can't afford a rideshare. The exercise is good for me since I sat at my desk all day. I'm almost completely caught up from my week away. As I walk home, I run through all the reasons I can't be William's mistress. I may not be perfect, but I can't be the good sex he has on the side. I deserve better than that. But maybe I'm fooling myself. He hasn't even asked me for that.

When I walk in the door, I quickly plug my computer in. It's just after seven, and I'm late. My phone line via my computer rings almost immediately.

"Hello, handsome."

"Hello, Cinnamon. I'm feeling horny tonight."

And so my evening goes. Someone knocks at my door just before nine, and I ignore it. If it's my landlord, I don't have my rent quite yet. If it's anyone else, I don't have time to talk to them. Tomorrow I'll get my direct deposit, and I'll be able to pay some of my bills. I'm still behind by over a month, but at least he'll have some money. My landlord's patience is running out.

It's a night of strange requests, but I just roll with it. Some people have some serious fetishes. I turn the computer off at one and crawl into bed. My throat is sore from so much moaning and talking. Tomorrow will be another day.

As I cry myself to sleep, I realize I can't do this much longer. I adore my friends, but it isn't enough to remain here. I know what I need to do, but I can't bring myself to do it.

chapter

twenty-four

WILLIAM

More clues come up with the helicopter crash, and the investigators certain that my dad was not in the crash, but where is he?

It's late, and my phone rings, making me jump. Hoping it's Quinn asking me to come over, I answer.

"Hello?"

I can hear something in the background, but no one speaks.

"Hello?" Still nothing. "Look, stop calling if you're not going to talk to me." Still no response. This is probably the fifth time I got this call, but this time it's very late.

This is getting ridiculous. I hate to silence my phone in case Quinn needs me, but when I've counted a dozen calls, this is bordering on ridiculous. I text Jim.

Me: I've had over a dozen phone calls and no one answers. Is there anything you can do to trace these?

Jim: We're on it. Is it this number they're calling?
Me: Yes.
Jim: If they call again, push *98.
Me: Okay.

I wait, and it takes about twenty minutes before my phone rings, and it's the same thing. I push *98, and then I text Jim.

Me: Okay, they just called, and I did as you asked.
Jim: We got it. We've also pulled your phone records. It seems to be coming from Philadelphia.

I sit up straight. Philadelphia. Is Harriett okay?

Me: Do you know where in Philadelphia?
Jim: Looks like we can narrow it down to Rittenhouse Square. Do you know that area?
Me: Yes. My family home is there. My stepmother moved out of the house, but my housekeeper is there. Do I call her and see if she's okay or do I call the police and have them do a wellness check?
Jim: Try calling her first.

I dial the house, and a sleepy Harriett answers the phone.

"Harriett, I'm so sorry if I've woken you. I think I keep getting calls from the house. Is everything okay?"

"I believe so. Marcus is here with me, and we're fast asleep."

"I'm so sorry I woke you. Do you think Brett or Jason could be in the house prank calling me?"

"We changed the locks a few days ago. I don't think so."

"Okay. I'm sorry I woke you."

"That's okay. Marcus is walking around the house. The alarm pad is lit up, so I know that's on."

"I have a feeling someone is playing a practical joke on me and has spoofed the location of the house and is calling me and then hanging up."

"I'm so sorry, Master William." I hear her talking to Marcus, but I can't make out what she's saying. "Marcus says the house is buttoned up tight."

"Thank you, Harriett. Again, I'm sorry I woke you both."

"Any time. I'll do a better search in the daylight and let you know if anything seems out of place."

"Goodnight."

This is really strange. I text Jim back.

Me: It's not my housekeeper. Could the location be spoofed?

Jim: I'm sure it's not impossible. We'll check it out.

It's after midnight, and the calls finally seem to end. I can't sleep. I wish Quinn was here. I see the pile of mail sitting on the table. I sort out the junk mail, and I'm stunned that leaves me with very little left.

There's a white envelope without a return address. I almost throw it out without opening it when I notice the canceled stamps. They're from Tanzania. I examine it carefully. It doesn't seem out of the ordinary, but it's strange. I debate opening it, but my curiosity gets the better of me, and I open it anyway.

Inside is a letter written in my father's handwriting. I read the note.

My dearest William,
If you are receiving this, something has happened to
me. I'm worried for my life. I discovered something at
the company, and I can't figure out what or who may
be behind it. I'm sending you this key. Everything I
know is in safe-deposit box 625 at Market Street Bank
on Market Street in San Francisco. Please know that I
love you very much. I'm sorry I didn't tell you more.

I put the letter down. What the hell? It's late, but I call Jim anyway.

"Hello, William. Still getting phone calls?"

"No. Something else has happened." I pause for a moment, trying to figure out what I want from Jim. "I opened an envelope that was postmarked from Tanzania. Inside was a letter that was in my father's handwriting, but it isn't signed, and it includes a key to a safe-deposit box at Market Street Bank on Market Street. I've never even heard of Market Street Bank." I run my hands through my hair. "He lives in Philadelphia and has to my knowledge never come out to visit me. I don't know when he might have been here in San Francisco. This is really strange."

"I agree it's strange. Can you read it to me?"

After I read it to him, he says, "I guess that means we meet at Market Street Bank in the morning when they open, and we see what's in the box."

"I don't have the death certificate. I'm not sure they'll allow me to access the box with only a key."

"Let's see what they say. We can try. The note is very strange. Are you sure it's in your father's writing?"

"Positive. I mean, it could be a counterfeit, but it does look very much like his writing."

"It's a private bank that opens at nine. We can meet there tomorrow morning, that is if you'd like me to go with you."

"As crazy as this sounds, I think I'd like a witness with me when I go in and see what's in the safe-deposit box."

"I'm happy to meet you there."

I think about it for a few brief moments. This could go sideways in so many ways. "I'll see you then."

I don't sleep well. Instead, I start to examine everything about my time at home and what I may have missed. When I wake, I realize I can't meet Quinn today for lunch. Shit. I need to have a conversation with her. It's early, but I text her anyway.

Me: I'm so sorry. I can't meet for lunch today. I've had strange calls from the house in Philly, and I got a strange piece of mail from my dad.

I see the little dots rotating. She's up early.

Quinn: No worries. Sorry about your dad. Let me know if I can do anything.
Me: Dinner tonight?
Quinn: I need to work. Sorry.
Me: Please?
Quinn: I really can't.
Me: I miss you.

And she doesn't respond.

After going for a good run, I get dressed and make it to the bank about a half hour early. I've walked past here two dozen times and never knew a bank was here. It's a discrete door, and there's no signage, but you can tell it's well secured. I see a Starbucks and head over for a cup of coffee. I'm waiting outside when I see Jim being dropped off by one of his team members.

"Are you ready?"

"As ready as I'll ever be."

We walk over, and I push the call button at the address. "Can I help you?" comes out of the intercom.

I look at Jim, and he nods. "Hello. My name is William Bettencourt. I have a safe-deposit box for your bank?" I show the camera the key and the door buzzes.

We walk in. There is a beautiful Asian woman sitting at the desk.

"Welcome to Market Street Bank. How may I help you?"

"I have a key to safe-deposit box 625."

"May I see your ID please?"

I hold my breath as I hand her my driver's license. She clicks a few buttons on her computer, and after a few moments, she says, "Thank you, Mr. Bettencourt. Please follow me."

She is thin and quite tall, made taller by her three-inch Manolo Blahniks. She walks me back to a giant safe, and the three of us go into the room with all the safe-deposit boxes. She points to box 625. It's a large box. I place my key in the lock, and she inserts hers and turns both. She removes the box and places it on the center table before leaving Jim and me alone.

Opening the box, I'm stunned at what I see. There are several VHS tapes and a stack of papers an inch thick. I glance through them, and I can't quite make out what they all mean. I start to ask a question, and Jim shakes his head. He opens his bag, and I put everything I can inside. We empty the box and close it up. I lock up the box, and we leave without saying a word.

As we exit the bank, Jim's team immediately pulls up, and we get in the car. When I start to say something, Jim holds a finger over his mouth, and I stay quiet. We drive the five blocks to his offices, and I follow him in to a soundproof room.

We begin looking through the papers. They don't make a lot of sense. There are affidavits of captains of ships, both men and women, but I can't make out what the cargo is. One of Jim's men brings in a device that they wave over the contents of the box, and it goes crazy as it passes over a piece the papers and tapes, indicating that there is a bug hidden somewhere inside.

"Sorry about that, but I noticed the listening devices in the vault, and I'm not sure what may be here, so I didn't want to give anything away."

I nod.

"Okay, let's look at what we have." Jim picks up a phone. "Can you bring in a television and a VHS player." He listens for a few moments. "I know VHS is old, but that is what we have. I believe we have both in the storeroom in the basement." He hangs up and shrugs at me. "VHS isn't exactly cutting edge."

I chuckle. "Hopefully it still works."

"It will slow us down, but we have other options if it doesn't."

There are pictures of young women in their early teens, if that, of all nationalities. I can't make heads or tails of this. "Do you know what this is all about?"

"Unfortunately, I think I do. We need to see the tapes, and we probably need to call the FBI and possibly get you and your father an attorney."

I'm dumbfounded. "What does all this mean? What do you see? These are VHS tapes, could they be old?"

"Possibly, but believe it or not, some people will use VHS for these kinds of films since they can't be shared easily."

"Does this mean what I think it does?"

"I think your father uncovered a sex trafficking ring."

chapter

twenty-five

QUINN

"Miss Faraday, you are almost ninety-days past due with your rent. I need you to become current in three days, or I will begin eviction proceedings."

I disconnect from the voice mail message. Shit. The tears fall, and they fall hard. Why is it that I've done everything right and it's still not good enough? I got good grades in school. I work hard, and I don't steal. I'm honest, and I try to treat others like I want to be treated. Why do I have the shittiest luck? I look to the heaven's and yell out, "What did I ever do to deserve all this?"

I have to be to work in a half hour. The voice mail from my landlord came in while I was working out. I haven't showered, and I need to get to work. My mind is racing. My school loans are due. I can forgo them again, but with the principal at almost two hundred thousand dollars, missing a payment is like adding four more. I'll never dig myself out of this debt. I feel completely defeated. Slowly, I make my way to the shower and get dressed in my typical uniform—black pants, a black turtle neck, and black boots. Throwing my hair up into a messy bun, I set out for the walk to work. As I walk, I work through all my options. I can ask for an advance on my bonus, but that would require approval by all the partners, and that is just too embarrassing, and there's a good chance they'd say no. As I see it, I need to come up with fifty thousand dollars in less than three days to cover my rent and bring all my bills current.

When I arrive, it's still early, but I see Mason sitting in his office. I wave to him. He motions me into his office. "William told me what happened in Philadelphia." I brace for the added bad news. "I'm glad you're okay. The partners and I truly value your contribution. In your paycheck yesterday you should've seen a 10 percent raise."

I'm shocked. I didn't even look at my bank balance. It's all too depressing. Ten percent is a big raise, but I quickly realize it won't dig me out of my troubles. "Thank you, I'm so grateful. It means a lot to me to be recognized for my hard work."

"I believe you know this, although it isn't common knowledge, Emerson is pregnant. It's going to be busy while she's out on her maternity leave."

I paint a smile on my face that I don't feel. "I understand. I'm happy to help and pitch in."

"Great. Thank you."

I've been dismissed. I stand to leave.

"One more thing. I'm really happy for you and William."

"Umm. Thank you?" I'm not sure what William has told him, but we're not anything more than friends. I smile and leave. I'm fuming. My personal life is exactly that. It's personal.

I see William arriving, and I march right into his office.

He smiles. "Good morning, sunshine. I've been missing you. Sorry about lunch today —"

I want to yell. I want to scream. Through clenched teeth, I say, "How dare you tell Mason we're dating?"

He blanches. "Well, err...."

"We are not dating. In fact, if you hadn't blackmailed me into going with you to Philadelphia, we wouldn't have ever seen each other naked. And let me assure you, you never will again." I'm on a roll. "I learned this morning that because I went with you, I will most likely be evicted from my apartment. I owe the world money, and you thought by telling the managing partner that we're fucking that it would make you look like a hero." I'm fighting back the tears. "After all I did for you, I can't believe you'd out me to Mason."

As I turn to leave, I hear William say, "I'm sorry —"

Before I stormed out, I saw what might have been hurt cross his eyes, but I'm too overwhelmed to think it through. I rush into the bathroom and burst into tears. I cry for the loss of my friends and my life as I know it. Here I have an amazing opportunity with my boss going out on maternity leave, and I'll be living in a homeless shelter—either that or.... It's been staring me in the face, and I haven't really wanted to do it, but it's time I start lining things up to move home to help my dad.

chapter

twenty-six

WILLIAM

I wanted to tell Quinn about what we found in the safe-deposit box, but she was so angry with me that I didn't get a chance. I had to tell Mason about our relationship because of my partnership agreement. Dillon and Emerson are married and partners, and while it happened before I joined the firm, I heard it was tough to get by Mason. I figured with Quinn and Mason having a history, I needed to warm him up. I didn't tell him that I plan on marrying her, only that I wanted his and the company's okay to see her.

I run through the conversation. She owes the world money, and she's looking at eviction. She was incredibly helpful in Philadelphia, and I owe her more than she knows. I did promise to pay her for coming with me, so I need to make this right. I do some quick research and figure out who owns the building she lives in. His number is unlisted, so I call Jim, and with a few clicks, he gives me his number. I make the call.

"Hello," a gruff male voice says into the phone.

"Yes, this is William Bettencourt. I'm calling on behalf of Quinn Faraday."

"She's behind over three months' rent."

"That's why I'm calling. What is the total?"

"Her monthly rent is $4,000. When she pays after the 5th, she owes another $500 and interest kicks in."

"What kind of payment world is that?"

"I'm starting eviction notice day after tomorrow if I don't have the past three months' rent."

"So she has told me. What is the amount?"

I hear a ten-key clicking and the tape going and going. "It looks like she owes $19,064.26."

I'm stunned into silence. No wonder she feels overwhelmed. Seven thousand dollars in late fees—I need to get her out of this apartment. The rent is unfortunately in line, but the terms are bad. "What is your banking information? You'll have that plus an additional $8,000 to cover the next two months."

He rattles off the banking information, and I put through a transfer from my savings.

"You should have the money in your account tomorrow. Please call her once you have it, and let her know that she doesn't owe you rent for the next two months. If you try to cheat her in any way, I will bring the force of the law down on you so hard, you won't ever be able to dig out."

"I'm not a liar. I'll let her know."

"No, you're just a cheat."

"I have a few other tenants who are late since you're in a generous mood."

"Not surprising given you are essentially a loan shark." I hang up. I want to relieve her of some of her school loans, but I know she may already be upset that I paid off some of her rent. I know she didn't tell me of her plight to get help but to make her point, and I need to tread carefully.

Looking at my phone, I see I have a voice mail; I'm not sure when I missed a call. The message is from Harriett. "Master William, Marcus and I have been through the house. We don't think anyone was here. We'll keep our eyes out."

I don't delete the message, but I hang up. This is all very strange. I'm due back at Jim's about three so we can watch the VHS tapes. I'm anxious to know if my dad uncovered a sex trafficking ring. Just the thought sours my stomach.

I work through lunch, and I watch Quinn do the same. I want to talk to her, but she won't even look at me, so I know I'm still firmly in the dog house. At two thirty, I pack up and head out to Jim's. He has a ride waiting for me downstairs. This can't be good.

When I arrive, they take me in through the garage and to a floor that I can't quite determine if it's above ground or below, but the lack of windows suggests it's below. Jim greets me. "We were able to get the tapes transferred to a digital copy, and we're set up. I've asked Thomas and Brian here to join us."

I extend my hand and say, "Nice to meet you."

We sit in what looks like a movie theater, and someone starts the video. It's a young girl with blonde hair and beautiful big blue eyes, and she can't be more than ten years old. I blanch as I see an old, withered hand caress her cheek. We watch as he removes her dress and then pulls down her panties. She stands looking at him scared. "I'm going to make you feel so good." He touches her genitals, and I can't take anymore. I run from the room and find a metal trash can. Ripping the lid off, I vomit, emptying my stomach of everything I've eaten today, and I'm still dry heaving when Brian joins me. "You okay?"

I shake my head.

"That's the right response. I've watched the six hours of tape already. They are much of the same. None of them are your father, if that makes you feel any better."

"Who are they?"

"We don't know, but we have pictures of about twenty different men. I'll get freeze-frames of them and see if you can identify them."

I nod. "What do we do after that?"

"This is where it gets tricky. We need to get the FBI and possibly Interpol involved. I would suggest that you retain an attorney used to dealing with the FBI, and we take it to them. I'd like to get a few more things figured out if we can, first."

"I'm good with that."

Jim walks up and puts his hand on my shoulder. "I'm sorry you had to see that. I have an update on your crank calls. Let's head up to my office."

I follow him upstairs and to his office. It has a wall of windows that overlook a bullpen of men and women working on computers. All are dressed in the company uniform—black cargo pants, military-style boots, black T-shirts, and the occasional sweater or sweatshirt. Jim points me to a set of chairs at a small table. I sit down.

"These are pictures of the accident site." The helicopter is a blackened mess of metal. I look at him expectantly.

"My team hiked down to the site, and here are the pictures."

I can see the inside of the cockpit, and it looks like the seats are blackened. "I'm assuming your team noticed the plants already growing into the cockpit in less than a month."

"You have a good eye. We think the accident is much older than they are reporting."

I sit back hard in the chair. "So chances are my father is alive?"

"We don't know. There was a second accident in the right time period that killed six people on their way to base camp. That may be our accident. We believe they used this accident because they were too lazy to climb to the other accident site."

"How will we find out?"

"My team has your father's DNA and dental records. Now we just need to find the other accident and get it in front of some people."

"What about the recording? Do you have any updates on that?"

"We compared the recording to your father, and we agree, it's a doctored tape. We believe that some of it comes from previous recordings spliced together. It's a setup though."

Well, at least this is good news. This whole thing is making me anxious—first the Ponzi scheme, then Lillian being strange, and now the sex tapes with minors. It's all too much. I'm not sure what to do at his point.

"Where are the pictures? I want to know if I can identify these motherfuckers."

"We'll have them for you by morning."

"What about the crank calls?"

"They're using burner phones that were sold here and in Philly. Each time we come close to triangulating them, the number changes."

"Great, we don't know much more. So I can leave?"

He nods. I stand and check my phone for the time. It's getting late. I walk out for a rideshare. I can't breathe. How the fuck did my father get involved in this shit?

As I wait for the rideshare, I listen to my voice mail, and it's Quinn. "I'm not happy with you, but thank you for paying my rent. I will repay you."

I direct the rideshare to Quinn's apartment. She's not home yet, so I use my time to consider what's going on and all the implications as I sit on the front step and wait for her.

"What are you doing here?" she asks in greeting.

"I needed to see you. I know you need to work tonight, but I'll pay you if you will just join me for dinner."

She looks at me, taking in my disheveled hair and my bloodshot eyes. "Come on upstairs."

I follow her. When she opens the door, she puts her computer and things over a chair close to the door and faces me. Trembling, I pull her into my arms. "Can we order in? Please?"

"Yes. Otherwise, we're stuck with peanut butter crackers and bananas."

"What are you interested in?"

"A steak actually. Is that too much?"

I laugh. "No, we can do that. Ruth Chris okay?"

She nods. "More than okay." We order two rib eyes, twice baked potatoes, sautéed mushrooms, and asparagus with Hollandaise sauce. When she isn't paying attention, I add a chocolate cake and a cheesecake for dessert. I find her in the kitchen. "It'll be here in about an hour."

"I'm not having sex with you," she informs me.

"I'm fine with that. I just need to talk to you."

We talk about what's been going on with my dad and how screwed up it all is.

"That is completely unbelievable. If you were to write this in a book, no one would believe you."

"Welcome to my life."

Dinner arrives. I watch Quinn dive in, and I love her enthusiasm for food. "This is so good. I didn't realize how much I missed a good steak."

"Make sure you save room for dessert."

She evaluates me carefully. "So talk."

I talk for over three hours, telling her all about what happened with Lillian, the tape I was given from the flight attendant, the crank calls, and the mail that was sent by my father.

"Holy shit. That's unbelievable."

"I don't know what to think."

"I can see why." She looks at me, and I can see tears in her eyes. "Thank you for paying my rent."

"I promised that I'd pay you for going. It's the least I can do since it's my fault you're behind."

"Uh, no, it isn't. It's the fact that my loans and rent are more than my take-home pay."

"You know you could always move in with me. That would eliminate your rent and leave you only with your school loans."

"That's very kind of you, but I can't do that."

I'm saying this all wrong. I'm too tired to say this right.

"I will pay you back the money you wired to my landlord," she says with great force.

"First, that isn't necessary. Think of it as payment for helping me with my predicament."

"I'm not a charity case. I will get you your money back."

I know I can't force it, but I'll work on her. After dessert, we're both fighting sleep. "Can I stay the night?"

She nods, and I follow her into the bedroom. We both strip to our underwear, and she tosses me a T-shirt, and we crawl into bed. I don't even care that sex is off the table. I only want to spend as much time with her as she'll let me. I'm determined to wear her down.

chapter

twenty-seven

QUINN

I'm truly grateful for what William did for me. Without the monkey on my back, I feel so much lighter. I feel like I can breathe. I was able to send a double payment for my school loan with this pay period, and I evaluated my finances. Even with the two-month reprieve, it doesn't look good.

There's really only one solution. Pulling up the company calendar, I put a meeting on Mason's calendar for eight. The email sends and almost immediately is accepted.

No going back now.

I look around my apartment. I don't have a lot. I have a semi-decent television, some expensive wireless speakers, my bed, and some bookshelves. There are a few things I want to take with me, but only a few. There's my car. It's worth money. It's currently uninsured, which is why it just sits in my parking space. After checking the Blue Book price, I'm actually surprised at how much I'll get for it. I'll have to buy another car, but at least now I'll have the money to do so. Pulling up Markslist, I list the car for sale. It now feels real.

After what feels like hours of tossing and turning, I finally get up and list all the things I need to do. Each time I'm close to drifting off, I think of one more thing. When my alarm sounds at six thirty, I'm slow to get out of bed. I fight back the tears and get ready and walk to work for my eight o'clock meeting with Mason.

He's already in the office when I arrive, so I put my things down, grab a cup of coffee, and make my way to his office.

"Hey, what's up?" Mason asks expectantly.

All of a sudden, I'm nervous. This is going to be harder than I thought. "My father is having some challenges, and I need to go home and be with him."

"You need to take some family leave?"

"No, I think I need to give notice. My two weeks' notice."

"Wait. You can come back after your dad is on the road to recovery."

"Thank you, but I guess I look at it this way, my career, my friends, my personal belongings, these are all rubber balls. If I drop them, they'll bounce back. Family is a glass ball. If I drop that, it'll break. I'm an only child. There isn't anyone else for my dad, and I can't convince him to come here, so I need to go to him."

"Do you think it would help if I talk to him? I can help you find a place down on the peninsula," Mason pleads.

"I'm not sure if William told you, but I have a second job."

"Why? Are we not paying you enough?"

"Mason, my rent and my school loans are more than my take home each month. That isn't your fault. I'm over thirty, and I want to live without a roommate. You know that I borrowed for grad school. I can't afford it here anymore. I know this puts you in a bad place, and I'm really sorry, but I need to go. I will do a really good transition memo so that everyone has everything they need to know."

"We'll throw you a big party, but it won't be a goodbye party, rather a see-you-soon party."

"Actually, I'm hoping that we just tell people I'll be back in a few weeks, but don't tell anyone I won't be coming back. I know that is asking you to lie, but I don't want anyone to make a big fuss, and I beg you not to tell the partners about my financial situation. It's truly embarrassing."

"I understand about wanting to be close to your dad. You know I'm in a similar boat with my mom, but I won't accept your resignation. When you're ready to come back, we'll find you an inexpensive and safe place to live, and we'll give you a raise. Please don't leave us."

"I don't think you understand. My second job is a phone sex operator. It most likely is a violation of the ethics policy."

"Phone sex?"

"Yes, men call in the evenings and want me to talk dirty to them. I don't use my real name, but I get paid by the minute."

"Does anyone know?"

"Yes. William knows. I was leaving him a message one night, and I accidentally didn't hang up, and he heard my side of a very embarrassing conversation."

"I see. Did he threaten you? Is that why you went to Philadelphia with him?"

"No, he needed someone to be his beard for his crazy stepmother. It was all good."

"So you've been supplementing your income with a second job, but no one knows it is you?"

"That's correct."

"Why do you think that's a reason to quit? I mean, there is someone here that is writing erotica and publishing it under a pen name, and that doesn't bother me. If they decide to do a book tour, then we might have to have a conversation, but from what you describe, it's legal what you're doing, and I know San Francisco is expensive."

I'm both shocked and grateful for his response. I paint a smile on my face. I can't let him convince me to stay. Working that many hours for years on end will put me in an early grave. "Please keep this between you and me, and I know the partners need to know, but can you wait until after I leave? I don't want anyone to make any fuss."

"Is this because you aren't a partner?"

I fight back the tears and shake my head. "No. I don't think I could afford to buy into partnership anyway. I love my job, and under different circumstances, I might think differently, but I want to be there for my dad."

"You'll always have a place at SHN."

I choke back tears. "Thank you." I stand and extend my hand, and we shake. Mason looks crestfallen.

When I get back to my desk, I begin the process of writing up the giant memo so that I can transition my dream job to someone else. Throughout the day, my phone rings and I take care of multiple issues, making notes in my memo so that nothing falls through the cracks. I have too much pride in my work to leave a job without a roadmap so that my clients don't see any disruption.

I'm going to miss my job. It's something I'm truly good at. I can manage crisis after crisis, loads of drama, and sometimes intrigue, and I love it.

I'm going to miss my friends. CeCe's wonderful, and I love Emerson and Cynthia. I'll miss the glasses of wine and the gossiping, eating, and going out shopping with them—I look, and they buy.

I'm going to miss this city. Despite the influx of tourists year-round, I will miss the fantastic views, the amazing restaurants, and all the fun things to do here.

The only good thing I can take comfort in is that I won't see William anymore—not that I don't want to see him, but it's so hard to be with him and not do anything he asks. He's only interested in friends with benefits, and I want more—I want it all. He's been out of town dealing with his father's mess, but he emails and calls every day. I think the distance will be good for me. If I stay, I know I'll be devastated if I have to watch him move on to someone else. I just don't think I could take it.

chapter

twenty-eight

WILLIAM

Jim, a few members of his team, and I fly back to Philadelphia so he can help me figure out videos and all the paperwork my father left behind. When he presents me with the photos of the men who are abusing the girls, I'm dumbfounded. Henry Gray is one of the men. My father's friend and my confidant—how is it possible?

I then identify the current president and chairman of the board of my father's company and three other board members. "What the hell kind of perverse company are we running that we have so many pedophiles?" I'm angry and disgusted. "How do they all work for my father's company?"

"Unfortunately, these guys are probably all part of some group, and since they hang out together socially, they hook each other up with employment and other things."

"I need to consult an attorney."

"Yes, you do. We now have the names of five of the twenty-three. I also think we need to loop in a public relations team because once it is determined that four of these guys are part of your father's company, it may very well tank the stock and the company. You could be looking at a total revolt of your products."

"I agree. A good PR team can help us, hopefully, mitigate the destruction." I look at the pictures of some of the other men, and I have to wonder if I know any of the others. "When do you want to go to the FBI?"

"I think we need to go soon."

I nod. "Let me make a phone call." I pull up the number of an attorney who has worked with our firm. Since it's a federal case, she can help us, but she may not have the time, and she may not be interested. "Marci Peterson, please."

"May I tell her who's calling?"

"This is William Bettencourt with SHN." I might as well name-drop, what harm can it do?

After a few moments, I hear, "Hello, William. How are you?"

"I'm well. Sorry to drop my company name, but I'm in Philadelphia and I'm in need of some representation when I meet with the FBI, and given I live in San Francisco, I thought it was more prudent you and I were close rather than have representation here in Philly."

She takes a big breath. "I see. Without going into too much detail, what can you tell me?"

"I have Jim Adelson here on the phone."

"Hi, Marci."

"Hey, Jim, we need to stop meeting like this."

I then proceed to walk her through my father's death along with what we found in the safe-deposit box—very high level and with minimal details. "Wow, that's quite a big deal."

"Marci, we'd like to go to the FBI by Friday. If these guys were on to Reginald Bettencourt, they most likely know we have the tapes and other information. We have protection on William twenty-four seven, but I'd feel a lot better if we could hand this over to the FBI."

"I understand, particularly if they were behind the crash of Reginald Bettencourt's helicopter. It's eleven thirty now. I can see what kind of flights I can get out of the Bay Area tonight. We can meet tomorrow and go see the FBI Civil Rights Unit in Philly. We'll also need to hire Philly representation, so that if we need to turn something around in Federal Court quickly, we can do so without me losing a day to go back and forth," Marci says.

"Marci, I have a plane at SFO. I think I'd like a few more of my team here, so I can bring everyone out together. They are flexible on departure time. What time works for you?" Jim asks.

"That would be incredible. Thank you. How about seven? I think I can wrap up here and move a few things around on my schedule for the remainder of the week," Marci shares as she thinks through everything she needs to get done.

"That would work. I'll have someone from my team pick you up at your home, or would you prefer your office?" Jim asks.

"Home is fine. I have your cell phone number. I'll text over my address, and that way they'll have both my phone and address."

"I'll also have the files and videos that we discussed brought to you by my team, so we won't have to worry about getting it to you safely, and you can view it on the plane," Jim offers.

"That would be so helpful. Thank you."

"Thank you, Marci. I'll set up a room for you here at the Rittenhouse Hotel. We can meet in my suite when you're up tomorrow morning," I tell her.

"I don't know that I'll be sleeping tonight," she teases.

We work through a few more details before we hang up. Jim quickly begins calling members of his team, letting them know they're wheels up at seven and giving them instructions to pick up Marci from her home by six thirty and drive her in.

There is so much anxiety in all the activity. I'd hate to see all the work my grandfather and father did go down the toilet, but if the company has more people involved than the four I recognized, then I'm not sure I care. Abusing young girls is completely unacceptable.

"So let's go take a look at your family home. The guys and I can make that our base of operations if that still works for you?" Jim suggests.

"Absolutely. I think Harriett will love having you there. She's a bit bored these days with the house empty." We walk outside, and the weather is incredible. "It's just across the park. You up for a walk?"

"Great idea. I did see in Gerald's reports he went running with you and Quinn a few times."

"Yes, that's another thing Quinn and I enjoy doing together."

Jim looks at me and smiles. "Gerald is staying in San Francisco with eyes on Quinn. Do you want me to pull him?"

"No. No way. I want her guarded tightly. She's way too important to get swept up in this mess."

Jim smirks at me. "I was only testing you. You're not only at the cliff, but I think you're close to going over."

"I'm not only over, but I'm swimming downstream already."

"Good to know. She's a great lady."

"That she is."

When we arrive at the house, I alert Harriett and ask her to join us. "Harriett, Jim, and his team are going to be here for a while. They can stay in the third-floor bedrooms, and if need be, you can move into the family suites on the second floor. In fact, please set Jim up in my father's room."

"Yes, sir. How many are you expecting?"

I look to Jim for that answer. "There are three of us here now. Tonight I have six more arriving. Are you able to accommodate that?"

"Without a doubt." Harriett beams, looking so excited to have reasonable guests. She scrutinizes him and apparently decides she needs to lay out her house rules. "There's no smoking in the house, so if any of your team need to smoke, they need to cross the street to the park." She looks him up and down in his black cargo pants and black T-shirt. "There are no feet up on the furniture, and I expect that your team does a modicum of help picking up after themselves."

"None of that should be an issue."

"I'll place a buffet breakfast out at 7:00 a.m. each morning and a lunch buffet out at noon. Both meals will change from day-to-day and will be served in the dining room. Dinner will be served each evening at 6:00 p.m. If anyone won't be able to make dinner, they need to let me know. I can order any drinks your team wants, and those are available along with any snacks they'd like." She looks around. "I'll send Marcus in, and he can help you run electrical and data lines into the sitting room for your teams if you'd like?"

Harriett is smart and efficient. She knows that nine people working together will need a lot of gear and the ability to work together closely. "That's a great idea."

"I'll make the beds each morning and do the housekeeping here. Linen will be washed every four days."

Jim's eyes bulge a bit. "Yes, ma'am. I know my team will be thrilled with all of the meals and attention. Please don't spoil them too much. They may want to move in permanently." Jim winks at her, and I know she'll do anything he asks. She's putty in his hands.

She picks up a small walkie-talkie from her apron pocket. "Marcus, I'm here with Master William and Mr. Jim in the sitting room. Can you please join us?"

"I'm on my way," says the voice over the radio.

In less than a minute, Marcus comes in with a tool belt that would be the envy of any carpenter I know. Wiping his hands on a towel, he nods to us. "How can I help you, gentlemen?"

"Marcus, I'd like you to meet Jim Adelson. He's with a security team, and they're going to set up shop here in the sitting room for a few days," I say.

Marcus looks Jim over carefully. "How many folks will be joining you?"

"There will be nine."

He nods and says to me, "I have a dozen wooden tables that your mother used for dinner parties years ago. They're rectangular and can seat four people at each table. I just refinished them earlier this summer."

I like how he's thinking. "Jim, these are roughly the size of an executive desk."

"That sounds perfect. You have a dozen?"

"Yes. We can move the furniture downstairs to the basement, and I can set up electrical and digital for you. I think, even if you have about three dozen machines, we can get you over a terabyte of connection speed per device."

Jim seems impressed.

Marcus looks to the ground. "Mr. Bettencourt often needed the high-power connections speed for his inventions, and I set that up a few years ago."

Jim smiles. "Okay then, when can we start setting up?"

"I have a few hired hands I can call, and we'll empty out the sitting room. I'm not sure when they can be here, but I don't expect it to take more than two or three hours."

Jim looks at Marcus. "Is it okay if I help? The two of us can clean this out—that is if you don't mind."

"Absolutely. I don't ask anyone to do anything I'm not willing to do myself," Marcus assures him.

"I can help too," I offer.

In less than forty-five minutes, the room is cleared of all furniture. We then bring up the tables. As we open the folding tables, Jim says, "These are nice wooden tables. You'd never guess they are folding tables." He runs his hand over the oak. "Very nice. Where did you get these?"

"I made them," Marcus says proudly.

In no time the room is set up. Harriett has made a really nice beef stew for dinner, and we eat well before we go back to work. It's after midnight when we're done. "The guys should be here before too long, and they'll be able to set up as soon as they arrive. Great. Marcus"—Jim extends his hand— "you're a real asset to our team. Thank you."

He blushes. "Not a problem, sir."

Jim and one of his team members escort me back to my suite at the Rittenhouse. I'm exhausted when I get there. Looking around the suite, I'm reminded of Quinn. I miss her more than I've ever missed anyone else. I order room service, and I call her while I wait.

Her voice mail answers. "Hey, it's me. I identified five of the guys in the pictures. I'm devastated that Henry Gray is one of them, and the other four are senior executives from Bettencourt Industries. Marci Peterson is coming in tonight with Jim's team, and I need to check with Greer on a good PR firm for when this breaks." I rub my face. "I miss you so much, and I wish you were here. I'm going to eat and go to bed, but call if you can. I'd love to hear your voice."

I hang up and hope that she's just on the other line and can call me back later. My dinner comes, and I eat the cheeseburger and fries but don't taste them. I make sure my phone is close as I crawl into bed, and I think I'm asleep before my head hits the pillows.

When my alarm sounds at six, I'm wasted and not really ready to get up. I check my phone and see no messages from Quinn. I'm sure it's because she didn't want to wake me, but I really wish she would have called — if only to hear her voice. Today's going to be a rough day.

My cold shower gets my blood pumping, and I'm grateful for the carafe of coffee that's been delivered to my suite, and I admire the breakfast set up the room service team has done. I need all the help I can get. It is exactly seven when the bell on my suite rings, and I see Marci standing there.

She extends her hand. "It's great to meet you face-to-face, I just wish it was under better circumstances."

"Thank you, it's great to finally meet you too. Cynthia, in my office, raves about you."

"That's very sweet of her."

"There's coffee, tea, bagels, fruit, yogurt, and whatever else over on the table. Please help yourself while we wait for Jim."

"I saw him earlier this morning. He was with his team getting their systems up and in place at what I understand is your family home."

"Yes. It's across the park."

"Why are you staying here?"

"Jim thought it would be a little more secure."

She nods. "We can probably start without him."

I wave her to the dining room table, and I take a seat and wait for her to get herself unpacked and ready. "Mr. Bettencourt, may I call you William or Will?"

"William is fine." I smile. She has this way about her that makes you feel at ease and ready to pour your heart out.

"I've had the chance to look through everything in the files. From what I understand, your father isn't on any of the videos."

"I only watched the first video and vomited, but Jim and his team went through and pulled stills of all the men, and I identified the ones I knew. None of them were my father."

She's taking notes. "Tell me about the five men you've identified."

"The first video was of my father's estate attorney, Henry Gray. He's been our family attorney for many years. He handled my mother's estate and has helped to manage the house here when it came into my possession after I turned twenty-five."

"Why didn't you take over running your own trust?"

"I didn't know I had inherited it. I'd always assumed my mother left her estate—which included the house—to my father."

She nods. "What's your relationship like with Mr. Gray?"

"I don't recall meeting him while I was growing up, but he's been my father's attorney for some time. When he called to tell me about the accident, he alerted me that my father included a clause in his will about me being married to collect my inheritance, which is why when I came a few weeks ago, I had Quinn Faraday join me."

"Is she your girlfriend?"

"I'd like her to be."

"She doesn't want to be your girlfriend?"

"I don't know." I need this line of questioning to move on.

"So he suggested you facilitate a lie?"

"I think it was more about my stepmother. She was trying to take the house and all of my inheritance. I'm certain that when it came down to it, he'd require my marriage. I think this was just a façade."

"And where is your stepmother now?"

"We're not sure. She was angry at not getting the entire inheritance, so she cashed out her half and disappeared."

"Has anyone called the police to report her missing?"

That alarms me. "No. She was very anxious for the money, so we figured she took it and ran."

"Do you think she could have been part of this sex ring and that's why she was so anxious to get out of town?"

I hadn't thought of that before. "I would hope not."

"Okay, tell me about the other four men you identified."

"They are Carl Carmichael; he's the CEO of Bettencourt Technologies. He's been CEO of the company for almost as long as I can remember. He ran the business side, and my father oversaw the innovation and technology. They were a great match."

"Is he married?"

"He was. I can't say for certain if he still is. I met with him a few weeks ago when I was in town and signed a few things I was asked to as part of my role on the board of directors."

"Did you read them over before you signed them?"

"Yes. They were about moving my father's stock to the trust his will set up."

"Did anything about him strike you as creepy?"

"No." I shake my head.

"The other three are board members with me on Bettencourt Industries. I don't know them beyond sitting in a room and attending stockholder meetings a few years ago."

Marci interviews me for three hours. Jim wanders through at one point and then leaves again. When the room service staff arrives to remove the breakfast items and replace it with some sandwiches, she looks at me and says, "Let's eat lunch, and then let's call the FBI and let them know we're coming in."

"Do you just call the main number and they put you through to someone?"

Marci laughs. "No, I had someone I know in the San Francisco office give me the name and direct dial of the person we need to meet with."

"How ugly is this going to get?"

"I'm not sure yet. Since you and your dad are not implicated at his point, you may be fine. The company may struggle."

"I get that." I sigh. "I have the name of a big-deal PR firm in New York to reach out to if we feel our internal staff and their PR company can't handle it, or more people at the company are involved."

"I'm curious to know if they know who any of the other men are."

"I'm just not involved with the company enough to know if they all aren't executive at Bettencourt Industries."

"I do find it odd that your father was surrounded by pedophiles and didn't know or, if he did know, didn't do anything about it."

"Well, I think it's the first option. But you'd have to know my dad to understand. He's a well-liked guy. Smart as a whip but probably has a really low emotional intelligence score. He doesn't read body language well or pay attention to things around him. His mind is always on his next invention. They're his babies."

"I have a brother like that," she sympathizes.

She picks up her phone and makes the call. "Hello, this is Marci Peterson. My client is ready to meet with you. Do you have time in about an hour?" She listens a few moments and nods her head. "Yes, I have your address. We'll see you then."

My palms feel wet all of a sudden, and my stomach does a summersault. "Now I'm nervous."

"Don't worry, you'll be fine. Now let's talk about what to expect."

She runs through everything, and then we walk down to meet Gerald who drives us into downtown to the Federal Building. When we get out of the car, I straighten my suit coat and take a deep breath. It's not like they're going to arrest me, but this very well could destroy everything my great-grandfather built. Taking a few more deep breaths, I collect myself, and we walk in. There's a large woman sitting behind the desk with two armed guards standing behind her.

"Good afternoon. I'm Marci Peterson. Terrence Wood is expecting us."

"Just a moment." She picks up the phone and announces us. When she's done, she asks for our ID's.

"I don't suppose you know Matilda in the San Francisco office?" Marci asks.

She looks up, surprised. "Yes, she's my cousin. I got her the job there."

"I knew you must be related. The resemblance is uncanny."

She hands us back our ID's and, as nice as can be, points us to the security check-in before the elevators. "Dana will meet you just beyond the metal detectors and will take you upstairs."

"Thank you, I can't wait to tell Matilda we met," Marci says.

"I'm going to email her right now," she says, and I swear she winked at Marci.

"Well, that was surprising."

We walk up to a conveyor belt and are asked to put our bags through the X-ray machine, and we walk through. Once we're through, a short, dark-haired woman approaches us and extends her hand. "Dana Bucannon."

"Nice to meet you, Ms. Bucannon. I'm Marci Peterson, and this is William Bettencourt." We follow her to the elevator and take it to the fourth floor. When we walk out, we're escorted to a room with no windows and a mirror on the wall. I know this is when it gets serious.

Terrance Wood walks in, as does Agent Michael McGraw and his unnamed partner. I'm surprised to see them. They introduce themselves, and the unnamed agent calls himself Brendan Phillips. I inform Marci, "Agents McGraw and Phillips are the ones who interviewed me regarding the supposed Ponzi scheme."

"I see. Are you both with the Civil Rights Unit or Financial Crimes?"

Agent McGraw looks at me and informs us, "We're with the CRU. We wanted to know what you knew."

After introductions, Marci begins. "Mr. Bettencourt recently learned of his father's death following a helicopter crash in Tanzania. He received a letter"—she passes the letter to them—"and a safe-deposit box key to a private bank in San Francisco. When he opened the box, this is what was inside." She pushes the box across the table at them. "We've digitized the videos and Mr. Bettencourt has identified five of the twenty-three men on the tapes." She sits quietly, and I'm uncomfortable as they stare at her before carefully looking through the box.

Agent Phillips hands the box to a member of his team, who leaves with it. Turning to me, he asks, "Mr. Bettencourt, tell me about yourself."

Marci had warned me they are going to ask me the same questions they've asked before, looking for inconsistencies. So, I walk them through what I do and where I live.

"What was your relationship with your father?" I know they've asked this each time I've met them, and Marci warned me they would do things like this to ruffle me. I'm glad she warned me since I answer the same question over and over.

"We weren't close. We also weren't estranged. We just didn't talk often. But this trip to Tanzania was a surprise. My father usually told me where he was going."

"Did he climb mountains often?"

"Yes, he's proudly climbed all the peaks over fourteen-thousand feet in the US and was working his way across the world."

"That's a lot of climbing."

"He enjoyed it. My father was an introvert and a bit of a loner."

"I see. Is your father on the tapes you provided?"

I bristle at the insult. "No, he's not. My own investigative team has questions about the accident and don't believe it was an accident but sabotage."

"Would it surprise you to find that we think so too?"

"Given the conversations with your team, no, I'm not surprised."

The agent who left early with what we provided steps in and asks to speak with Agent Wood, and he steps out. Agent McGraw remains behind. "You stand to gain from your father's death."

"Maybe. I have to marry my girlfriend and, well, she isn't really my girlfriend, rather a coworker. But also, I have a trust that I got from my mother on my twenty-fifth birthday, which includes the house on Rittenhouse Square. Money isn't a motivator to me. And, I might add, I had no idea my father was going to Tanzania."

"So you say. Your witness is a pedophile."

I cringe at the thought. "You can't get a rise out of me on this."

Agent Wood returns. "Ms. Peterson, Mr. Bettencourt, it appears the information you provided us has closed several holes for us. We will review it further and be making arrests."

That was quick. Now it all seems so real. I'm worried about the company and the stockholders. "Do you have a timeline? Since part of the leadership team at Bettencourt Industries will be arrested, I'd like to have a public relations firm ready to save the company that my great-grandfather worked so hard to build."

"I suggest you begin that soon, as we don't want to waste too much time."

"I understand." Almost as an afterthought, I add, "I believe my father was killed because he found this information. He knew he was in trouble when he sent me the key."

"I think that may be a fair assessment."

We stand to leave.

"We have your information. I suspect that we'll be in touch," Agent McGraw warns me.

"Thank you."

We are escorted down the elevators and to the waiting car. Once we're inside, Marci grasps my hand. "You did fantastic in there."

"I don't feel like it, but thanks." I unbutton my coat and sit back. My stomach is unsettled, and my stress levels are through the roof.

"I'll fly home today. I think Jim's team is sticking around for a few days," Marci informs me.

"That's my understanding. I'm going to catch the train into New York City and will be staying in Philly until this thing breaks. We'll need to find a new CEO and quickly."

"I think you'll have a great spin for the PR agency with what happened to your dad. I don't feel the stock will lose too much. Much will depend on your next steps."

I call Quinn and only get her voice mail. I wish she'd talk to me. I know I've not been super attentive, but I have a shit load going on. I hope she understands.

Given what I now know, I put a call into Dillon. He answers after the first ring. "Hey, man, how's it going?"

"It's going. How are things there?"

"It's going here too. What's up?"

"I just learned that the CEO and three of twelve members of the board of Bettencourt Industries are going to be arrested in the next few days for human trafficking."

Dillon whistles. "Wow, that can't be good."

"No, it won't be. The theory is that my dad was a deep-throat in all this, and it appears he's behind getting them arrested, only they killed him before he could finish passing the information along."

"Ah, man. That really bites."

"You're the best at analyzing the market. Do you think this is going to destroy Bettencourt Industries or do you think that, given my dad was behind ratting them out, that it might just save the company?"

I hear him clicking on the keyboard. "The CEO owns 10 percent of the shares. There's a slew of executives who own another 10 percent combined. Your father owned or controlled 40 percent, and the remaining 40 percent are publicly traded. We have to believe that once this hits, the CEO's going to need cash and will want to sell his 10 percent, but the board would have to sign off on that."

"And the company has the ability to buy them back at a specific cost, but I'll have to look at his agreement. We won't be out any golden parachute, but he may have to forfeit the shares due to an ethics clause."

"So I'm not sure it's going to take you down when the arrests happen, but I do think if it isn't handled right, it could go into a death spiral in a few months."

"Agreed. Greer has me talking to the best crisis public relations firm in the country, and I'm going to meet with them in the morning."

"Good luck, man. When are you back?"

"I'll be working from here for the next two or three weeks. Once this shit hits the fan, we'll have to get a few things taken care of—like finding a new CEO."

"I'll have Emerson reach out to you. We may have some candidates she can push your way."

"I didn't think about that, thanks."

We hang up, and I call the PR agency and set a time to meet with them in Manhattan tomorrow morning at 9:00 a.m. That means catching the 6:05 a.m. train into Penn Station in New York and catching a rideshare over to their offices.

I let Jim know my plans. "I'd rather we drive you than you take the train."

"I understand, but the traffic is so bad we'd have to go tonight."

"I'll figure out an alternative."

"Let me know. I need to be down on 5th Avenue by nine."

I try Quinn again and get her voice mail. I'm disappointed, but I can't think about it for very long because, before I know it, Harriet is putting a plate underneath my nose. "You have to eat."

"This smells amazing. I can eat with everyone else." I start to stand.

"They've all eaten. You've been so busy you missed dinner."

"It's more jetlag than anything else." I take a few bites. "Harriett, I miss your amazing cooking so much."

"Well, you and Quinn should hurry up and have some babies so I can cook for you every night."

"I'm not sure that's in our future."

"Sure, it is. You love her, and she loves you—I could see it the way the two of you looked at each other. It's like what your parents had so many years ago." She turns and heads out the door, leaving me to consider what she said. I do love her, but I'm fairly positive that she doesn't feel the same.

Jim arrives just as I'm finishing up. "Harriett is a great chef. I wonder if I can get her to move to San Francisco and take care of my team all the time."

I give him a look of warning. "You can ask, but I don't think she'd go."

He shrugs. "I have to at least try. Of course, she's going to fatten my team up at this rate." He quickly changes subjects. "Listen, we've chartered a helicopter to take you into Manhattan. We'll land at the Downtown Manhattan Heliport where we'll move you to a Suburban and then take you to your destination. We'll leave here tomorrow at seven."

Okay, I'm not sure I've ever commuted to New York via a helicopter. "This should be interesting."

I try Quinn a few more times, and I decide that I'll call when she gets off work, but somehow, I fall asleep watching *SportsCenter*. I wake with a start and look at my watch, and it's after three in the morning. Shit! I text Quinn.

Me: I miss you so much. I'm not sure what I did, but whatever it was I'm sorry. Please talk to me.
Quinn: You didn't do anything. I'm just super busy getting some things done. It's crazy busy right now.
Me: Can I call you?

I wait, and she doesn't respond immediately. Then I see the rotating dots.

Quinn: Yes.

My heart beats triple time while the number connects. "Hey."

"Hey yourself, what are you doing up so late?"

"It's been so crazy here. I'm heading into New York in a few hours to meet with the PR team to help handle the disaster that's going to come raining down on the company." We discuss everything that happened. I feel so much better talking to her.

"What about you? What has you so busy?"

"I have two companies going public next week. I need to do all the prep work for that. And I think they're getting close to the mole, so that has everyone on pins and needles. You know, same old same old." The line is quiet for a moment. I should tell her how I feel about her, but I really want to do it face-to-face. She murmurs, "I do wish you were here."

"Do you want to come out this weekend and spend it with me?"

"I don't know if I can. Can I reserve the right to change my mind?"

"Absolutely."

I need to tell her how much she means to me. "I miss you."

"I miss you, too."

"What are you wearing?" Okay, I couldn't help myself. When she snickers into the phone, I know I have her.

"My pink lacey thong and matching bralette."

I groan. I know exactly what she's talking about. The pink is the perfect color against her skin and is see-through. The bra scoops low, and her areola's peek out, hiding the nipples behind it. The thong is see-through as well, and I can make out her hairless slit. When she turns around, the small ribbon in the back disappears between her ass cheeks, and when she wore that the last time, it took all my self-control not to bend her over the closest chair and fuck her hard. My cock comes to life.

"What would you like me to do to you if you were here?" she asks in a coquettish voice.

"It isn't what you would do to me, but what I'd like to do to you," I growl.

"Tell me what you're wearing?"

"I'm in my gray sweatpants and a T-shirt—a Carolina basketball shirt."

"Is your cock hard?" she rasps.

"It is now."

"Just imagine me between your legs helping you to remove your sweatpants and boxers. God, your cock is huge. I hold it tight at the base and lick the underside, just the way you like."

Just the thought has my hands grasping my cock, and I begin stroking myself. "Does it make you wet?"

"Yes… and my nipples are achingly hard… Please play with them."

I'm breathing heavy as I stroke myself. "Can I lick them?"

"As long as you bite and pull, too."

"Are you playing with yourself?"

Her breathing is ragged. "Yes… my tongue is licking the end of your cock, and I can taste your precum. Mmmm… it tastes so good."

I can hear her moving, and it turns me on to know she's playing with herself, too.

"I can hardly get it all in my mouth. Guide me on your cock. Fuck my mouth. Show me how fast you want it. That's it, baby, you can go faster. Ohh. You taste so good. I'm massaging your balls. Give me what I want…"

"I'm going to come," I announce.

"Send it down my throat," she murmurs.

I reach for some tissues and groan loudly as I spurt. "Jesus, woman… you're amazing." Now it's my turn to get her off. "Do you want to come for me?"

"Please…"

"I'm going to slip those panties off."

"Mmm…"

"I'm opening your legs wide. You have the most beautiful pussy. It's glistening and begging to be sucked and fucked. Imagine my fingers running up and down your slit. I'm leaning over, and I take a deep breath. Fuck! You smell divine as I lick from the bottom to the top. You taste like honey. I stop at your hard nub and suck it hard into my mouth. I love you writhing beneath me."

"Finger fuck me at the same time," she begs.

"Your wish is my command. I'm inserting two fingers to stretch you wide as I suck." I can hear her breath increasing. I whisper, "Come for me, baby. Come all over my face."

An animalistic groan comes from her, and my dick is hard again. Breathing hard into the phone, she shares, "I've never actually had a real orgasm with anyone on the phone."

"I've never had real phone sex. You have quite the talent, but I have to say, it isn't as good as you being here with me."

"I know," she says wistfully.

The phone is quiet a few moments. I think of her perfect tits and her legs wrapped around me as I drill deep inside her. I need her with me, of that I have no doubts.

"I'm tired, so you must be exhausted. I'd better go to bed," she says.

"Goodnight, Quinn."

"Goodnight."

As I hang up, I feel like she's holding something back from me, but I get it, it's crazy busy, and I wouldn't mind getting off this crazy train.

I drag myself to the bedroom and fall into bed. I don't sleep well and struggle to get up to meet Jim.

He hands me a cup of coffee. "You look like you could use this."

Taking it from him, I mumble, "Thanks. I fell asleep last night in front of the television, but I finally got to talk to Quinn last night after three."

"That's quite the short night. You ready for this?"

"As ready as I'll ever be."

The helicopter ride is faster than a car, but really, we're just cutting short all the traffic lights. We arrive at the Downtown Manhattan Heliport in less than an hour. It then takes us another hour to navigate the downtown traffic, so between all the other prep we make it just in time.

Jim joins me for the meeting. Greer has asked someone she knows and trusts to make the introduction. "Vanessa Morgan?"

"William." She holds me by my upper arm and brings me in for air kisses. "So wonderful to meet you."

"Thank you for making the introduction and helping us out." Since my team at Bettencourt Industries isn't in the loop, Vanessa and her team will act as our team until it can be handed off.

We're getting to know one another when a deep baritone voice says, "Vanessa! So wonderful to see you."

"Jeremy, I'd like you to meet William Bettencourt."

He extends his hand and I shake it firmly. "Please join me and my team in the conference room."

I follow him down the hall and am shocked. There's an army of ten people at our disposal. When Greer wants all the stops pulled out, she pulls them out! They make introductions, and I only catch what some of them do: media relations, corporate governance, brand management, and several others.

As we take our seat, we're provided with coffee and water. Jeremy turns to me. "You have the floor. I was told you have a problem."

I walk them through how I came to be the majority shareholder, my father's sudden death and the suspected murder, the safe-deposit box in San Francisco, and my meeting with the FBI. No one asks any questions as I share with them what Bettencourt Industries is currently facing and that I can't go to anyone in the company currently because I don't know who they're going to arrest.

When I'm finished, the woman across the table from me breaks the silence. "Wow. I'm Liz Crown, and I'll be heading this up and be your point of contact. I'm sure we have a lot of questions, so bear with us."

I nod. "I'll do my best to answer them."

"You know the names of five of the twenty-plus pedophiles—one is your CEO and three sit on your board. There could be others you can't identify."

"That's correct."

"William, I'm Neil Rube, and I'm with research. That's good news because they may not make it a flashy arrest if they want them to turn others in."

"I got the impression from the FBI they could name most of the perpetrators. I could be wrong."

"I'm Adam Warner with media relations. This will be a significant bust for the FBI; they're most likely going to go big. We'll want to plan for that. We can get you on all the morning shows and really play up your backstory about your dad dying to protect the children despite what it would do to the company."

"That's great. That's exactly what I was hoping for."

The meeting runs for four hours. I'm drained but finally feel exhilarated. I have a path, and it leads to a light at the end of the tunnel. We agree to multiple meetings over the next few days, a few here, but most will be over video conferencing.

Jeremy walks us out. "Are you staying in The City tonight?"

"No, I'll head back to Philly tonight."

"Would you like a drink before you go?"

"Thank you, but I'll have to pass." As tired as I am, I'm just interested in getting back to my hotel in Philadelphia.

"Next time then." He turns to Vanessa. "I'm looking forward to working with you again. Maybe I'll be able to convince you to finally bring your team over."

"We'll see." We get onto the elevator, and she walks us down. "I love that man, but they work too hard. Crisis management firms like this run on high-octane fuel all the time. I don't mind spurts of busy, but I like to be at home with my husband a lot more."

"I agree," I share.

She walks us to our waiting car and says, "This is going to work out. It will have a few hard days, but it'll all be fine."

"Thanks, Vanessa. I'll talk to you in the morning."

Jim and I make our way back to the heliport, and I ask, "You were very quiet in there. What did you think?"

"I didn't have much to say, but I do think we need to play down your dad's death just in case he's alive."

"Agreed."

chapter

twenty-nine

QUINN

Today's my last day here at SHN. Nobody but Mason knows that I'm leaving for good, they just think I'm taking some time off. He's offered to take me to lunch today. I know he's hoping to change my mind, but I can't. My apartment is empty. Everything I own that doesn't fit into my suitcase is gone or given away, minus the last few boxes, which will be picked up by the Boys and Girls Club.

My landlord was beyond livid when I gave him notice. I figure he has over a month rent since I gave him essentially six weeks' notice. He'll have someone living here within a week, and he'll come out ahead. Rentals move quickly in The City.

I've wrapped up all of the notes on my open clients here at the office and indicated what may need to be done next. My responsibilities have been dispersed among my team, but I've left detailed instructions with Emerson just in case someone wins the lottery and never returns to work. I met today with her and walked her through everything.

"I'm really sorry to do this to you," I say.

"You don't worry about us, or me for that matter. You worry about your dad. I know I look like I'm going to go any day now," she rubs her big pregnant belly, "but I'm all good. You go home. Take care of your dad. We'll be here when you're ready to come back. Maybe you being away for a little while will get Mason to figure out how much we need you in a partnership role, and maybe William will realize he needs to pee or get off the pot and make your relationship more serious. None of this sneaking around BS."

I adore Emerson, but William will move on quickly. If he wants his dad's company, he'll need to marry soon. "I am not looking for a serious relationship from William."

"Everyone else thinks the two of you look really good together. You should reconsider your position — well, maybe after your dad gets to feeling better."

"William has a lot going on right now," I confide in her.

"Yes, he does. I don't know all of the details, but I do know some, and I don't envy where he's at. Boy, did his dad leave him with quite the quagmire."

I nod enthusiastically. "That he did. And just wait, it's going to get a lot worse before it gets better." I give her a big hug. As I walk out of her office, my team has come in from all over the Bay Area. They've brought my favorite pistachio macarons, and they promise to keep in touch. Emerson insists, "It'll only be for a couple of months."

She doesn't know that I'm not coming back. As I wrap things up, I write a note to William. My cell phone is a company cell phone, and I told Mason that William was looking for a new phone, and since my phone is newer than his, I'll leave my phone for him.

Dear William,
Thank you for everything. I'll miss you most of all.
Quinn

I attach it to my cell phone and hide it in his top desk drawer so he'll see it when he returns. I'm trying not to cry, but it's getting so hard. As I fight back the tears, the phone suddenly rings; I see CeCe is calling.

"Hey, lady! Would you like to join me at Quince tonight for dinner? I see they have a roast duck on the tasting menu, and it will be highly decadent? My treat?"

"I wish I could. I'm flying out first thing in the morning, and I have a ton to get done. Thank you so much for your generous offer."

"Can I give you a ride to the airport? Please, let me do something. I'm not going to see you for a few months, and you're going to fall in love and get a tan."

I laugh so hard. "First, that's very sweet of you. I've got a ride all set up. Second, I won't have time to meet anyone. And third, you know I have two shades—white and red. There is no such thing as tan."

We're both giggling at this point. How do I tell her how much she means to me without telling her I don't plan on coming back? Everyone thinks they'll just call or email me while I'm gone, but I won't be giving them my new phone number. I just think a clean break is best for all of us— particularly me. I'll miss them so much, but their lives will move on, and they'll forget me quickly.

CeCe resigns herself that I'm not going to budge. "We're going to miss you. Who can I dish the dirt on about Mason and Annabelle?"

"I think just about everyone here would do that."

"Can we come for a visit?"

"Of course. That sounds fun. Once I get settled, we'll figure something out." I hate lying to her, but the truth is, it's too embarrassing to be moving home to my dad's because I'm broke. And she could write a check for the debt and go shopping at Cartier for a diamond tiara. No, it's important for me to have a clean break. Putting the phone back in the drawer, I leave, shutting the lights off, and walk back to my cubicle for the last time.

No one is quite sure where my dad lives. They think Fort Lauderdale or Miami, but in reality, he lives closer to the Alabama border at the top of the Gulf in Pensacola.

When people have moved on to their other things, I casually leave. I really am embarrassed that I'm moving home. I'm thirty-one years old. I walk home for the last time. My hands are buried in my pockets. It's a cool and brisk summer evening, typical San Francisco. I fight back the tears. What did Mark Twain say again? "The coldest summer... no, coldest winter I ever spent was summer in San Francisco." He sure did coin that correctly.

When I open my apartment door, I see not much is left. I have a blanket and pillow for my last night, and in the morning, I'll put it outside for someone who is homeless. I'll enjoy my last night here in San Francisco, drinking a decent California wine from a paper cup and sleeping on the floor.

It's kind of strange being without a cell phone, no television, internet, radio, nothing. I'm totally broken off from the world. At least I still have my Kindle. I open it up and read my book until I can't keep my eyes open anymore. Every time I read these steamy novels, I think of William and all the things that I love doing with him. By far, he's the one I will miss the most.

* * *

chapter

thirty

QUINN

I have an early flight into Atlanta. At least it's direct. My seat is in the back of the airplane next to the window. As the plane speeds down the runway, the tears fall hard. When the wheels leave the ground, we do one last turn away from San Francisco, and I watch the Bay Bridge become tiny behind me. The lady next to me starts up a conversation and spends the next six hours telling me all about her daughter, her amazing husband, and their new grandchildren. Putting my own issues behind me, I enjoy the pictures and the conversation.

When we land, I collect my things and head to the rideshare that will take me to a used car dealership. I bought the car last week online. It's a sensible silver Toyota Camry. My dad should be able to fit in the front seat as I shuttle him from appointment to appointment. It was easier than renting a car to drive off the lot. Before leaving Atlanta, I pick up a pay-as-you-go cell phone and activate it. I need something in case I get lost or stranded.

It's rush hour, so I find a diner and order myself a cheeseburger and fries for dinner, and I pull out my Kindle and read for two hours to let the traffic pass. The drive is roughly five hours, and there's no use in extending the drive if I don't have to.

Driving to my dad's house, I go through the various stages of grief. I deny that the move is going to bother me. That being there for my dad is the real reason I'm moving home. Then I remember the colossal amount of debt I have. Selling all my things didn't even make one month's payment in my loans. Mason was kind and paid out my bonus early, so that will give me time to find a job.

I move to anger. I'm mad that the cost of education is so high in the United States. Sure, I could have transferred to another less expensive school as an undergraduate when my dad got sick, but we thought he'd recover quickly. We had no idea how long it would take for him to get better, and we didn't think he'd blow through all his savings and investments. And sure, I could have gone to a much less expensive business school, but Stanford is one of the best and comes with a healthy price tag.

Then bargaining begins. I think, if I can find a good job, I can get my loans paid off in five years and I can always move back to San Francisco, or I can move to another large city like New York or Chicago and start over. Being in Florida and climbing out of debt and being here for my dad is really all that matters.

Crossing over the Florida state line, the depression hits. It's hot and humid, and I swear I hear the buzz of a mosquito around my head. I'm driving eighty-five miles an hour and a mosquito flies into my car. They love me. That's another thing to hate about Florida. There are hurricanes, and their state bird is the mosquito. When I looked, I didn't see one exciting job. What if I've moved for nothing? What if the only job I can find is being a barista at a coffee shop, and then I'll barely make the interest payments.

As I enter the town of Pensacola, I realize it isn't going to be so bad. There is a Marine air station here, so there will be cute pilots to look at. I'll figure it all out. I don't have to figure it out tonight, tomorrow, or even next week. Everything will somehow work out.

The outside light is on. It's after one and my dad's waiting up for me. I knock, and he rips the door open. "Quinnie!" He scoops me into a giant hug like I'm a little girl, and I feel so safe being home. Yes, Florida is now home.

"Daddy, you shouldn't have waited up for me."

"I sleep quite fine in my chair, so who says I waited up for you?" He holds me back and says, "Look at you. You look positively beautiful. Just like your mother."

I pull him in for another hug. I don't ever want to let go. "You look pretty good yourself." He looks a little older, but he looks pretty healthy, and that makes me feel good. Maggie is all excited that there is a new person in the house. Getting down on one knee, I give her lots of love. "Why, hello there. Aren't you the sweetest thing? I bet you bring in all the ladies with that lopsided grin and those big brown eyes."

"I don't know about the ladies, but she does bring in the people. She's just a happy dog. I love that about her. She makes me happy." He picks up my bag. "What do you have in here? Lead pipes?"

"Just my clothes."

"How long are you staying?"

"For a while. I'm taking some time away from San Francisco. I put my things in storage, and I thought I'd find a job here locally."

"Did you get fired?"

"No, Dad! San Francisco is just too expensive. I want to own a house one day. I want to be debt free."

"All right, we'll talk about that in the morning."

"I don't want to keep you up, but after a long day of travel, I'm exhausted."

"Here's your room." He puts my suitcase down and gives me one last hug. "I'm so glad you're here, no matter how long you plan on staying."

I step in, and it is beautifully decorated in shade of dark purple and gray. He's had help. Maybe there's hope for his love life after all. "Thanks, Dad."

Lying in bed, I can't believe I'm here in Florida. I can't believe I had to move home to dig myself out of debt, and I realize the stages of grief have started again. I cry, and I dream of William. I miss him so damn much.

It will get easier. It must.

chapter

thirty-one

WILLIAM

I haven't talked to Quinn in over a week. I finally broke down and asked Mason where she was, and he was evasive. Something's up. I've been getting minor updates from the FBI, so I know they are getting close.

I just wish Quinn was here to hold my hand. She calms me down when I don't even know that I'm anxious, and right now I'm very anxious.

The phone rings and the number's blocked. I glance at the clock and see it's after three in the morning. My heart beats a little faster knowing this must be her calling me. "Hey."

"This is Agent McGraw."

I sit up straight. "Yes?"

"We've contacted the media. They'll be meeting us here at our offices in ten minutes, and we'll make forty-seven arrests in the Philadelphia area and another hundred and eighty-three across the country."

My heart stops. How can it be that there are so many despicable people who'd trade the innocence of a young girl for a second of pleasure? The bile in my stomach starts to rise. I think I'm going to be sick. "Thank you, Agent McGraw."

"We wouldn't be here without your dad and you. We'll talk again."

Unfortunately, I know he's right. I'll be a star witness in all the various cases. What a mess.

He hangs up the phone, and I immediately contact my crisis manager. She answers, sounding alert. "Liz, they'll begin making arrests within the hour. They've contacted the media, and it will begin to go out shortly."

"I'm on it. We'll have a message out to your shareholders the second it hits the wires. Most likely we'll start a round of interviews with you with some of the morning shows. When can you be here?"

"I'll make it to you within three hours." We've put a smooth plan in place. I call Jim and his team and let them know we need to get moving. Then I call Vanessa, who will meet me at the heliport and will be with me all day.

I lie back in my bed and stare at the ceiling. My stomach hurts, and my heart beats triple time. That means our stock is going to take a tumble. This is it. I'm convinced these are the motherfuckers who killed my father, and I'm grateful they are going to pay.

I meet Jim downstairs twenty minutes later. "Let the fun begin."

I'm exhausted by the time I fall into bed at the Ritz-Carlton later that night. I did four morning shows, had a call with the stockholders, we did a press junket with print media, and I didn't have one minute to myself in over thirty hours. Vanessa and Accurate Communications ensure that my father was the hero and that I, too, was a hero. Putting the young girls above the company meant more and stock prices be damned. We actually closed three dollars a share higher.

"Mission accomplished," Jeremy Fielding proclaimed over dinner.

Today would have been better with Quinn. I finally reached out to Emerson after returning to my hotel room. "You've had quite the day."

"I know Greer was working her magic with our clients because of me. I'm so sorry."

"She loves this, but really this has been helpful. You're a hero. You saved countless numbers of young girls."

"It's really gross that I got to be a hero of something I wish never existed."

"Me too. I'm sorry about your stepmother."

"They haven't found her yet. She knew that the shit was going to hit the fan, so she bolted out of town. It seems her job was to keep an eye on my dad or these men were going to hurt her, but I think she was the one behind my dad changing his will, and I'm pretty sure she orchestrated the crash that killed my dad."

"I hope they find her and fry her."

"I do too." I need to gracefully figure out how to pivot the conversation to Quinn.

In the silence, Emerson asks, "Have you talked to Quinn?'

I'm relieved she opened the door for me. "No. I've tried, but I can't get ahold of her. Do you know where she is?"

"You didn't know she went home to take care of her father?"

I sit up straight. "No. She didn't tell me that. Where is he? I'll go to her. I need to be there to help her."

"You're in love with her."

"I am, and I've tried to tell her, but she changes the subject every time I start to go there. Where is she? I need to get to her."

"We don't know. She left her cell phone behind. She told everyone that she was only taking a few weeks or months off to help her dad, but she cleared everything out of her cubical. I don't think she's coming back."

My stomach crashes to the floor. "No. That can't be. I need to talk to her. I know she feels she can't get ahead, but I've told her she can live with me rent free and work to pay her loans off. Christ, I'd pay her loans off if she'd let me."

"I think Mason knows. We just need to get him to tell us."

"I'll be back in the office in a few days. Thanks, Emerson." Before I say goodbye, I realize I don't know how she's doing. "I'm sorry, I didn't even ask. How are you doing?"

"Well, the little guy is growing. They measured his head and are worried he won't come naturally."

"It's a boy?"

"It is, but don't tell anyone. We're debating names. I want to name him after Dillon's dad, but Dillon wants to name him some strange old philosophers' names."

I laugh. "That sounds just like Dillon. I do hope you win out."

"I will if I have to fill out the birth certificate without him. I'm way too emotional already."

"I can't wait to meet the little guy."

"Well, he needs to hold on a bit longer. It's a little early yet."

"I understand. Thanks for your help, Emerson. I'll see you in a few days."

"See you soon."

I have a few more days of press coverage and some post-action things to get done. I've met with the board in Philadelphia. We ended up losing seven people from the leadership team. That was really disappointing. We agreed to meet with the three candidates that the recruiters at SHN identified for the CEO position. I know one of them, and if we were to get him, we'd be far ahead of where we were. Bettencourt Industries is going to be fine.

I fly back to San Francisco with Jim and his team. Midway through the flight, I sit down with Jim. "I need your help with finding Quinn. She moved home to her dad's in Florida. I think she's in the Miami/Fort Lauderdale area. Can you help me?"

He nods. "I've been notified that the FBI is going to launch their Trojan horse into the hackers this week. I'll get someone on it, but you and I are going to be busier than we've ever been."

I'm sure my eyes bug out of my head. He's right, it will be busy, but wouldn't it be great to have all of this behind us?

From the plane Wi-Fi, I email Mason, letting him know I should be in the office in the morning. I'm determined to bring Quinn back, and if I need to, I'll get her dad set up here too. I won't let her get away. She's the one.

I'm early to the office; it isn't even seven when I arrive, but the office is buzzing. The mole has really affected us greatly, and the entire company is ready for it to be over. We have a company-wide meeting at eight in the big conference room, and everyone is here.

I get caught up on a few things as I prepare for the all-hands-on-deck meeting. When I open the desk drawer, I find a note from Quinn attached to her cell phone. I open it up and read it. Fuck! She's definitely not coming back. Mason knows where she is, and I'm determined to find her.

Like so many others, I grab a coffee in the kitchen and head into the conference room. I'm stopped along the way with lots of "Welcome Back's" and people saying they've seen me on television. A few of the females are a little too friendly, but I only have eyes for Quinn, and she's not here. Mason and Cameron arrive with a tall woman with short curly hair.

After Mason gets the room to quiet down, he says, "All right everyone. Today's the day. Thanks to Quinn and Francie spotting the high-signs of our hacker friends, Cameron and Parker, along with the FBI Cybercrimes unit, was able to plant a Trojan horse in their system. They've been monitoring their site and watching and waiting. But before I give too much away, I'd like to introduce you to Special Agent in Charge, Cora Perry."

There is some polite clapping around the room.

"Thank you for allowing me to be here. Your coffee sure beats federal government coffee." Several people snicker. "Six weeks ago, this Trojan horse went into place. We were able to mirror over twenty-two computers in what we've decided is a hacking farm. We found their location in the East Bay, and we watched and identified better than forty employees coming and going. This morning we executed search and arrest warrants across the Bay Area, and by this afternoon, they will be in one location but unable to see or talk to anyone else."

A hand rises in the air. "Are they Russian-related?"

"Some are. But some are Americans, while others are Chinese nationals. Our hacker farm was not discriminatory."

"Do you know who is behind this and did you catch them?" Dillon asks.

"We know that Adam and Eve are behind this, but currently we aren't sure if we have them in custody or not," Cora tells us. "But in my experience, if they're not one of those arrested, given the number of people we've arrested, we'll see several who will turn them in in hopes of avoiding jail time. We have a light at the end of the tunnel."

There's a celebration around the room, but Mason looks up and says, "When we get this all wrapped up, we'll celebrate. In the meantime, we have four companies going public in the next thirty days. Let's keep our eye on the ball and make sure we stay aware. If you see something, say something."

We all file out of the conference room and begin our day.

chapter

thirty-two

WILLIAM

It's been three weeks, and yet I still don't know where Quinn is. I've sat with Mason, and he swears all he knows is that she's in Florida. That's driving me crazy. I've checked every major city and suburb in Florida looking for Faraday. There are over four hundred Faradays listed in the white pages between Fort Lauderdale and Miami alone. I called a few, but I've not had any luck.

Why didn't I ask her father's first name? What a self-centered jerk I was to not even ask where he lived in Florida. I thought I'd have more time. Hell, I thought I'd be flying home with her to meet her dad. Damn it! I don't want to keep pestering Jim, but I need to know where she is. She isn't doing anything to hit a credit card or her social security number. It's as if by moving home she's fallen off the grid.

I dream of her often, and last night was no exception. Sure, sometimes they are her look of pure ecstasy, but often they are of her laughing and her look of awe as we explored Independence Hall. Last night I dreamed we were walking a dog down the beach. We were holding hands and just talking. When I woke up, my chest hurt. I miss my friend.

This morning I work out hard and listen to the voice mail again. It's becoming my morning ritual so I can hear her voice. In the office, I sit through two meetings, and I follow up with the deals I have in progress. To the outside, I look fine, but on the inside, I feel like I'm incomplete without her.

Today seems to be a particularly hard day. I'm unable to concentrate on my work. I need some fresh air. I need coffee. Sure, the breakroom has amazing coffee, but if I walk to Starbucks, I can get a decent cup and the fresh air I so desperately need. With my coat buttoned up tight and my hands buried in my pockets, I walk with my head down. It's a typical gray and drizzling day. I love it here, but I hate the gray days.

After I've ordered my drink, I wait for them to call my name. I'm staring down at my cell phone reading the Silicon Valley Business Journal when a gentleman stands next to me a little closer than I like. I step aside, but he follows. I look up at him and start to say something, but the words get lodged in my throat.

It can't be. Those eyes. A smile cracks on his face.

"Hi," he says.

"What the hell? What...?" I pull him into a huge hug. "Dad, I thought...." and then the tears begin to fall. His hair is much lighter, and he has a beard. I could have passed him on the street a thousand times and thought he looked similar to my dad, but he's different enough that I wouldn't have thought it was him.

"I know. I'm sorry. It's a long story."

"Let's talk. Here. We can sit over at that table," I beg.

He looks around, surveying the people in the store. "We can sit for a short time, and then I need to get going. I've been watching you for a while. I'm so proud of you. You did what I wanted to do, but I was too worried about so many things."

They call my name, and I pick up my drink. Then they call the name "Felix," and he gets his drink.

We sit down, and I eagerly stare at him across the table, not knowing where to start. I have so many questions, so many things to tell him, but I can only come up with one right now. "Felix?"

He shrugs. "It's all I could think of when they asked."

"Where have you been?"

"It all happened so quickly. I told Lillian that I was going to Tanzania to go climb Kilimanjaro. I went through the process of planning a trip, but my real plan was to actually fly here and talk to you. I suspected that things weren't going right with Lillian and haven't been for a while. I was spending more and more time at the suite in the Rittenhouse. She didn't like that. I explained that after the trip I would move home again, so she relented. I flew here under an assumed name and put the evidence I had in the safe-deposit box and included your name on the box. I was at your house waiting for you to return when I saw an alert on my phone that my helicopter went down in Tanzania, and they were pronouncing me dead."

"Holy shit. Did you suspect foul play?"

He nods, fingering the side of the cardboard sleeve on the cup. "I did. You saw what was on those tapes. I couldn't trust anyone, but Lillian was the only one who knew where I was going. It made no sense at all." He glances at his watch. "I should go."

I reach out and grab his arm before he can leave. "Wait. We need to get this figured out. Do you want to stay at my place?"

"I don't want to put you in any danger." He looks around frantically. No one is paying any attention to us.

"Dad," I say in a yelling whisper, "we need to get this taken care of. Those men are in jail. I outed them with the evidence *you* provided me."

He relaxes and smiles at me. "It goes deeper. I continued to dig after everyone thought I was dead."

I stand, and he does too. "Then we're going to my lawyer, and we're walking her through everything you know, and we're going to tell the world that you're still alive."

"I'll meet you there," he assures me. I don't trust him. I can tell he's scared.

"We can do this together, Dad, and we're going to do it now."

I grasp his arm and walk us outside to a rideshare. As we drive over, I text Mason.

Me: An emergency has come up, and I'll be back as soon as I can.
Mason: No problem. News on Quinn?
Me: No. I'll call you as soon as I can.

Then I quickly call Marci. She answers on the third ring. "Sorry to bother you. I'm on my way in. Something's come up, and I think you'll need to clear your calendar for this afternoon."

"I'll be here."

"We're walking up now."

We step out of our ride and rush into the building. "Where is your bodyguard?" my dad says as it occurs to him that I'm without a member of Jim's team.

Guiding him through the lobby and up the elevator, I answer, "I haven't needed one since everyone was arrested."

"You're the heir to a fortune; you should always have a bodyguard with you."

I'm not going to argue with him. We walk into the lobby of her firm, and she's waiting to escort us back to a conference room. She starts with a room full of windows. "Marci, can we have one of the small conference rooms in the back? One with no windows."

She looks at me puzzled. "Of course."

She escorts us to the back and shuts the door behind us. "Why the cloak and dagger?"

"Marci, I'd like to introduce you to my father, Reginald Bettencourt."

My father extends his hand, and she's not sure if she should take it.

"Really?" she questions, looking at him skeptically.

"He's not dead," I confirm for her.

"Yeah, I can see that," she mutters. "Let's sit down and figure out what's going on."

We sit around a large table, and I watch my dad unravel an even bigger conspiracy beyond human trafficking but also drugs, gambling, prostitution, and much more.

I'm stunned. "How did you figure this all out?"

He smiles. "It's amazing what you can figure out when everyone thinks you're dead."

Marci looks at her watch. "It's after four thirty. We need to loop our friends in with the FBI. Let me see who can come over. This conference room is going to get tight."

She leaves and is gone all of fifteen minutes. When she returns, two agents are with her. There really isn't room for me, so I excuse myself. As I leave, I look at my dad, seeing he's really nervous. "Dad, I love you. I'm going to meet someone from work. I'll be back." He visibly relaxes, and I walk into the neighboring conference room and call Mason.

"Is everything all right?" Mason asks.

"It is. I just had a huge surprise. How about a beer? I'm in the financial district."

"I'll be right there. How does McCoy's Pub sound?"

"I'll be there waiting. What'll I order you?"

"How about a Guinness."

"See you soon."

I let the receptionist know where I'm headed. They're going to be a while, so I walk the two blocks to the bar. The wood paneling and small front windows make the bar dark, but it's perfect. I see an open booth in the back and take it. When the buxom waitress arrives, I order two pints of Guinness and wait. This place is going to be crazy busy in less than a half hour with people stopping on their way home from work. Mason joins me just as the two glasses are put on the table.

"What's going on?"

"I'm sorry I just left today. I needed some fresh air and went for a walk to Starbucks. I was approached by a man who," I lean in and whisper, "is my father. He's alive."

Mason sits back and whistles. "Are you sure?"

"Of course I am. It's my dad after all."

He shakes his head. "I didn't mean that. I'm just stunned."

"Me too. He's meeting with Marci and the FBI. He has more information on more than the human trafficking ring. He's been sleuthing around and asking questions. He's uncovered a much larger criminal enterprise."

"Holy shit. The world thinks he's dead, so they may just keep him that way," Mason warns.

I hadn't thought of that. "I hope not. I don't want the seat on the board, and I'm not interested in living in the house I grew up in, even if it has been in my family for generations. We have something good going. I want to see where it goes."

"We'll figure it out. Don't worry. And you need to do what you need to do."

We've just finished a second beer when my cell phone pings.

Marci: Come on back.
Me: Be right there.

"I need to get back. Keep this between us for now."

"No problem. I'll lock up your office, and unless I hear from you, I'll see you in the morning."

"Can you do me a favor? Can you please put some pressure on Jim to get me Quinn's contact information? I need to, if nothing else, let her know I love her. If she doesn't want to be with me, I can deal with that but not knowing is killing me."

Mason nods. "I'll see what I can do."

I walk into Marci's office, and my dad's not there. "Where did he go?"

"The FBI has him in a safe house. I've called Jim, and your bodyguard will be here in twenty minutes. While we wait, let's talk about what we decided."

She leads me back to the conference room. "Your dad is going to remain dead for the time being. He has uncovered a lot with his network of friends—"

"But what about everything else?"

"You've got this under control. In a few days, he'll have an encrypted phone, and the lines of communication will open between the two of you. Your father is going to take down an international criminal organization that looks like it covers almost every continent."

She must be exaggerating. "What do I do now?"

"You go about your life for the time being. You'll remain on the board of your father's company. He knows where Lillian is, and she'll be arrested tonight."

"Wow, that's great news."

"He did mention that the inheritance that was given to Lillian was set up so that he could track her. He was thrilled that you couldn't care less about the money. He also said he likes Quinn and talked to her at one point. I guess she was walking around a park and she was admiring a statue. He also thought you should know that she flew to Atlanta, bought a silver Toyota Camry, and drove to her father's home in Pensacola, Florida."

I shake my head and smile. "I've been looking for her since she left, and no one knew where she was. I need to go to Florida."

"Only if you go with your bodyguard. Your father believes you're in danger, and you just might be. The world knows you and your dad took down a human trafficking ring."

"If they don't know he's alive, then they won't know I'm behind anything."

Marci smiles. "He's your dad. On some of these things, he may be right on. Take the bodyguard to Florida." As almost an afterthought, she adds, "He also said, if you get a bunch of hang-ups from burner phones, he's thinking of you."

I should have known. I miss my dad.

While I wait for my bodyguard, I text Mason.

Me: She's in Pensacola. I'm going to fly in tomorrow.
Mason: She's crazy if she doesn't come back.
Me: Agreed.

chapter

thirty-three

QUINN

Waking up in the guest bedroom at my father's has been fun, but this isn't a vacation like my dad thinks. I'm here for a while. The heat borders on oppressive. The humidity makes me feel like I can never get dry. I have a fine ring of wet hair constantly. And my hair... it's a disaster. I look like a furry dog. I keep it in a ponytail, but that gives me a headache after a while.

I hear the news going in the kitchen. They're highlighting the legal maneuvering of those caught in the human trafficking ring. From what I can tell from the news report, they're pleading out to avoid public hearings, which is good news for William. He won't have to testify. They remind everyone that William and his dead father brought down the ring.

The scary part is that they believe that this has been going on for years. I can't even imagine. Young runaways, girls from impoverished countries promised an escape, and flat out kidnappings—there is no way to see this as anything other than tragic. I'm proud of William for having the courage to put a stop to it. His company teetered for a while, but I could see some heavy Greer influence on making sure the focus was on that the moral high ground was where they wanted to be.

I read in the paper that they expected William to assume the position as chairman of the company, but I've been reading the business paper in Philadelphia, and it looks like they found someone from Silicon Valley to come in. I'm so happy for William. He can try to go back to his unassuming life in San Francisco.

I walk into the kitchen in search of a cold glass of orange juice and a slice of toast. I'm in the kitchen when my dad announces, "Here she is. Would you like a cup of coffee?"

I would, but these days I drink it over ice. I nod and grab the pot I brewed last night and tucked into the fridge.

"What's your plan today?"

"I guess I should start looking for a job that will make me some money to pay my bills while I continue to look for a job more in line with my skills."

"Are you staying here because of me? Because, sweetheart, I'm doing great. Maggie and I wander the beach, which keeps my stress and blood pressure low. Everything is going well."

I sit down at the table. It's time to confess. "No, Dad. Right now I don't have anywhere to go."

"What do you mean? You said you weren't fired."

"I wasn't. I quit."

"But you love your job, why would you quit?"

I take a deep breath. "I couldn't afford to live in San Francisco anymore. My rent was more than a paycheck, and I make good money."

"You could live in a less expensive apartment."

"I do stay in a less expensive apartment. I'm not in a trendy neighborhood, but I do live where it's safe."

"What about getting a roommate?"

He doesn't understand. His rent for his two-bedroom apartment two blocks from the beach is less than a thousand dollars a month. "I'm too old for a roommate."

"Okay, I know this isn't very father like, but what about a male roommate in a one-bedroom apartment?"

I laugh. "Are you condoning premarital sex?"

"I'm not naïve, I know you've had sex. Probably with that boy you went to Philadelphia with."

"Okay…" How do I explain this to my dad? "San Francisco is like most cities. It's roughly 51 percent female. The problem is that half of the 49 percent of the male population is not interested in my female anatomy. That means the other half are interested. But in my experience, when roughly 25 percent aren't in San Francisco for serious relationships but to make a lot of money, it doesn't always lead to fulfilling relationships. They aren't looking to settle down. Only to have fun."

"And you don't want to have fun?"

"I do, but I also want a family." Maggie puts her head in my lap. "And a dog."

"Okay, I'm your dad. It's my job to worry about you."

I stand and give him a nice kiss on the cheek. "I love you, and I love that you worry about me. I'm going to take a shower and then go find myself a short-term job."

I stop by three different Starbucks and leave applications. It's been a long time since I've had to apply for work. I leave Emerson's contact information for a reference. I hate that she may be called. That'll blow the fact that I'm not coming back, but I need to do something while I look for a long-term job.

When I return to my dad's place, there's a big black Mercedes in his visitor spot. "Hmm. He must have one of his lady friends over for a visit." Oh, gwad! That's why he wants me out; he wants to resume his playboy ways. Duh! I'm putting a cramp in his style. I'll talk to him. We can figure this out. I park a few blocks away from his building and walk back. At least it isn't cold and raining. Well, the humidity is at 98 percent, so it might as well rain.

I walk in and announce myself loudly so that he has time to disengage from his girlfriend. Then I spot Gerald. "What are you doing here?"

He shrugs. I hear my dad say, "You have a visitor. Come on in here."

I round the corner and immediately see William. The heat must not affect him. He looks delicious with his hair combed just right, a blue linen plaid Polo shirt, and white linen shorts. "What are you doing here?" I ask before I even have a chance to process he's here.

"I came to talk to you. I've been here getting to know your dad. You didn't tell me that you were born here in Pensacola."

"Yes, he was stationed at the military base here in town. He was a pilot in the Marine Corps."

"You didn't tell me a lot of things."

I see my dad gather up the dog and leave. "I... I... I couldn't stand the idea of seeing you date other women. It would have shattered me."

"Why would I date anyone else? Quinn, I love you. I've been trying to tell you that for weeks before you left. I know my life is a complete mess with my dad and all the stuff with his company, but I need you in my life. Please? If you want to remain here close to your dad, I'll move here. I'll start my own firm here in north Florida."

"No, I can't ask you to do that. SHN needs you. You need to go back to them, and I'm going to stay here for a while. I'm looking for a job that matches my skills, and I'll pay off my school loans."

"I told you, you can live with me and pay off your loans. Hell, if you'd let me, I'd pay them off for you, and then you wouldn't have to worry about it."

I can't argue with him any longer. He doesn't understand that he will break me when our relationship ends. We can't build a relationship on hiding a secret from everyone.

I try to crack a smile. "Let's go for a walk. Pensacola Beach is two blocks away, and it's a beautiful white sandy beach."

He claps his hand to his thighs and stands. "Okay. I get it. You're worried that I don't actually love you, but I do. I'm standing here before you." He pulls me into his arms and presses his soft lips to mine. When his tongue brushes mine, the jolts of electricity shoot right to my core. "I love you, Quinn Faraday, and I always will. My life is incomplete without you."

I rest my head on his chest, and I can hear his heart racing. "Let's walk. It's a brilliant day."

He takes my hand, and with Gerald behind us, we walk to the beach. He tells me what's been going on, and I'm stunned as he walks me through his dad showing up, Lillian being found and arrested.

"What was she doing with the sex trafficking ring?"

"She was being blackmailed by the CEO of the company to manage my dad. She decided if she got rid of my dad, she would get rid of the blackmail and get all my dad's money and could run away."

"I guess you messed that up a little bit." I smile at him and squeeze his hand.

"Yes, she pulled her boys into it, and now they're all going to a federal penitentiary for quite a while."

"That must make you feel pretty good."

"It does, and at SHN we may be seeing the light at the end of the tunnel with Adam and Eve since they arrested all those in their hacking farm. You were pivotal in deploying of the Trojan horse into their system."

"So that must mean they caught the mole. Who are Adam and Eve?"

"We don't know. They weren't arrested, and while everyone who ever worked with them was ready to turn them in, they don't know their names."

"Oh, you've got to be joking! Will this ever end?"

He chuckles. "You sound like Dillon."

We watch the sun set, and the views are amazing. The military jets take off above us. "Boy, that's pretty loud."

I nod. "I love that sound. My dad used to call it 'the sound of freedom.'"

"Let's get you some dinner. Where can we go?"

"Let's check on my dad and make sure he isn't planning a big feast or something else."

"I'm down with whatever you want to do." He reaches for my hand, and we walk back to my dad's apartment holding hands.

When we walk in, my dad says, "I didn't think I was going to see you again tonight."

"Dad, I wouldn't just disappear on you."

"Well, I just ordered Chinese for one. Why don't you kids head out for dinner? And maybe I'll see you for breakfast in the morning."

WILLIAM

I can't help but be excited to see her again. She has a warm glow about her, and I know it's the sun. Before I left for Pensacola, I got a text message from CeCe.

CeCe: Bring our girl home.

That's my plan, but I have a feeling that she isn't going to budge. Not without help. After talking to her, I know that she still isn't sold on coming back.

Me: I need some reinforcements. Can you come and bring some help?
CeCe: We'll leave tonight and be there for breakfast.
Me: Perfect.

I send over her dad's address and let her know I'm staying at the Portofino.

When Quinn walks out of her room in my favorite sundress, it takes everything I have not to take her hard and fast, but I know if I did, I'd lose all the goodwill I've built with her dad and with her.

"You look beautiful."

"Thank you. There's a beachside shack that sells fried clams and fries in pages of today's newspaper over by the ocean. Would that work?"

"Sounds amazing."

"That stuff will kill you," my dad announces from the kitchen.

We laugh. "One night will be okay." And I wink.

Gerald walks behind us as we head back to the beach.

"It's quite beautiful here. Look, that house here is for sale. We could buy it and live here. I'm sure there's even a guest house for your dad." I'm not joking.

"The cost of living is pretty low here, but I still think waterfront property is pricey."

"I'd do anything for you. You just need to ask."

She smiles but doesn't respond. "Here we are."

It's a shack on the beach. From the roof line are two chalkboard menus. "How does the family size order sound?"

"That's a lot of food, but you and Gerald might be pretty hungry."

I look over at Gerald, and he nods his approval, so I step up and order. I'm shocked when it costs me twenty dollars. Not because that's expensive, but because I'm worried it won't be enough food. Boy am I wrong, and I mean I'm seriously wrong. There is enough food to feed an army.

"I warned you it was a lot of food."

We drink our beers with our fried clams and barely make it halfway through. Gerald sits at another table, and I keep offering him more food, but he declines. "We're going to waste so much food."

"We can wrap it up and give it to a homeless person."

"I like that idea."

We get it wrapped up and walk along the beach. It doesn't take long to hand off our leftovers to a grateful person.

"You really are very thoughtful," I tell her.

"I try. So do you."

"Where is your mother? You never really talk about her."

"We were never particularly close. She really struggled with the life in the Marine Corps. A lot of traveling and long absences. When my dad got sick, she was there through it all. She took him to all his appointments and was really the rock for him. Once they pronounced him cancer-free, she decided she wanted to go live in Arizona, so she moved there without my dad. Today she paints and lives alone. I talk to her every now and then, but really, we aren't close. Probably similar to how things were with your dad growing up."

"I'm sorry."

She stops and shrugs. "I came to peace with my relationship with my mother a long time ago. She did the best she could but really needed my dad a lot more than he was available to her."

I lean down and softly kiss her lips. God, how I've missed her. "I'm staying at the Portofino. Please stay with me tonight. Please?"

She agrees but not without adding, "I can't go back to San Francisco with you."

"I reserve the right to change your mind."

She nods, and it gives me hope. When we arrive at the Portofino, I escort her to my room. Gerald disappears into his room next door. He knows if I'm going to leave, I'll alert him.

The floor-to-ceiling windows in my suite showcase the beauty of the Gulf. I turn to look at Quinn and see the awe on her face. Every time I see her, she's even more beautiful. The golden glow of the full moon only heightens her exquisiteness. My cock, which has been hard for hours, is anxious for her body. "You look positively enchanting."

She steps in and kisses me. Our kisses start off soft and subtle but quickly become hard and feral. Pulling back, she yanks her dress off, leaving her in a sexy pink demi-cup bra and little pink panties. Sliding her arms around my neck, she flattens herself against my front before tilting her head up and capturing my lips. She takes every bit of what I'm giving and meets me with a hot passion that leaves me needy.

She unbuttons my shorts, and they fall to pool at my feet. I help her out by pulling my shirt over my head. My cock is hard and begging to be touched, but I don't want tonight to be about me. I want it to be all about her.

Leaning forward, I brush my nose along hers, wanting to take things slow, and yet not. Moving down her body, I press my mouth and nose to her sex, breathing in deeply and then glancing up at Quinn as she stiffens. Her eyes close as I flick my tongue over her panty-covered mound.

"God," she groans and pushes my head away. "Too much."

I take her wrist in my hand and lick along the inside of her thigh. "Not nearly enough. Relax and let me taste you."

She's almost shaking by the time I tug her sexy panties off. I splay my fingers over her stomach and glide it up to her breasts. Her nipples are hard and wanting as they strain against her bra, and she arches her back into me as I play with the hard nubs. Trapping my hand against her breast, she opens her legs as she beckons me to enjoy her wet slit.

She tastes like honey, and I lap up everything she offers. My fingers probe her tight channel as I lick and taste, her muscles grasping and holding me inside. I hum to cause a slight vibration, and she moans out her pleasure, filling my mouth with more of her sweet nectar.

She's the whole deal, the perfect woman as far as I'm concerned. It's scary to think that something so close to perfection is in my grasp, and yet there's a high chance I could very well fuck it all up tonight.

* * *

Mirrors cover the walls behind us, reflecting the moon and water below, setting an erotic scene. I lay her on the couch overlooking the water and take her foot in my hands, massaging one and then the other. Her moans make my cock hard as a baseball bat as it peeks out of my boxers.

Opening her eyes, she sees it waving at her and smiles. "I think something is looking for some attention."

I tear my boxers off and lift my hips. Bending over, she takes my cock deep into her mouth, swirling her tongue around the hard, bulbous head while stroking my balls. She swallows me deep, going up and down while looking right at me. I watch, enraptured, feeling her tongue flatten so she can take more of my length deep into her throat. When she pulls up, she flicks at the tip. What an incredible sensation.

One hand cups my balls and plays with them while the other holds my cock steady at the base as she moves it in and out of her delicate mouth. Fire spreads through my veins as she works me slowly. Pure, hot, unadulterated lust consumes me. God help me, I want her. I won't let myself come in her mouth. It's too early in my plans for the evening.

I caress her warm, soft skin as I spoon her overlooking the view. I whisper in her ear, "I love you, Quinn. I always have, and I always will."

Rolling over to look at me, she says without hesitation, "I love you, William. I always have and always will."

My cock is poking at the apex of her thighs, but I need to see her. I roll her on her back and position myself on top of her, my fingers finding her slit. She's wet and ready for me. As she lifts her hips up to meet mine, there's a look of pure need on her face. I slide my cock into her slowly, leaning down on my forearms so I can be close to her face, which I intend to cover in kisses.

Seated firmly inside her, our bodies one, I whisper, "I love you."

I slowly move through her, never wanting to leave. Her pussy hugs my cock perfectly, and with every thrust inside her, I want to come. But I ride it out, looking into her eyes and moving slowly, a major tease for us both. Seeing she's close, I pick up the rhythm, methodically slamming my cock into her.

At some point, we move to the bed, and we spend long stretches of time just feeling each other's skin, running our hands over every inch of the other's body, memorizing curves, lines, and angles. We make love again, and then we fall asleep. We somehow manage to order in room service, which we leisurely enjoy before turning back to each other once again. It's an evening and early morning of love, sex, and sleep, with maybe a little food and a lot of Quinn.

When I wake, the bed is empty. I wander to the living room and find her sitting on the couch freshly showered and dressed, drinking a cup of coffee. She has the advantage of living in this time zone. "I need to get home."

"I understand. Let me take a shower." I can't help but feel deflated. We are so good together. Why can't she let it happen? I hear the familiar sound of my cell phone alerting me of a text.

CeCe: Reinforcements have arrived. See you shortly.
Me: We'll be there in twenty minutes. She's being stubborn.
CeCe: We're ready.

I send a quick text to Gerald, letting him know we're heading out in twenty minutes, and he tells me he'll be ready. I hop in the shower, and I quickly dress. I look at myself in the mirror and know I'm ready for the fight of my life.

Gerald knocks on the door just as I exit the bedroom, and he leads us to the car. We hold hands as we ride back to her dad's. I can hear our friends as we arrive. She looks at me puzzled.

"I called in reinforcements."

She walks into her dad's, and everyone greets her with hugs. I'm amazed. We're missing Emerson, Dillon, and Mason, but everyone else is here.

"I hear someone is being difficult about returning to San Francisco to her job as a partner and her friends as well… maybe a boyfriend too," CeCe's announces.

"What do you think we can do to convince her otherwise?" Greer asks.

"Well, I'm almost positive that the jobs she applied for at Starbucks isn't going to be enough for her brilliance," Bella announces.

Quinn smiles and shakes her head.

"Mason is working with the FBI to catch our hackers, so he couldn't be here himself, but he wanted to make sure I gave this to you." Cameron hands her a stack of papers.

She stares at it a moment, looking shocked. Then her head shoots up. "This is a partnership agreement. I can't afford to buy into the partnership."

"We know that. You'll see that the plan is that you get a nominal raise, the remainder of what would be a partner's salary will go toward paying your entry into partnership." Cameron takes the agreement and opens it to the payment terms. "You will receive bonuses. A small percentage will go to you, and the remainder will go toward buying into the partnership."

"My leaving had nothing to do with being a partner. Don't get me wrong, I love this, but I want more than San Francisco offers," she explains, choking back tears.

It's now or never. I take both of her hands in mine and look her in the eyes. "Quinn Lea Faraday, I've loved you from the moment I heard your voice mail. There's been no other. When you were gone, I realized that you make me a whole person. I can't live without you. If you won't move back to San Francisco and prefer to stay here in Pensacola, I'll stay here, but all I ask is that you marry me and be with me forever. I need you. Please say yes."

I pull my mother's engagement ring out of my pocket. "This is my mother's ring. Quinn, will you marry me?"

Her eyes tear up, and her hand goes to her mouth. She doesn't answer, and I hear her father say, "He asked me last night, Quinnie. Don't stay here for me. Follow your heart. I think your love with William shines brighter than any star. You have my permission. Plus, I want grandbabies." Everyone laughs.

"I love you so much, William. Yes, I will marry you."

chapter

thirty-five

QUINN

On the flight back to San Francisco with my friends, we continue the last seventy-two hours of celebration. We moved from the house to the beach, we roasted clams, drank beer, and even splashed in the water. My dad even joined us for most of the afternoon.

During one of CeCe's walks, she met a nice woman who she introduced to my dad. Her name is Vivian, and she's a widow of a Marine pilot. They have a lot in common. CeCe has a knack for matchmaking, and she's convinced she knows these things. For example, she knows her prince isn't the one for her. He's fun, but I do hope she meets the right guy soon.

Everyone is so happy. William pulls me in, and it feels so right. "Are you okay leaving your dad behind? I wasn't kidding. I'll move to Pensacola, or I'm really fine buying a condo close to us in San Francisco where he can live. When we have kids, he'll want to be close."

I smile at William. "Let's do a few things before we start having kids."

"Shall we christen one of the bedrooms on the plane?"

"Everyone here would know," I admonish.

He kisses my head. "Do you think they think you're a virgin?"

I laugh.

"I mean, not only did you date the managing partner, but I do have proof of your naughty mind that I love so very much. Plus, rumor has it I'm a ladies' man...."

"Oh, you're funny. Just remember, you *were* a ladies' man. From now on, you can look, but you cannot touch."

"I only have hands to touch you."

We land and head back to William's place. When we get there, he hands me a business card. "CeCe thought you might want this."

I'm at a loss. "Who is this?"

"Her designer. You can make the condo all yours. Even decorate with pink flowers if that is what you want."

That's not my style, but I might tease him a bit. "Good to know. Maybe not pink flowers, but how about rainbows?" I watch him paint a tight smile on his face and nod. I can't torture him much longer. "I'm just kidding. I'm not in any hurry to make changes."

"Thank you for coming back with me."

"I can't wait to meet your dad."

"He tells me he met you already."

"He did? When?"

"He met you when you were admiring the public art in Rittenhouse Square, and you actually were looking at a piece that was done by his father."

"I remember that man. That was him? He was so sweet."

"You made quite an impression on him, and without him, I still wouldn't know where you were."

I lean in and kiss him. "Guess we'll have to find a way to thank him."

He cringes. "I can get behind a lot of things when I'm naked, but not with my dad."

"Eww! No. I meant have him over. Cook food for him. Maybe make his favorite dessert."

"Oh. Sorry."

"You really thought I want you and your dad together?"

"Well, I've heard your stories about—" Her eyes are bugging out, I'm over the line.

"No! That was only fiction. Not my desires."

QUINN

We christen the new bed, the couch, and the kitchen table. I love how insatiable he can be when it comes to being with me. Tomorrow is going to be my first day back to work. Most people won't know that I quit and am coming back. I'm excited. I still have my school loans, but the mole is in reach, I have the man of my dreams, I have a job I love, and I have wonderful friends. I couldn't be luckier.

I love his bed. It's huge, warm, and it overlooks the bay. We fall asleep tangled in each other's arms. Our plan is to go for a run in the morning.

William's phone is ringing. I look at the bedside table, and the clock tells me it's just after three. "This can't be good," I say as I wipe the sleep from my eyes and shake away the cobwebs from my head.

"Hello," William grumbles into the phone, sounding barely awake. He sits up, and I immediately know this isn't good news. I reach for him, and he grasps my hand so tightly it almost hurts. "Okay, we're on our way."

He disconnects the call. "That was CeCe. Mason's in the hospital. He's just had a heart attack, and Annabelle is missing."

Read an excerpt from:

Fascination

Venture Capitalist
Book 9

by Ainsley St Claire

(And, don't forget to sign-up for our newsletter/readers group. Don't miss a release or sale.)

chapter

one

CECE

Sinking into the bath full of bubbles and smelling of lavender, feels so good, and I'm able to relax for just a moment. Today has flat-out sucked. Why do so many people feel the need to forward me the links and the downloads of the gossip rags?

I'm so mad at Frederic right now. If he wanted to break up with me, he should have grown a fucking pair and told me. He didn't have to take an eighteen-year-old porn star out to a heavily press-covered event.

His messages afterward were stunning.

"Please, baby. Savanah and I are only friends."

Yeah, right.

I guess I could own some of it. I haven't been feeling it with him for a while, and we were both just hanging on. But damn, it still smarts to be dumped on television.

Asshole!

With cucumber slices over my eyes, the stress begins to evaporate. My phone rings, and normally I wouldn't answer while I'm de-stressing in the bath, Frederic's been blocked, but my best friend, Emerson, is due any moment with her first child. This just may be it. Besides, Frederic's been blocked, so I'm pretty sure I don't have to worry about dealing with him.

"Hello?"

"Caroline, it's Evelyn."

Crap. Work call. I spent most of the day with Evelyn. I'm kicking myself for not having checked the caller ID. "Hi, what's up?"

"I'm here at the San Francisco General Hospital with my boyfriend. We think he broke his arm. Umm... I just saw them wheel your friend Mason Sullivan in from an ambulance."

I sit up straight, splashing water all over the floor, but I don't care. "Are you sure?"

"I'm fairly positive."

"Thanks, Evelyn." We hang up, and I immediately call his cell phone. "Please pick up. Mason, please pick up," I whisper to myself.

"Hello?" A male voice answers, but it isn't Mason.

"May I speak with Mason, please?"

"I'm sorry, who is this?"

"It's his friend Caroline."

"This is Detective Lenning. Are you related to Mason?"

My mind is racing. "No... may I please speak with him?"

"Do you know how I can get in touch with someone who's related to him?"

"His mother lives in Ohio. I'm one of his best friends. Where is Mason?" I dread his answer, wondering, praying, hoping that he's not at the hospital.

"Caroline, Mason is currently unable to speak right now. He's at San Francisco General Hospital. We need to reach a family member. Do you know his mother's name?"

"I can't remember right now. I'm on my way. Where is his girlfriend, Annabelle Ryan?"

"We can't be sure."

I quickly throw some clothes on and call for a rideshare. While in the car, I call Dillon.

"Hello. Boy, do you have good timing."

"Dillon, Mason's at San Francisco General. All I know is that they wheeled him in on a gurney. No one knows where Annabelle is."

"We're on our way there now. Emerson's water just broke."

"Oh my God! I'll check on Mason and be right there."

I hear a scream in the background. Obviously, Emerson is having some serious contractions.

"I have to go," Dillon says in a rush.

"No worries. I get it."

"CeCe, let me know the minute you know anything about Mason."

Fighting back the tears, I tell him, "I will."

I disconnect the call and call Cameron.

He answers with "Did Emerson have her baby?"

"She's going in now, but the reason I'm calling is because Mason's at the hospital."

"What? Why?"

"I don't know, but a detective answered his phone when I called, and Annabelle can't be found. I'm on my way."

"Hadlee and I will be right there, too." I hear him tell Hadlee what's going on, and she jumps on the phone.

"What do you know?"

"Nothing really. Just that Evelyn from my office called and says she saw Mason brought into the hospital, and when I called Dillon, he said Emerson is in labor and they were on their way to the hospital."

"Okay, Cameron wants me to tell you he's calling Cynthia, Christopher, and William. I'll call Greer as soon as we hang up, and you call Trey. I'll call and use my credentials and find out where he is, and I'll text everyone."

I can breathe a tiny bit easier. "Thank you."

I disconnect the call and phone my twin brother.

"Hey," he answers.

"Hi. Please let Sara know that Mason's in the hospital."

"Is he okay?"

"We don't know." I hear him call for Sara and tell her.

"We're on our way," He says, and I can't hold back my tears. "Ces, he's going to be okay. I saw the rags, and I know today has been terrible, but I promise a big hug when I see you."

"Can you call Mom and Dad? They'll want to know."

"Yep, I got that. See you in a few."

"Hadlee will send a group text out as soon as she knows something." The rideshare pulls up to the emergency room entrance. "I love you, big brother."

"I love you, too."

We're hardly at a stop when I open the door and race up to the information desk, pushing myself to the front of the line. "Hello, Mason Sullivan was just brought in?"

"You'll need to get in line. I can only help one person at a time," the tired-looking receptionist says.

As I step in line and take a few deep breaths, trying to calm myself, my cell phone pings with a text.

Hadlee: Mason's in surgery on the fourth floor. His doctor is Jordan Severs. She's an amazing heart surgeon. Everyone, let's meet at the fourth-floor surgical waiting room.

This hospital is huge. Where the hell is the fourth-floor surgical waiting room? I see a janitor and figure he probably knows the hospital better than any information lady.

"Excuse me. I need to get to the fourth-floor surgical waiting room. Can you tell me how to get there?"

He smiles at me. "Yes. You take the green line on the floor to the elevators and head up to the fourth-floor. Once you get out there, you need to watch the signs. It's about as far away from the elevators as you can get, but you'll find it. If you get lost, there are plenty of people who can help you."

"Thank you so much. I appreciate your help."

I race off, following the green line, and he's right, the walk to the waiting room is as long as it can be. Once I arrive, I let the nurses know that I'm here for Mason Sullivan.

A man approaches me. "You're here for Mason Sullivan?"

I turn and size him up quickly. As I begin to answer, Cynthia arrives with her fiancé in two steps behind her. "CeCe? Is Mason okay?" She turns and her eyes widen. "Detective Lenning? What are you doing here?"

"Miss Hathaway? I wish we were meeting under better circumstances."

"Did the Russian mob do this?"

He holds up his hand. "You must be the woman who called Mason not long ago."

"That was me. My name is Caroline Arnault." I extend my hand, and he takes it cautiously.

"What made you call Mason at that particular time?"

"I received a call from someone who works for me. She was here with her boyfriend in the emergency room and saw him come in."

"I see." Turning to Cynthia, he asks, "And who alerted you?"

We hear them before we see them, and up rush my brother Trey and his wife, Sara; Cameron and his fiancée, Hadlee; Greer with her husband, Andy; William and his fiancée, Quinn; and bringing up the rear, Christopher and his wife, Bella.

"I called Cameron, and between the two of us, we alerted everyone else," I answer.

"Did you tell anyone who isn't here?"

I look around at the group. "No... wait. Yes, I alerted Dillon and Emerson first, but they were on their way here because Emerson's water broke."

The girls go crazy.

Detective Lenning is becoming visibly agitated. "Miss Arnault, when we spoke, you asked about his girlfriend—" He searches through his notes. "—a Miss Annabelle Ryan?"

"Yes." I don't know where he's going with this, but I'm not going to help him.

"Did you call her?"

I shake my head.

"Why not?"

I shrug. "I guess I figured she already knew."

"Why would she know?"

"Because they live together?"

I begin to feel bad for not calling her. They live together, and while she may not be our favorite person, she loves Mason. I'm sure of it, and she should be told.

Me: Annabelle, Mason is here at San Francisco General. We don't know much, but we're here. Come as soon as you can.

William speaks up. "Detective Lenning, why are you here asking questions? Is there something we need to be aware of?"

"No, nothing," he shares. Turning back to me, he asks, "Did you recall the name of his mother?"

"His mother's name is Janice Sullivan Harris of Canton, Ohio," I tell him, able to remember now that some of the panic has worn off.

He has Mason's phone in his hands and scans through the contacts. "Excuse me."

"Mason's going to be pissed if he calls her," Cameron mutters.

I know he's right, but she is his mother and should probably be here. My parents arrive. They are pretty close to Mason.

I'm a complete wreck as we wait. Sara and Greer take seats next to me, holding my hands. All the things I've wanted to say to him circle in my mind, and if he dies, I'm going to be more than disappointed in him. I'm going to chase him down in hell and kill him again!

Hadlee has disappeared, and Annabelle hasn't responded to my text, so I decide to call her. It goes right to voice mail. "Annabelle, this is CeCe. Mason is here at San Francisco General. We don't know anything. Please call when you get a chance or come down. We are in the fourth-floor surgical waiting room."

Cynthia puts her arm around me as I disconnect the call. "He's strong. He's going to be okay."

"Thanks. Annabelle's phone rings right to her voice mail. I should try the house."

She nods, and I call the main line at Mason's house. Fighting back the tears, I virtually repeat the same message on that answering machine. I hope she can get here soon.

It seems to take forever for Hadlee to return; when she does, she's in scrubs.

"They aren't telling us much. We don't know what's happened. He has an irregular heart rate and shortness of breath. His EKG was bad, and they're trying to stabilize him and determine if they need to do surgery. It looks like they're going to induce a medical coma so they can run tests." Hadlee looks at me. "Let's go get some coffee. It's going to be a long night."

My heart is beating triple time. A coma? That seems extreme. What happened? "I'm okay here. I can wait."

Cameron puts his arms around me. "Come on, CeCe, you look exhausted and in need of some food."

I paint a smile on my face. "I'll be fine."

Looking around the room, I see that everyone is as stressed as I am. Hoping they will follow my lead, I clap my hands together and say, "All right, everyone, Mason would not be happy to know that we are out here worrying about him. Let's head down to Labor and Delivery and see how Emerson is doing."

Everyone seems to perk up, and a few of my friends even smile as we walk to the other side of the hospital in search of our other friend and partner. Emerson is bringing the very first baby into our group of friends.

When we arrive, the nurses recognize Hadlee but won't let the rest of us in. After a few minutes, Dillon walks out looking grim.

"How ya doin'?" Cameron asks.

"Baby is not moving into the birth canal. The docs are giving the baby a few minutes to figure it out on his own or they'll begin prepping her for a C-section."

"I see the baby's stubborn just like his parents," Sara sympathizes.

"Maybe." Dillon grins. "Any word on Mason?"

"We don't know much, but Detective Lenning is here and investigating."

"Was it a car accident?"

I shrug. I'm following Cameron's lead and not wanting to stress Dillon about Mason's situation. He needs to focus on Emerson and his new baby. "I'm hoping Hadlee can find out more from her side."

"You guys can wait here or, of course, with Mason. I can text you as soon as the baby arrives."

I give Dillon a big hug and whisper in his ear, "You tell Emerson we're here and cheering for her. We can't wait to see your little bundle."

We wander back to the ICU waiting area. The hours tick by even slower than normal. I stand, I sit, I read my social media. Everyone I care about is here with me, but I'm worried about Mason, and I'm mad at Annabelle for not being here. Where could she be?

Everyone's phone pings at the same time.

Dillon: When you can, come meet Liam Michael Healy, born at 10:22 p.m. at 7lbs, 8 oz. Mom is a rock star and doing great!

We celebrate the new addition to our team. I can't wait to meet the little guy.

"Hadlee, you go first to visit, and we can follow in less than overwhelming groups," Greer says.

"I think we can go in small groups of four," Hadlee informs us.

I stop listening to them. I know Mason's doctor is going to be out any minute.

It is just Cynthia and me waiting when a petite woman steps out. "Caroline?"

I stand. "Yes, that's me."

"Hello, I'm Jordan Severs, Mason's doctor."

"How's he doing?"

"We can't be sure why Mason had a heart attack, but he seems to be doing well. We've put him in a medically induced coma for a few days. He needs to recover. Once things settle down, everyone can visit him. It will be good for him to hear you all talking to him."

"Thank you," I whisper as I fight back the tears. *Mason, you'd better pull through this. I have a lot to tell you, and if you think you can die, you'd better think again.*

"He's strong. This coma will only last a few days."

You can preorder *Fascination* and read CeCe and her man's story on Amazon.

THANK YOU!

Okay, I know, I dropped a bomb at the end of this book. Don't be too mad at me. There is one more book in the series, and I know you're going to love it.

Thank you for taking the time to read *Enchanted*, and if this is your first book you've read in the series, I hope you'll consider reading the others. These stories ramble around in my head and pour out of my fingers as I write. I'm grateful for the opportunity to share them with you. Thank you for giving me your time so I can share them with you. If you like it well enough, please write a review on your favorite review site – you can find me on Amazon, Goodreads, and Bookbub. This is one of the ways that others will see my books. If you want to know the exact date of a new release or know what's going on with my books, join my newsletter. I try to send only one a month, but if I'm releasing a book, you might get a second.

I grew up the daughter of a Marine pilot, and Quinn's dad is exactly my dad—kind and would do anything for me. While he has never read any of my books (I won't let him), he is my biggest fan and has regaled me with stories of people he's met that will be downloading my books. My mother is nothing like Quinn's. My amazing mother always has the knack of telling me how to keep going when Amazon does something that frustrates me—they seem to get the ship moving left and divert to the right without telling anyone.

I met my husband almost fifteen years ago. We met through an online dating site. We were two busy professionals who needed a little help being introduced. I thank my lucky stars that I met Daniel. He's my first beta reader and critique. He's amazingly supportive. He'll take the boys to the park after dinner so I can write for an hour or just let me talk through my story. I can't tell you how grateful I am that we met—in fifteen years, we've bought two homes, had two kids, lived in two countries, and driven each other crazy. I'm the luckiest girl around!

My editors from Hot Tree Editing are amazing. Donna is the heartbeat at Hot Tree. She moves my manuscripts around to the various editors, and without her, my work would be full of mistakes and typos. My content editor, Barbara, really helped to keep me on track. She warned me you'd hate the ending, but I promised not to make you wait too long for the final installment in the series. Virginia did the heavy lifting with this book and my line edit. She makes sure all those commas and apostrophes are in the right place, and she's wonderful at smoothing out the rough spots. And Kim and Sue, my wonderful beta readers who always find the last few missing periods, commas, and things that don't make sense.

Aria Tran at Resplendent Media does an outstanding job with my covers. I adore her and all her work. I highly recommend her!

And to my friends, Gayle, Erin, Carol, Marcia, my college BFFs Darren and Nicole, THANK YOU! These ladies (and one guy) listen to me talk unending about my books, let me talk through the plot points that sounded so good when I mapped out the series and now make no sense as I'm writing. You are my biggest fans and greatest support. Thank you for listening even when I'm pretty sure you're over me talking about it.

With that, September will be here soon. Enjoy your summer, and I can't wait to share with you all the fun with CeCe and her man.

Thanks again!

XOXO
A.

WHERE TO FIND AINSLEY

If you are interested in sneak peaks, random cocktail recipes that show up in my stories, or just the simple reminder to read the next book in the series, please join my reading group:

www.ainsleystclaire.com

Join Ainsley's newsletter

Follow Ainsley on Bookbub

Like Ainsley St Claire on Facebook

Join Ainsley's Naughty Readers group

Follow Ainsley St Claire on Twitter

Follow Ainsley St Claire on Goodreads

Visit Ainsley's website for her current booklist

I love to hear from you directly, too. Please feel free to email me at ainsley@ainsleystclaire.com or check out her website www.ainsleystclaire.com for updates.

ALSO BY AINSLEY ST CLAIRE

Forbidden Love (Venture Capitalist Book 1) Available on Amazon
(Emerson and Dillon's story) He's an eligible billionaire. She's his alluring employee. Will they cross the line from boardroom to bedroom?

Promise (Venture Capitalist Book 2) Available on Amazon
(Sara and Trey's story) She's reclaiming her past. He's a billionaire dodging the spotlight. Can a romance of high achievers succeed in a world hungry for scandal?

Desire (Venture Capitalist Book 3) Available on Amazon
(Cameron and Hadlee's story) She used to be in the 1%. He's a self-made billionaire. Will one hot night fuel love's startup?

Temptation (Venture Capitalist Book 4) Available on Amazon
(Greer and Andy's story) She helps her clients become millionaires and billionaires. He transforms grapes into wine. Can they find more than love at the bottom of a glass?

Obsession (Venture Capitalist Book 5) Available on Amazon (Cynthia and Todd's story) With hitmen hot on their heels, can Cynthia and Todd keep their love alive before the mob bankrupts their future?

Flawless (Venture Capitalist Book 6) Available on Amazon (Constance and Parker's story) A woman with a secret. A tech wizard on the trail of hackers. A tycoon's dying revelation threatens everything.

Longing (Venture Capitalist Book 7) Available on Amazon (Bella and Christopher's story) She's a biotech researcher in race with time for a cure. If she pauses to have a life, will she lose the race? He's in desperate need of a deal. Will he put his job over his career?

Enchanted (Venture Capitalist Book 8) Available on Amazon (Quinn and William's story) San Francisco has become too expensive to call home so Quinn can't help but take a second job to make ends meet and payoff her expensive school loans. Women don't hold his interest past a week, until she accidentally leaves me a voice mail so hot it melts his phone. Can they find a way to each other?

Fascination (Venture Capitalist Book 9) Available for preorder on Amazon
(CeCe and her man's story) CeCe's prince charming is caught in public with a girls lips on his you know what. People think her life is easy - they couldn't be more wrong. Dating is near impossible with the paparazzi following her everywhere. Any sane man would run from that. So, when a competitor steals her company's entire fall line, down to names and packaging, he's the only one who can prevent her from moving to a tropical island.

In a Perfect World Available on Amazon
Soulmates and true love. They believed in it once… back
when they were twenty. As college students, Kat Moore and
Pete Wilder meet and unknowingly change their lives forever.
Despite living on opposite sides of the country, they develop a
love for one another that never seems to work out. (Women's
fiction)

Coming Soon

Gifted (A Holiday Story)
November 2019

House of Cards (Tech Billionaires Book 1)
February 2020

Tilted (Tech Billionaires Book 2)
April 2020

ABOUT AINSLEY

Ainsley St Claire is a Contemporary Romantic Suspense Author and Adventurer on a lifelong mission to craft sultry storylines and steamy love scenes that captivate her readers. To date, she is best known for her Venture Capitalist series.

An avid reader since the age of four, Ainsley's love of books knew no genre. After reading, came her love of writing, fully immersing herself in the colorful, impassioned world of romantic suspense.

Ainsley's passion immediately shifted to a vocation when during a night of terrible insomnia, her first book came to her. Ultimately, this is what inspired her to take that next big step. The moment she wrote her first story, the rest was history.

When she isn't being a bookworm or typing away her next story on her computer, Ainsley enjoys spending quality family time with her loved ones. She is happily married to her amazing soulmate and is a proud mother of two rambunctious boys. She is also a scotch aficionada and lover of good food (especially melt-in-your-mouth, velvety chocolate). Outside of books, family, and food, Ainsley is a professional sports spectator and an equally terrible golfer and tennis player.

Made in the USA
Columbia, SC
24 July 2019